BOOK TWO IN THE RECKLESS SERIES

NYSSA KATHRYN

An NW Partners Book
Cover by Deranged Doctor Design
Developmentally and Copy Edited by Kelli Collins
Line Edited by Jessica Snyder
Proofread by Amanda Cuff and Jen Katemi
Cover Photography by Madison Maltby Photography

❀ Created with Vellum

It's a long-awaited homecoming...but not everyone's happy about her return.

Five years ago, Tilly Taylor's father did something that cost her everything. Her home. Her friends. And all the trust she'd ever earned. Now she's back, and ready to prove to everyone that she's nothing like Martin Taylor. Unfortunately, the small town of Misty Peak doesn't forgive or forget so easily. And when a murder occurs at Tilly's new workplace, proving her innocence gets even harder.

Kayden Walker likes his solitude. That's why working in the mountains suits him so well. They're his sanctuary. His safe place. So when a woman he doesn't trust is hired to work alongside him, it's an adjustment he doesn't want to make. Only, no matter how much he tries to keep Tilly at a safe distance, he can't seem to get her sad green eyes out of his head. Despite their families' unfortunate history, Kayden finds himself playing savior to the last woman he should want to protect.

When dangerous things continue happening in his mountains, keeping her close becomes vital—for Tilly's safety and for Kayden's heart. Someone doesn't want her home...and they'll go to great lengths to make sure she's gone.

ACKNOWLEDGMENTS

Thank you to my amazing team who helped me make this story the one it is. Kelli, Jessica, Amanda and Jen—you're a team that others could only dream to have. Thank you.

Thank you to my ARC team and readers. Your support and willingness to step into every world I write about is everything.

And to my family—you're my world. My reason. And you inspire me every day to work hard. I wouldn't be able to do this without you.

Twenty-five-year-old Macy Hodgkin, murdered in the Smoky Mountains on the edge of Misty Peak.

Murdered…Macy was *murdered* right here in the mountains surrounding the Misty Peak Visitors Center.

Tilly Taylor read the news report again and again. A week had passed since the woman's stabbing and it still didn't feel real. Macy had worked in the café here at the visitors center. She was nice. Friendly. What on earth could have led to someone wanting to kill her?

Tilly scrubbed her hands over her eyes as she switched her gaze back to the second screen. A million emails sat unopened in her inbox, but she knew what each of them said…or the gist of them, at least. They were from worried tourists wanting to know if the mountains were safe.

Were they? Well, the sheriff's office hadn't found the murderer. What they *had* found was an open safe in the room right beside her office, which was completely empty. A safe no one had any idea about. Hell, they'd even contacted Linda, the former office manager, who had already been on her cruise halfway across the world. She'd sounded just as shocked as them, claiming she'd never heard of or seen the safe, and she'd been the office manager for over twenty years. *And* the office manager before her was deceased.

So how had this robber known about the safe, and how had that ended with the murder of Macy?

Tilly massaged her temple. This was not how she'd pictured her first month working at the Misty Peak Visitors Center. She was supposed to be scheduling tours through the mountains. Transferring Linda's old-school paper trail filing system to a streamlined online system. And she was doing all that, just not fast enough because this devastating murder was taking up a lot of her time…and energy.

Five years. She'd left Misty Peak five years ago, but before that, this small town had been her home since birth, and there'd *never* been a murder here in all that time.

God, the move back here had been hard enough. So much harder than she'd expected. She missed her simpler life back in Cleveland. She missed her cute corner office. The coworkers with whom she'd built good relationships.

Yet here she was…back in a town where no one wanted her.

It was strange how this place had once felt like home, but now…now it only felt like home when she was in the mountains. But then, Cleveland had stopped feeling like home when she'd lost her mother.

The quiet of her office slipped over her as she looked at the framed photo on one of the shelves. Her and her mother stood in front of their Christmas tree. It had been their last Christmas together…only they hadn't known it then.

An ache throbbed in her chest.

This town was not only where she'd grown up, it was where her mother had grown up. Where her mother had birthed and raised her. It *would* be her home again. It had to be.

Taking a deep breath, she clicked into the first email just as her phone rang. She straightened at the sight of Roy Pierce's name, a local carpenter.

She answered on the second ring. "Tilly speaking."

"Hi, Tilly, sorry it's taken me a few days to return your call. We've been backed up here. You left a message about some windows?"

"Yes. I have two that need replacing, both at the front of the house, one in the living room and one in the bedroom. The glass has completely shattered. For the moment, I've just boarded them up with wooden planks, but I wouldn't say I've done a good job." And boy had that been an ordeal. She was not "handy," something she'd learned the hard way. "It's pretty cold in my house, so I would be grateful if you could come as soon as possible."

"Yeah, I can imagine. How did it happen?"

She cringed. "The house was vacant for a few years." Five. Five years. That was a few, right? "And I guess some people broke in by shattering the windows during that time. There are quite a few other things that need fixing, but the windows are the priority."

A few other things. That was the understatement of the century. The house had been a mess when she'd returned. So much worse than she'd expected. It had been the first of many disappointments upon returning to Misty Peak. She'd cleaned up as much as she could, but it was slow going, especially when she was struggling to get contractors to help her. To get *anyone* to help her.

"Yeah, after what happened to Macy, the entire town's on high alert. Good security's important." He cleared his throat. "I may have some availability in the coming week, but I need to come by and measure up first. What's your address?"

She wrinkled her nose, almost not wanting to tell him. "Two Turner Court."

A heavy silence fell across the line, and Tilly's heart sank because she knew what was coming next. The same thing that had come with countless other contractors she'd called.

"Two Turner Court?" he repeated. "That's the old Taylor house. What did you say your name was?"

Her fingers tightened on the phone. "Tilly."

"Tilly…Matilda Taylor. As in, Martin's daughter?"

She scrubbed a hand over her face, knowing just by the tone of his voice she wasn't going to get this man's help. "Uh, yeah. I'm his daughter, but—"

"You know what, I'm gonna need to check with my boys. They may have already scheduled something in that free spot. I'll get back to you."

He hung up before she could get a word in. And she knew he wouldn't be getting back to her.

Frustration punched her in the gut, not just because *another* contractor had hung up on her after looking into both local contractors and those in surrounding towns—but because she was so tired. Tired of trying to convince this town she wasn't her father.

He'd hurt people in Misty Peak. Not physically, but some would say what he'd done was worse. He'd robbed them of their entire life savings, then run. And the second he'd done that, she'd lost everyone. This town's affection. Their trust.

God, she hated him for what he'd done.

She blinked back the tears, refusing to let them fall. She *would not* cry over this. Roy not wanting to replace her windows was a small setback, but she'd find a way around it. What she needed was coffee. A big, gigantic cup of double shot coffee.

With a sigh, she rose from her desk and crossed to the foyer. Her office was right beyond the front desk, where Pixie, the young receptionist, worked. On one of her first days, Tilly had confided in her that she'd lost her mother six months ago to cancer, and Pixie had shared that she'd lost her father less than a year ago, also to cancer.

Pixie glanced up from behind the desk and offered a small smile. "Hey, are you doing okay?"

Did she see the mild panic and disappointment on her face? "Yeah, just finding my feet in this town while reassuring the next few months of tourists that these mountains are safe when really, I have no idea if they are."

Pixie cringed. "Sorry. If it makes you feel better, I've tackled my fair share of phone calls."

"So we can be miserable together?"

The other woman lifted a shoulder. "Better than suffering alone."

She laughed. "Thanks. I'm just popping into the café for a coffee and to check on Elle. Do you need anything?"

She shook her head. "No, thanks. I've had two already and it's not even ten."

Ha. Sometimes she was up to her third by nine. "No problem."

The foyer of the visitors center was one large room with a door on each side, one that led to the parking lot, the other to the deck, the café, and the mountains beyond. There was also a small eco center that displayed some local artifacts.

Tilly exited the back door and stepped onto the deck. The second she saw the mountains, the ache in her chest eased. Because those mountains...they were so familiar. They were comfort. They were home. How many memories did she have of growing up in those woods? How many times had her mother taken her on hikes so the two of them could just get lost? Too often, and not often enough.

She sighed as she moved across the deck and stepped into the café. A family sat at a table to the right, with a couple to the left. The place had a dozen tables scattered around the room and a few more on the deck, with the counter at the back right.

The café was definitely a perk of working here. Fresh coffee right beside her office? Heck yes.

She stepped up to the counter. "Hi, Elle, how are you doing today?"

Elle and Macy had been the only two employees of the café, and they'd been good friends as well.

Pain laced Elle's eyes, but she blinked it away. "I'm doing okay. Still in a bit of shock, but that's to be expected." She swallowed. "Has Eastern said anything about finding the person responsible?"

Tilly shook her head. "No, sorry. He's just told me that he and his deputies are working on it."

The other woman nodded, disappointment drawing the corners of her lips down. "What can I get you?"

"A latte, double shot, extra hot, please."

"You got it." She turned toward the machine.

"Remember to let me know when you're ready for me to start looking for a new worker in here." She intentionally didn't use the words, "Macy's replacement."

Elle nodded quickly...too quickly. "I will. Take my mind off things. Tell me how you're finding it here."

Did the woman want the honest truth or a pretty lie? "There's been a lot of...tidying up to do with the job. Mostly of the online systems."

"Yeah, Linda was kind of old school. Very passionate though."

And obviously very open-minded, because she'd chosen Tilly to take her place even though she knew who her father was. "I'm really glad I'm here though. I've loved these mountains since I was a kid."

"Me too." Elle sighed. "There's something almost magical about them."

Elle had grown up in Misty Peak too. She was few years younger than Tilly. Maybe that was why she'd never shown her any of the hostility that other locals had.

"Have you been working here for long?" Tilly asked.

Elle popped a lid on the cup and pushed it across the counter.

"Since I was eighteen. So I'm kind of part of the furniture. Macy started at the same time as me…"

When that same sad expression crossed Elle's face, Tilly reached across the counter and placed a hand over hers. "I'm sorry. If there's anything I can do, just let me know."

"Thank you."

Tilly was just taking her hand away when the door to the café opened and four large men stepped inside. Not just large—massive. The four guys who made up the search and rescue team. Jake, Hendrix, Theo, and Kayden. They also ran tours.

They all looked up, but the only person to smile at her was Jake. That wasn't unusual. If looks could kill, the other three would be searing holes right into her chest.

Great. Just what her day needed.

She gave Jake a small smile before looking back to Elle and holding out her card. The second she'd paid, she stepped away from the counter. As she rounded Kayden, she was met by the most intoxicating scent of trees and spice and something so incredibly male. It made a tiny shudder course down her spine and heated her skin.

Damn her and her reaction to the man. He'd made it very clear he did not like her, yet she reacted to him just by walking past.

She was just nearing the door when a hand touched her arm. She turned to see Jake smiling down at her.

Her brows rose. "Hey."

He grinned at her, a lock of his shaggy blond hair falling over his eyes. "Hey, Tilly. Just thought I'd check in on how you're doing, what with you still being fairly new here and all."

That was nice of him, and man, she needed nice right now. "I'm okay. Making some progress on the new systems. I'm getting the roster ready for the four of you guys for the next month."

His grin widened. "So if I bribe you, I might get the better roster?"

She chuckled. "No bribing necessary. Just tell me what you want, and I'll try to make it work. Although, the odd Sugar and Spice cupcake would not be turned down."

"Ah, a fellow Sugar and Spice fan. I should have known, a woman after my own heart."

"I think Mrs. Sandler is the one after all our hearts."

He chuckled, and the sound was deep and warm. "I think you're right. Well, I should get back to the guys. We're about to go on a team training run, but if you still want me to walk you to your car at night—"

She shook her head. After what had happened to Macy, Jake had insisted on accompanying her to her car every afternoon for the last week. It was sweet. "I'm okay. But thank you."

He nudged her shoulder before heading back to the counter.

At least not everyone in this town hated her. But then, Jake wasn't a local, he'd only gotten here a few months before her.

She was about to turn back toward the door when someone near the counter caught her attention.

Kayden. He was looking straight at her...and he didn't look happy.

CHAPTER 2

*K*ayden Walker forced his gaze away from the exchange between Tilly, their new center manager, and Jake, the newest member of the SAR team. The two of them stood close. So close that if she reached out, she'd touch him. And for some reason, that grated on his nerves.

It shouldn't. Just like the fact Jake had spent a chunk of his time walking Tilly to her car each evening shouldn't annoy him. Hell, he should be happy the new guy was looking after an employee, shouldn't he? Especially after what had happened to Macy.

Something hard and uncomfortable coiled in his gut. Someone had killed the woman, stabbed her right here in his mountains after breaking into a safe no one had known existed. And his brother, the town sheriff, still hadn't found the asshole, meaning the perp was still out there.

Tilly laughed, and the sound made Kayden's stomach twist. It was light and airy and took up far too much of his attention.

Without his damn permission, his focus shifted back to them, and suddenly he couldn't take his eyes off her. Because when she smiled, the shadows around her eyes lifted, and for a moment she looked ten years younger. Like the weight of the world wasn't pressing down on her.

Fuck, he needed to stop looking at her. Not just because she was the new manager but because of who her father was and what he'd done to Kayden's family.

Jake bumped her shoulder and turned. Kayden was moments from dragging his eyes away when her beautiful moss-green gaze collided with his.

Look away, Kayden. Stop staring like a fucking creep.

It wasn't just her eyes that were beautiful though. It was the dusting of freckles across her nose that reminded him of the stars in the night sky. It was the pale skin that made her look far too delicate.

"Here you go, guys. Going out for a training run?"

Finally, Kayden forced his attention to Elle behind the counter as she pushed four shots of espresso toward him and his team.

"Thanks, Elle." Jesus, why was his voice so gruff? He cleared his throat. "Yeah, we're doing a run through the mountains."

They tried to do the run weekly, always with a backpack full of equipment. Although in the craziness of the last week since Macy, they'd missed the last one.

"How are you doing?" he asked, forcing gentleness into his voice.

She sucked in a visible breath before answering. "As okay as I can be, I guess. I keep thinking…"

"What?"

Her gaze flicked to Theo and Hendrix, who'd already grabbed their espressos and stepped away from the counter, before shifting back to him. "I feel guilty that it was her and not me. I mean, I do the schedule for the café. I scheduled her to close that afternoon. I didn't know she was staying back to do some extra cleaning and prep work, but still…"

Kayden shook his head. "You can't do that. We don't know the circumstances of what happened that night yet." Keyword...yet. Because they would find out, one way or the other.

She nodded quickly. "Thanks. Well, have a good run."

Kayden dipped his head before turning and moving back to the guys.

"Not sure this will cut it," Theo said in a hushed voice to Hendrix as he shot his espresso back. "I need about ten to make me feel alive."

"Well, maybe you should have gone easier on the alcohol last night," Hendrix replied just as quietly.

Kayden frowned as he moved to stand with them. "You got plastered on a work night?"

Theo's eyes widened. In a normal job, that might not be so bad. But they worked in search and rescue. Every one of them needed to be at their best in case they were sent out to save someone at a moment's notice.

"Not plastered," Theo spluttered, running his fingers through his hair. "I just played some poker with the guys and had a couple drinks. I'm fine."

Kayden narrowed his eyes, but before he could say anything, Jake returned to the group and Theo turned his attention to him. "What were you doing with *her*?"

"Talking. Why?"

"We told you what she did."

"No. You told me what her *father* did. And I didn't grow up in this town. Her family didn't do anything to me. Plus, she's cute."

The woman wasn't cute. She was fucking gorgeous.

Kayden shot back his own espresso. "Let's go."

They always had the shot of caffeine before they left. They'd started it as a way to give them a boost before the long run, but it had become somewhat of a tradition.

Kayden stepped outside and led the guys to the small shed just off the side of the deck, where they all grabbed their backpacks full of equipment. The things were damn heavy, but Kayden barely noticed. He'd had to travel with more than this during his time as a Pararescue Specialist in the Air Force. Hell, PJs had to do some of the most dangerous extractions in the most hostile environments in the world. Everything from parachuting from low-altitude planes to repelling off mountains. Jobs where he'd barely gotten out with his life.

He threw on his backpack and started moving.

The guys were quick to follow, Jake coming up to his side. "You in a rush this morning, Kayden?"

"The sooner we leave, the sooner we'll get back. Were you drinking with the other two last night?"

Jake's brows shot up. "No. I play poker with them sometimes but never drink. And never on a work night."

Kayden didn't miss that the man didn't deny Hendrix had been drinking too.

As the team leader, it was Kayden's responsibility to make sure everyone was at their best at work, and that meant it was his job to give Theo a warning for his behavior. That shit wasn't okay. It couldn't be. Not when they had lives on the line.

Jake cleared his throat. "So…you know much about Tilly?"

Kayden sped up his run. "We went to school together, but she was a couple grades behind me, so I wouldn't say I know her."

"Her father stole from people, right? Was an investment broker, but instead of investing the money, he took it and ran?"

Images of his own father's face when he'd told them that Martin Taylor had taken his money flashed through his mind. The disappointment when he'd revealed he'd had to sell their family home. The pain at admitting he'd re-mortgaged his bar and moved into the apartment above it.

"Yeah," Kayden confirmed, "that's what happened."

"But it wasn't her, right? She wasn't a part of it?"

"I don't know. Her and her mother left town a month later, and she only returned a couple months ago. I don't know if she's had contact with her father. If she knew what he was doing. Those are questions for her." Questions he hadn't asked yet.

Jake seemed to consider that for a moment. "Okay, yeah, thanks for the info."

Kayden increased his pace again, trying like hell to outrun those green eyes. Why was it this hard? Because they were so wide and vulnerable that he felt like he'd been sucker punched every time they met his?

When they passed the spot where Macy's body had been found, the blood in his veins moved faster. Theo and Hendrix had been the ones to find her, and the scene had been fucking gruesome, even for Kayden, who'd seen a lot in his thirty-six years.

For the rest of the run, Kayden didn't speak to his team. He dipped his head and focused on putting one foot in front of the other. Of wiping his mind of everything but his job.

He loved these mountains and he loved to move his body. Usually, when he put the two together, his mind would go blank and he could just feel at peace.

Today, that wasn't the case. There was too much going on with Macy's murder and Tilly's return.

The run usually took a couple hours. Today, Kayden finished it in one and a half, way ahead of the other guys. He went straight to the equipment shed and dropped off his pack before heading back to the center.

Pixie smiled at him from behind the desk as he stepped inside. "Hey, Kayden. Good run?"

"Yeah, it was good." A damn lie. He'd been racing as if he could somehow outrun everything that plagued him.

He moved into the office and straight to the cabinet. He'd just pulled off his shirt when a gasp sounded behind him. He turned to see Tilly standing there, mouth open, green eyes on his chest.

"I...you're..." She shook her head, her gaze finally lifting to meet his. "I'm sorry, I was just getting some water. I'll leave you to change."

Fuck, how had he forgotten this wasn't Linda's office anymore?

He pulled a clean shirt from the shelf. "It's fine. I just need to throw this on." He tugged it over his head. "Linda let me keep clean shirts in here, but I'll move them."

He should have already done it, but with everything going on, he just hadn't.

"No. That's okay. If that's the easiest place for you to keep them, you can continue." She opened her mouth, looking like she wanted to say more, only to snap her lips shut.

"You sure?" he asked.

She nodded, a lock of light brown, almost blond, hair falling into her eyes, and damn if his hand didn't twitch to shift it behind her ear.

Jesus, what was going on with him?

"Okay. Thanks." He moved toward the door, only to stop when she didn't move out of the way. As it was, she blocked the exit.

It took about three beats for her to realize. "Oh, God, sorry."

She stepped to the side, and when he brushed past her, all he was aware of was her scent. Sweet like honey, with a hint of fresh strawberries.

He was about to leave when he suddenly stopped. "Before I go, are you doing okay with everything?"

"Everything?"

"Macy."

"Macy...right. Um, yeah. I didn't really know her. Are *you* okay?"

No. He was frustrated and mad as hell that this had happened in his mountains. "I will be...when we find the killer. Stay safe, okay?"

She nodded slowly, then he stepped out of the room.

<h1 style="text-align:center">CHAPTER 3</h1>

*T*illy had ogled him. In a didn't-even-try-to-hide-it kind of way. The width of his shoulders. The thickness of the muscles across his chest. She'd taken it all in, in the most obvious way.

Argh. And then she'd just stood in his way like some kind of zombie psychopath.

Jesus Christ. She pulled up in front of her house and dropped her head to the wheel. How was she supposed to see him tomorrow? And the next day and the day after that?

Groaning, she slid out of her car and walked toward the house, her gaze drawn to the surrounding mountains. At least her home offered her a fraction of peace. The trees. The greenery.

A cool breeze brushed over her face, almost distracting her from the windows. Still broken...and they'd remain that way until she found someone to fix them. *If* she found someone to fix them.

Man, the hastily placed boards made her home cold. But then, the broken heating system didn't help...another thing she couldn't get fixed.

The old floorboards groaned beneath her feet as she stepped inside. The house was big, and back in the day it would have been quite grand. But after years of neglect, it was not looking so grand. There was an open living and kitchen area to the right and a bedroom and bathroom to the left with more rooms upstairs.

Her first day here, she'd almost turned back around and driven away. Because of the stench and the trash and the dirty flooring. The broken windows had been just one of her problems. Water had gotten inside, none of the lights had worked, the walls had been graffitied and the bathroom trashed.

Her entire first week had been spent scrubbing every surface, fixing the little things that she could, like replacing lights, painting the walls, and changing the locks. It had been backbreaking, and there was still so much to do, but day by day, this house was starting to feel like her old childhood home again.

She moved into the bedroom and dropped her bag on the bed. All she wanted to do was collapse into it and sleep, but she needed to shower and eat and all that other adult stuff that she had no energy for, then maybe she could devour a tub of Ben and Jerry's ice cream on the couch with a good sitcom.

In the bathroom, she caught her reflection in the mirror, and yep, she looked as tired as she felt. Exhaustion from endless emails and phone calls from tourists canceling tours and visits.

After stripping off her clothes, she stepped into the shower. This was the room she'd scrubbed the hardest because, well, it had been in the worst condition. She wasn't sure if it was because squatters had stayed here, people had intentionally trashed it, or maybe even wild animals had gotten inside. Hell, maybe all three. Whatever it was, the room had made her gag more than once.

When she stood inside the shower, the warm water beat down on her shoulders, allowing some of her tense muscles to relax. She'd run into Theo and Hendrix a couple of times today, and each time, she'd been met with the same passive hostility. Aggressive glares and barely even a hello...the way they looked at her made her feel like a bug to be squashed under their shoes.

No matter how hard she tried to tell herself it didn't affect her, it still hurt. Some days she just wanted to scream at people that she was innocent. That she'd had no part in what her father had done, and she shouldn't be punished by association.

But even if she stood smack dab in the middle of town and screamed those words at the top of her lungs, there would *still* be people who wouldn't believe her. They needed someone to blame, and with the absence of her father, that someone was her.

When the air around her started to mist and her fingers grew wrinkly, she stepped out of the shower and into the bedroom. It had been her parents' bedroom, and yeah, it was strange staying in it now. But when she'd arrived, *her* bedroom had smelled of dead animal, and that smell still lingered a bit.

She'd just pulled on a pair of yoga pants and a T-shirt when something sounded from the front of the house. She paused to listen with a frown.

Was that a car stopping out front? Her driveway was long and the house pretty isolated—people only stopped here if they were visiting.

She hadn't moved a muscle when soft, crashing thuds sounded against the house.

What the hell?

Her feet were moving before she could stop herself. She ran to the front door and pulled it open to see the tail end of a car pulling down her drive. And there, on her front door, was wet egg and broken shell.

Really? Locals were going so far as to *egg her house* now? And not just any eggs—rotten eggs, if the smell was anything to go by.

God, *now* she wanted to scream. Either that or cry. She slammed her door closed and moved back into the house.

They were trying to run her out of town. Well, guess what, jerks? She wasn't going anywhere. This was her home. This was where she'd grown up, and she had nothing to be ashamed of. Absolutely nothing!

An hour…it took her an entire freaking hour to clean the egg from her house. Too long. By the time she was done, she was angry and frustrated and about a million other things. Why hadn't she gotten the plate numbers? Reported them to the sheriff's office? At least Eastern, the town sheriff, didn't seem to hate her and would likely do something.

Because she hadn't been thinking. Shock had stopped her from doing anything but staring at the egg.

She was about to move to the bathroom for her second shower of the evening—because, yeah, she stunk—when her phone beeped with a message. She lifted it to see her friend's name on the screen.

Harper: Hey, if you're free, come down to the bar. It's quiet, so I can take a break and have a drink with you. It's been too long since we caught up.

Harper was new in town. She'd gotten a job at the local bar, Meridian, and had been kind to Tilly since their first meeting. They'd become instant friends, something Tilly had really needed. Hell, something she *still* really needed.

Tilly: Be there within the hour.

* * *

KAYDEN LIFTED his beer to his mouth. It had been a long-ass day. After his run, he'd taken a group of tourists on a hike, then finally given Theo that warning. It had not been taken well.

Kayden didn't give a shit how the guy reacted though. Being part of the Misty Peak SAR team wasn't voluntary, it was paid. It was also highly competitive. If Theo couldn't show up to work in a good state, there were a dozen guys who would eagerly take his place.

"Tough day?"

Kayden glanced at his brother Cody. After their father's cancer had taken hold, Cody had taken over the running of his bar. He was good at it, being a people person. They also had two brothers still serving in the military, Eastern, who was town sheriff; and a sister, Nylah, who'd moved to Cradle Mountain, Idaho, several months ago.

"You could say that," Kayden finally answered. "Theo showed up for work hungover."

"Why did he do that?"

"Who the hell knows? But he probably got drunk because he was losing at poker."

Cody scowled. "I'm guessing you had a word with him."

"Yep. He wasn't too happy about it either. Didn't say it so much with his words as with the glare I received."

Cody shook his head as he threw a dishrag over his shoulder. "Doesn't matter if he's happy with it or not. You're team leader—what you say goes."

Maybe that was the problem. Kayden had only gotten home from the military less than a year ago and had been given the job of SAR team leader from the get-go, while Theo had been working at the place for years and hadn't even been considered.

Incidences like this were the reason.

Kayden set his beer down. "How are you and Harper doing?"

Cody glanced down the bar to where she was serving drinks. "We're good. Harper's a damn warrior to have recovered so quickly from everything she went through."

Kayden nodded. His brother wasn't wrong. A few weeks ago, Harper had been targeted not only by a local but also her own family. You'd never know that by looking at her now though. "I'm sure it helps that she has you by her side."

"Nowhere I'd rather be." Cody turned back to him. "That woman is my world. I would move heaven and earth to make her happy."

While he could appreciate that his brother did look happy

with Harper, he didn't understand it. Maybe because Kayden didn't date. Why, exactly, he wasn't sure. Because no woman had ever made him want more than one night? Because he found it damn hard to trust people outside of his family?

When Harper approached Cody, his arms went around her like he had to be touching her. "Are you doing okay?"

She nodded, her eyes soft. "I'm doing great. Do you mind if I take a small break to have a drink with Tilly?"

Kayden's spine straightened. Tilly was here? He looked over his shoulder, and sure enough, the woman stood by the door. Her green eyes bore into him, feeling like an arrow in his chest.

"Take as long as you want," Cody said.

Harper crossed the floor of the bar. It wasn't until she met her friend that Tilly looked away, and damn, why was it only then that Kayden felt like he could breathe?

He swiveled back toward the bar and took a big swig of beer, feeling his brother's eyes on him before he spoke.

"Everything okay?"

"It's great." A damn lie.

Cody scoffed. "Okay, new question. You being nice to her at work?"

"When am I not nice?"

"All the time. You can be an asshole, and you know it."

"I'm not being an asshole to her." Hell, even if he wanted to, her big green eyes wouldn't allow it, because even though she tried to come off as tough, he saw the fragility beneath her exterior.

"Good."

"Cody," Tim, the new bartender, called from the other side of the bar. "Could I grab your help with something?"

"Sure." Cody gave Kayden a look of warning before heading off.

What did his brother think? That he'd intentionally make her life hell at work? He wasn't a *complete* jackass.

Kayden sipped his beer again. He came here a few times a week to see Cody, and sometimes Eastern would meet them here when he had someone looking after Avery. Kayden also came to get away from the quiet of his house. He didn't usually mind the quiet, but sometimes it got loud, and he had to get out. Maybe that was because after so many years of serving in the Air Force he was used to noise. To having people around him.

Half an hour passed, his brother stopping to chat every so often, before Kayden rose and turned—only to bump straight into Tilly.

She gasped and pulled back. "Oh, God, sorry. I was heading to the bathroom."

"You're fine, Matilda. I didn't see you, either."

"Tilly. People call me Tilly."

He knew that…still, he'd been calling her Matilda. Because using Tilly felt intimate for some reason.

There was an awkward pause before he cleared his throat. "How have you found working at the visitors center?"

Her brows rose like she was surprised he'd asked. Which was fair. He hadn't taken much of an interest before now. "It's good. Busy. There's a lot to do. But I like working in the mountains and being involved in the running of the center."

"The mountains are pretty awesome."

She smiled. "They're why people don't leave Misty Peak."

"You left." The words were out before he could stop them, and they had the small smile dropping from her face.

"I did." Another heavy pause before she cleared her throat. "Well…I'll leave you to it."

She started to walk away when some guys passed behind her, one bumping her in the back so roughly that she fell forward. She would have hit the floor if Kayden hadn't grabbed her and tugged her back up.

"Hey! You okay?" he asked.

She nodded quickly.

Anger pulsed through Kayden's veins, not just at the way the guy had knocked into her with no apology but because he'd muttered something under his breath before chuckling.

"What did you say?" Kayden growled loudly.

The guy paused and looked at him. "Nothing."

He started to walk away a second time, but Kayden grabbed him by the shirt and tugged him back. "Hey. You bump into a woman, you apologize."

A soft hand touched his arm. "Kayden…it's okay."

"There you go," the guy said, a cocky grin on his face. "She says it's okay."

He tried to pull away, but Kayden tugged him closer. "*I say, it's not. Apologize.*"

Some of the humor left his face, and an angry sneer took its place. "She gonna apologize for stealing from my family? Or better yet, she gonna return the goddamn money?"

Tilly stiffened beside him.

"This isn't about that." Kayden inched closer. "This is about you pushing a woman in the back."

"Not just *any* woman…*her*. A Taylor. The daughter of a thief."

"Everything okay here?"

Kayden ignored Cody's question as his brother came to stand beside him, all of his focus on the asshole in front of him. He had no time for men who physically assaulted women, and shoving Tilly in the back *had* been assault.

"Last chance," Kayden said in a voice so quiet that there was no missing the thread of violence. "Apologize to her before I do something to you that *you* won't get an apology for."

The man's eyes narrowed, and for a moment he seemed to be considering his options.

Was this asshole even dumber than he looked?

His friend bumped his shoulder. "Just say sorry so we can get out of here, man." Obviously the smarter of the two.

Finally, the jerk looked back at Tilly. "I'm sorry."

It wasn't sincere. Not even close. But Cody touched his arm. "Step back, Kay."

Reluctantly, Kayden released his shirt. "Do it again, and you *will* be sorry."

The guy's eyes narrowed for a second time, and it was a moment before he turned away, but even then, Kayden waited until he was a good few feet away before turning back to Tilly. "Are you okay?"

"I'm fine. Thank you, but you didn't have to do that."

"He shoved you and laughed." What the fuck did she *think* he'd do? Allow that kind of behavior right in front of him?

"I know, but saying something just makes it all worse sometimes."

What the hell was she talking about? "Has this happened before?" With the same asshole or someone else? Did Kayden need to turn around and kick his ass?

She opened her mouth, clearly about to say something, but then closed it and shook her head. "Don't worry about it. Thank you for your help, Kayden."

Then she was striding to the bathroom before he could push for more information.

CHAPTER 4

A trickling sound pricked at Tilly's sleep, causing her to groan as she rolled from her back to her side. It almost sounded like drops of water hitting a surface but coming from inside her house.

Christ, what time was it?

Slowly, she peeled her eyes open to see darkness. Thanks to the boarded-over window, there wasn't even a hint of light in the room. Blindly, she reached for her phone on the bedside table, shoving other items aside before her fingers wrapped around her cell.

Three thirty. Too. Freaking. Early.

The consistent trickling continued to echo throughout the house.

With a groan, she forced herself to turn on the bedside lamp before crawling out of bed. The coldness of the floorboards slipped up her legs, but it wasn't just the floor that was cold.

Jesus, she really needed to find someone to fix the heat in this house. Maybe she'd just pay someone from out of town an exorbitant amount of money to drive down here to do the work.

She grabbed her robe, which felt far too thin, and slung it over her shoulders before stepping out of the bedroom. The second she switched on the living room light, she saw it.

Water trickling from the ceiling light fixture. From the freaking light? What the hell?

Quickly, she turned the light off, not sure if having it on would cause some sort of electrical short circuit, and instead used the flashlight on her phone.

Great. This was just what she needed.

Water pooled on her coffee table...her brand-new coffee table. Everything was soaking wet. Fantastic.

In the hall closet, she grabbed a handful of towels, then got a bucket from the laundry room. Back in the living room, she placed the bucket under the dripping water and started wiping up the mess on the table.

The water squished beneath her feet on the rug. Her poor rug...another new item. Would it dry okay or would she have to buy a new one?

When the table was dry and the rug as dry as she was going to get it, she climbed onto the coffee table and attempted to inspect the ceiling light more closely.

Okay, the water wasn't coming through the actual light. It appeared to be coming through a gap on the side. Still, it was close enough to the light that it was something she didn't want to mess with.

Lifting her phone so it was closer to the hole, she rose to her toes to have a closer look—but because her feet were damp, her foot slipped. A yelp screeched from her lungs as she fell back-ward. She swung her arm behind her to catch herself, only to have pain blast throughout her arm as she landed hard on the floor.

Goddamn, that hurt!

Grabbing her elbow, she groaned and rolled to her side. For a moment, she just breathed through the ache.

Should she go to a doctor? Was anything even open at this

time in Misty Peak? Of course, the hospital would be, but a sore shoulder barely classified as an emergency. And even if she did want to go to the hospital, there was no one to call to drive her. Most people had at least one person they could ask, but the only person she had was Harper, and the woman had recently gone through a huge ordeal. She couldn't call her at this hour.

It was fine. There was no way it was broken, because she'd be in a lot more pain, right? She just had to get herself off the floor, ice it, and get back to sleep, then with a bit of luck, she'd be okay to drive herself to work in a few hours.

Emotion welled in her chest, but she pushed it down. She'd been through tougher situations, and she'd get through this too.

Words her mother had spoken to her flashed in her head... words originally spoken by Mary Anne Radmacher that Tilly repeated to herself time and again when things got hard and heavy.

"Courage doesn't always roar. Sometimes courage is the little voice at the end of the day that says I'll try again tomorrow."

That was what she needed to do...try again tomorrow. Or technically, later today.

Slowly, she forced herself to her feet. Ice, sleep, work...then she'd call for a doctor's appointment. She'd be okay.

* * *

"Found her."

Kayden lifted his radio at the sound of Jake's voice. "Where was she?"

"She'd veered off path and ended up close to the eastern boundary, near the cliff edge."

Damn. "Is she okay?"

Wind sounded over the line before Jake answered. "A bit rattled but uninjured. I'll bring her back."

"Need backup?"

"Nah, I got it."

Kayden set his radio back in his holster. The fifteen-year-old tourist had been missing for a good hour after she'd split up from her family…too long.

He turned back toward the visitors center. It was only ten a.m., but he'd learned it was never too early for someone to get off track and need finding. That was the thing about being part of a SAR team, you could be called down here at any moment of any day, even on a day off.

Wind brushed across his face, his feet sinking into the path as he moved. After a heavy night of rainfall, the mountains were wet and cold. They were beautiful, but if you weren't familiar with them and got lost for too long, they wouldn't be kind, especially considering some of the steep declines in the area.

He sped up his steps as a few drops of water fell onto his shoulders. He didn't mind the wet and cold though. In fact, often he welcomed it. It kept him alert.

When he entered the visitors center, Pixie was stepping out of the eco room, her mouth spreading into a wide smile as she lowered behind her desk. "Hey, Kayden. I heard you guys found the girl who went off-trail."

"Jake did. He's bringing her back now. Are her parents in the café?"

"Yeah, they're waiting for her. Elle made them coffees, but I doubt they've touched them. They're pretty anxious."

"Understandable. Can you make sure she has some water and dry towels waiting?"

"Of course." She moved out to the deck.

The office door was ajar. He placed his hand on the wood and was about to push inside when he stopped and cursed under his breath. Goddammit, how did he keep forgetting? It wasn't Linda's office anymore. In fact, she was far away on her around-the-world cruise. He couldn't just enter whenever he wanted.

"Really? No appointments until next week?" Tilly's hushed

voice just reached his ears. "Okay, yeah, that will have to do then. Um, maybe I can leave my number in case you have a cancellation before then?"

Kayden was about to go when he heard Tilly hang up. He knocked, and there was a brief pause before she spoke.

"Come in."

He pushed the door open to see Tilly sitting at her desk, seat turned toward him. "Hey, Kayden." Her voice didn't have its usual ring, and dark circles shadowed her eyes.

"Hey, do you have next month's schedule for our team tours?"

"I do. I just finished it last night." She swiveled her seat back toward her screen and tapped a few keys. When she moved her arm to use the mouse, he noticed she flinched, and her movement was almost rigid.

"I tried to accommodate what everyone requested, but if anything needs changing, just let me know." She hit print, but when she went to reach for the sheet, she gasped and tugged her arm back.

He frowned and shot forward. "Hey. You okay?"

Her breaths were loud as she cradled her arm. "Yeah, I just…I had a small fall this morning and hurt my shoulder."

"How bad is it?"

"I'm not sure. I can't seem to get a doctor's appointment."

That's who she was on the phone with as he'd walked in. "Can I have a look at it?"

Her brows rose as she stared at him from where she sat. "You want to look at my shoulder?"

"I'm not a doctor, but I know more than basic first aid and have provided medical attention to quite a few people in my time before getting them to emergency services." Understatement of the century. In his line of work, a lot of people needed emergency medical care right away.

"Um…okay, sure."

He crouched in front of her chair and touched her shoulder.

She flinched, but he wasn't sure if that was more because she'd *expected* pain than because he'd actually caused it. Tentatively, he touched around the joint, taking note of which areas and movements seemed to incite pain.

"You said you fell?"

She nodded. "Yeah, off my coffee table."

What the hell? "What were you doing on your coffee table?"

"I was…looking at something."

There was definitely a story there, but she didn't want to share. Did it have anything to do with the circles shadowing her eyes? "Did you get any tingling or numbness when you fell?"

"No. Just pain to the shoulder. It's a dull ache until I extend my arm, then it becomes a sharp pain." She looked at him. "Do you know what it might be?"

"I don't think you've fractured or dislocated anything, because you can still move it. You may have a small rotator cuff tear."

"That sounds bad."

He was so close that her warm breath brushed his face on every word, and for some damn reason, it sent his blood raging through his veins. "Not if it's minor. It should heal on its own. You'll know within a week because it will start feeling better, but I wouldn't be lifting anything heavy."

Even after his examination, his hands remained on her shoulder as he massaged out some of the tension. At her groan, his own muscles tensed. Because that sound…it seeped inside him and did something to his chest.

"My shoulder has been killing me all morning, but when you touch it, it almost feels good."

"I'm glad I can help." He tilted his head. "Other than the shoulder, are you doing okay?" Memories of that asshole bumping into her a few nights ago flashed through his mind. Of her words about how speaking up makes it worse.

Her gaze clashed with his, a million different emotions

running through it, but none of which he could name. "Why do you ask?"

"You look tired."

"I did this at three thirty this morning and couldn't get back to sleep."

"Why were you up at three thirty this morning?"

She opened and closed her mouth. "Just a small leak issue."

"Anything I can help with?"

Something that looked like hope lit her eyes, and for a moment he thought she might say yes. Then a knock sounded at the door.

"Hey, is Kayden in—" Pixie stopped, eyes widening as she took in the two of them. "Oh…sorry. Am I interrupting something?"

Kayden rose to his feet and opened his mouth to respond, but Tilly spoke first. "No, Pixie, you're not. What can I help you with?"

Her gaze shifted between them before settling back on him. "I just wanted to let Kayden know that everything's ready for the girl's return."

Kayden dipped his head. "Great."

She focused on Tilly. "I also need some help with the new system, if that's okay, Tilly?"

"Of course." Tilly rose from her seat. "Thank you, Kayden. I really appreciate your help."

She gave him one final smile before disappearing out of the office…and Kayden was left wondering why the hell he felt disappointed to not be touching her anymore.

CHAPTER 5

Cool air whipped across Tilly's skin as she walked through the mountains, her feet sinking into the wet dirt on each step. Often, she liked to jog, but with her still injured shoulder, a power walk it was.

Man, it was beautiful out here. If there was one place that could bring her peace when peace was the last thing she should feel, it was the Smoky Mountains. The smell of the cool, fresh air, the mist on cold mornings that made the paths look almost magical.

When she was little, she'd pretended the mist was clouds and she was in the sky. Her mother, of course, had gone along with it, like every other game. She'd always made Tilly feel like she was the most important person in the world. Like everything about her was just the way it was supposed to be.

For a while, she'd thought that was the case for every child. That every mother treated their daughter like she was the center of their universe. It was only as she'd gotten older and noticed parents only half listening to their kids and barely making eye contact that she'd realized it wasn't always the case.

Yeah, she was lucky. Or at least…had been lucky.

Her heart clenched and she sped up her steps. There were mountains around her house, but the paths weren't as well maintained as they were here near the visitor's center.

A week had passed since she'd hurt her shoulder, and she finally felt like she could move again without aching pain.

Kayden's beautiful blue eyes flashed in her head and she almost stumbled. The way he'd touched her, soothed her pain…it had felt so much better than it probably should have. Since then, he'd checked in on her here and there, but she still felt the invisible wall between them. In the way his eyes shuttered and the emotions blanked from his face.

And she knew why.

Kayden's father had been one of the most loved members of this town…and her father had betrayed him. Taken all his savings and run.

She pressed a hand to her chest, as if that could somehow alleviate the tightness. It wasn't her betrayal, yet sometimes she suspected he blamed her. He'd defended her at the bar and checked on her shoulder at work, but that was probably just because he was a good person. He loved his family. Protected them at all costs. And her family had hurt his.

Did he need her to tell him that she hadn't seen her father since he'd left this town? That a part of her was happy about that, because she wanted nothing to do with him, yet there was also this other part of her that wanted answers? Wanted to know if the money was worth everything it had cost him?

She sucked in a sharp breath as she rounded a bend, almost walking straight into a large chest. She gasped and grabbed onto his arms to stop herself from falling.

Jake grabbed her hips to steady her. "Whoa, Tilly! Sorry, I almost ran into you there."

Air whipped through her lungs. "I guess we both had the same idea this morning—a walk through the mountains before work."

Well, hers was a walk. Jake had clearly been running.

"On a beautiful morning like this, why wouldn't we take advantage? I've got to tell you though, I'm not used to all the rain and cold."

She set her hands on her hips as he stepped back. "Where are you from again?"

"Arizona."

"What made you come over here?"

"Saw the job advertised and needed a change. I'm just lucky Kayden and Linda hired me."

She smiled at him. "They must have seen something in you."

"The desperation in my eyes?"

She laughed. She liked Jake. He was funny, easy to talk to, and she never felt like she was battling the ghost of her father with him.

"Hey, how's your shoulder?" he asked.

Somehow, word had gotten around that she'd hurt herself. Well, not somehow…Pixie. The woman liked to gossip.

"It's good, actually. A lot better than it was, which is lucky, because getting in to see a doctor proved harder than I'd thought."

She tried to tell herself it was just because they were busy and had nothing to do with who she was or who her father was, but there was a small whisper in her head that questioned if that was true. In the end, she hadn't seen anyone, because the lady who worked at the desk in the practice had rescheduled her appointment twice, so she'd just told them not to worry about it.

"I'm glad. I was a bit jealous when I heard Kayden got to be your knight in shining armor. If you ever need another, don't hesitate to shout out."

Was he flirting with her? It kind of felt like it, but then, she was pretty out of practice, so she couldn't be certain.

Jake's gaze rose above her head. "And be careful in these

mountains by yourself… After what happened to Macy, we all need to be on alert."

"Thanks, I will." Although, she doubted anything would happen in the light of day, particularly when Macy seemed to have interrupted a robbery gone wrong.

He winked before jogging around her.

She moved forward again, but this time at a slower pace. She'd just reached the deck when the door opened, and Hendrix and Theo stepped out.

A tightness formed in her chest, but she ignored it, offering them both a smile. "Hey, guys."

Hendrix dipped his head, while Theo just glanced at her and looked away. They didn't even try to hide their dislike for her, especially Theo. Was it so hard to give a small hello to a colleague?

With a sigh, she stepped in to see Pixie behind the desk.

The woman rose to her feet. "Hey, I'm glad you're here."

Well, at least someone was.

"Can you cover the desk for me while I grab a coffee?" Pixie continued. "I am dying of caffeine withdrawal right now."

Tilly glanced down at her active wear. She'd been planning to change before starting her day, but she'd still have time for that later. "Sure."

"You're a lifesaver. An electrician should be here any minute to do some work in the café."

"Got it."

Pixie headed out, and Tilly was about to round the desk when the door to the parking lot opened, and an older man walked in. The second his eyes fell on her, they narrowed.

"Matilda Taylor. I heard you got a job here."

She swallowed, forcing her spine to straighten despite the flicker of nerves trickling through her at the disdain in the man's eyes. "I go by Tilly, and yes, I'm the office manager. How can I help you?"

He laughed, but there wasn't any humor in the sound. "Help me like your dad helped me?"

Tilly's stomach dropped, but she was careful to keep her unease off her face. She opened her mouth, but the man spoke first.

"You shouldn't even be here," he growled, stepping toward her. "Why did you come back? To remind everyone what we lost five years ago?"

She took an involuntary step back, hating the way the guy closed the distance between them so quickly. "Sir, if there's nothing I can help you with, then I need to ask you to leave."

Another humorless laugh. "Ask *me* to leave? The entire damn town is *screaming* for you to be gone, yet you don't seem to be going anywhere."

He'd closed a bit more of the space between them when the door behind her opened. She turned her head to see Kayden in the doorway, gaze assessing as he glanced between them.

"Harry," Kayden said almost too quietly, brows knitted together. "What's going on here?"

"I was called in to take a look at an electrical fault in the café. Didn't realize I'd be running into Taylor's kid." When he looked at her again, there was so much hate in his eyes that she couldn't stop the shudder from rolling down her spine.

* * *

Every protective instinct in Kayden shot to life at the way Harry Jacobs looked at Tilly—with the threat of violence in his eyes. Like he wouldn't hesitate to show her just how much he disliked her.

He moved to Tilly's side, almost touching her, needing to be close.

"You know where the café is, but I'll still walk you," Kayden said carefully, ignoring Harry's words and the way he referred to Tilly as "Taylor's kid."

Everyone in town knew Harry's hatred for Martin Taylor was strong—five years later and he still talked about it enough around town. And Kayden did not want that hatred to spill over into violence toward Tilly. Not in his visitors center. Not anywhere.

Harry's hands fisted and he didn't move, his eyes remaining on Tilly.

"*Harry.*" At Kayden's firm, raised voice, Harry finally shifted his attention to him. "You gonna come fix that electrical fault in the café, or do I need to call someone else?"

A muscle in the electrician's cheek ticked. "I'm coming."

Kayden made sure to remain between him and Tilly as Harry made his way toward the door. He waited until they were on the deck, halfway to the café, to grab Harry's arm and pull him to a stop.

"What the hell was that?"

Anger scowled the man's face. "How can you ask me that? You know what her father did to me. What he did to *your* father too!"

"You were scaring her, and you know it."

"Why the hell do you care?"

Fury filled Kayden's veins. If the guy didn't know the answer to that, then he was stupider than he looked. No man had the right to make a woman feel physically threatened, and Harry had definitely used his height and breadth to do exactly that.

"You know what? I don't think this job's a good fit for you. You can go."

"Are you kidding me?" Harry spluttered. "You're sending me away for a *Taylor*?" He said Tilly's last name like it was acid on his tongue.

"I'm sending you away because you made a staff member feel unsafe, and that's unacceptable."

"You know what? Fuck you, Kayden! You don't want me doing this job, then I don't want to fucking be here."

He stormed back toward the visitors center and Kayden followed, sticking close. When he passed the front desk that Tilly was now sitting behind, Kayden inched that bit closer, in case he tried anything. Thankfully, he didn't so much as look at her as he crashed out into the parking lot.

Kayden's muscles remained tight, and it took him a moment to turn and look at Tilly. She was on her feet again, gaze shifting between the door and back to him.

"He's not doing the work?" she finally asked, breaking the silence.

"No. I'll call someone else."

"I can do it—"

"No." Kayden's quick response made something he couldn't name cross over Tilly's face. "I'll call in a favor."

She nodded.

"And Tilly, maybe it would be better if you didn't work at the front desk."

Immediately, he wanted to take the words back, because even though it was clear she tried to keep her features neutral, he saw that flicker of pain deepen on her expressive face before she quietly said, "Good idea."

Fuck. He was wording it all wrong. He stepped toward her, but the door opened and Pixie stepped in, coffee in hand.

"Sorry I took so long. I got stuck telling Elle about my epic weekend and I forgot the time." Pixie stopped, a frown creasing her brow as her gaze shifted between them. "Is everything okay?"

Tilly nodded. "Yes, everything's absolutely fine."

"Harry didn't show up?"

Kayden shoved a hand into his pocket. "He had to leave. I'll get someone else."

"Leave?" Pixie asked, brows raised. "Elle said the work's pretty urgent."

Tilly's frown deepened, and he could just about see her blaming herself for this. It wasn't her fault. Harry was an asshole, and Kayden would be making sure he never stepped foot in this place again.

"I'll fix it," Kayden said, turning and leaving, the sadness on Tilly's face roiling in his gut.

CHAPTER 6

Tilly's gaze shifted to the clock for what had to be the hundredth time. She was so ready for this awful day to be over. Past ready. She'd been feeling so good after her walk through the mountains, the best she'd felt in a while. But then Harry had stepped in, and she hadn't been able to get his visit out of her head. The hatred in his eyes. The way he'd closed in on her like she was a bug he needed to squash.

You'd think that would be the worst her day could get, but nope, Kayden's words after that had pretty much been the icing on the cake...

Maybe it would be better if you didn't work at the front desk.

She massaged her temple, that whispered voice in her head returning to her, reminding her that she wasn't welcome here. That maybe it had been a mistake to return. Maybe she should have just stayed in Cleveland and sold her mother's house here.

The idea of selling that house though, of never returning to these mountains...it hurt. Made an ache beat through her chest and press down on her.

"Hey."

Her head shot up at Elle's voice from the doorway. "Elle. Hey. Everything all right?"

"Yeah, café's closed and I'm just heading out. I noticed your light on and thought I'd come in and check that you were okay. I heard Harry wasn't that great to you."

Had Kayden told her? It didn't matter. "I'm fine. But I am very excited to get into bed, eat a bucketload of chocolate chip ice cream, and say goodbye to this day."

Sympathy darkened the woman's eyes. "I'm sorry some people are so awful. If you ever need a friend to eat that ice cream with you, I have a massive sweet tooth and am great at trash-talking closed-minded townspeople."

Despite everything, Tilly laughed. "Thank you. I'll keep that in mind. Did the other electrician come out?"

There was a small grimace from the other woman. "No. Hopefully tomorrow."

Tilly swallowed the guilt. "I'm—"

"Don't say sorry. Not your fault." She gave her a smile. "Have a good night, Tilly."

With a sigh, she turned off her computer and packed her bag, then switched off all the lights and headed outside to lock up. The light trickle of rain fell on her shoulders as she dipped her chin and jogged to her car. She was just about to unlock the doors when a text message came through on her phone.

Got your message, Matilda. Unfortunately, we have no availability to come out to your place and fix the leak at the moment. Nick.

That was another contractor who was "unavailable to help." No explanation why. No possibility of future availability.

And this goddamn rain was never-ending. At this rate, she'd just have a permanent bucket in her living room...a bucket that kept overflowing and spilling onto her rug.

Gritting her teeth, she opened her car door and dropped behind the wheel. She'd just slipped the key into the ignition and turned it when...nothing happened. The car didn't start.

What the hell?

She tried again—same result.

Really? Now her car was giving her trouble? It wasn't enough that everyone in this goddamn town hated her, her house was falling apart, and no one would help her...now her *car* had to betray her too?

Suddenly, everything felt like too much, and even though she hated crying, hated anything that made her feel weak, tears she couldn't stop pressed at her eyes, and for once, she couldn't blink them away. She dropped her head to the wheel and let the tears fall.

She kept telling herself life here would get better, things would get easier. But when? When would anything feel like she wasn't fighting an uphill battle?

She scrunched her eyes closed, the tightness in her chest making her breaths come out short and choppy. She should be stronger than this, right? All the unkind comments and looks should be like water off her back. But the thing was, she was still mourning the loss of her mother, still trying to find her place in the world without her best friend, and it all felt so freaking hard.

The knock at the window had her shooting upright.

Kayden.

He stood on the other side of the glass, his brows tugged together, not seeming to notice the water falling on his head and shoulders. She'd thought he'd left already.

Oh, God, and now he was seeing her sitting in her car crying.

Quickly, she scrubbed the tears from her face, undid her seat belt, and climbed out.

"Are you okay?" His deep, raspy voice slid through her veins, warming some of the cold that had taken root inside her.

"My car won't start." It sounded as pathetic a thing to be crying about as it actually was.

His gaze shifted to her car, then back to her. The intensity in his eyes...it almost felt like he could see everything she wasn't saying. That this wasn't just about the car. This was the accumulation of all the little things that had built up since she'd arrived in Misty Peak. This was the last drop in her personal ocean.

He tilted his head toward his truck. "Come on, I'll give you a ride home."

"But what about my car?"

"Give me your key and I'll take care of it."

Her brows shot up. "Really?"

"Really."

A part of her wanted to say no. That it wasn't his responsibility, and he shouldn't have to go out of his way to help her out of pity. But standing here in the rain, while it felt like the entire world's problems beat down on her, she suddenly *wanted* him to help her. Was almost desperate for *anyone* to help.

She pulled the car key off the chain and handed it to him, and despite everything, just the small brush of his skin against hers sent awareness running up her arm.

He pocketed the key before placing a hand on the small of her back and leading her toward his truck. His hand was so big, his fingers took up almost the entire width of her back.

The second she slipped into the passenger seat, all she wanted to do was close her eyes and let the exhaustion of the day weigh her down.

Maybe Kayden felt that, because he was silent for most of the drive, just letting her sit and watch the rain hit the windshield in repeated splatters. He didn't even ask for directions to her house. Maybe the entire town already knew where the infamous Taylor family had lived.

"You doing okay over there?" he finally asked, his voice cutting through the quiet.

She turned her head to look at him. His fingers wrapped tightly around the wheel, the veins standing out on his hands. The man was all strength. "Not really. I didn't think coming back here would be easy, but I also didn't think it would be quite so hard."

"Why'd you come then?"

There was no malice in his question, just genuine interest. "Because this is home. This is where my mother raised me. Where most of my memories with her live. And she always wanted to come back, but she couldn't. So I'm doing it for her."

"Why can't she come back?"

Tilly brushed her fingers over a crease in her pants. "She died a few months ago. An aggressive form of brain cancer."

Kayden's jaw visibly tightened. "Shit, Tilly. I'm sorry."

"Me too."

* * *

KAYDEN'S HAND twitched to reach across and touch Tilly. Her hand. Her thigh. Offer her some form of comfort, not just at the news that her mother had passed but also her admission that coming home had been so hard.

The sadness in her eyes when she'd looked up from behind the wheel…fuck, it had gutted him.

"I know what you mean about these mountains being home," he said quietly, feeling her eyes on him from the passenger seat. "Even while I was away serving, every time I came back here, it was like this weight was lifted off my chest. A weight I didn't even realize I was carrying until it was gone."

"My mom used to call it magic."

"She wasn't wrong."

"Do you miss it? Serving? You were in the Air Force, right?"

"Yeah, I was." *Did* he miss it? It wasn't something anyone had asked him since he got out. "I guess some days I do. I miss the guys and the banter and the hit of adrenaline from extracting someone from a dangerous situation. But I don't regret leaving. I got out six months before Dad died, and I wouldn't take back that time for anything."

"I'm sorry about your dad. He was a good man."

Kayden took his eyes off the road to look at her, and something in his chest shifted. Because she understood. She knew the pain of losing a parent. It was incomparable to anything else, and that hole was never filled, it was just an empty space inside him that he had to learn to live with.

"He *was* a good man," Kayden said quietly. "And not a day goes by where he isn't missed." He cleared his throat. "Turner Court, right?"

"Turner Court."

They were quiet for the rest of the drive. When he pulled into her drive, his fingers tightened on the wheel at how isolated the property was. Too isolated for a single woman, especially one who was so disliked in this town.

Then he saw the house…

"Why are your windows boarded up?"

"The glass was already broken when I got back to town," she said, exhaustion slipping into her voice as she released her seat belt. "I guess people broke in at some point over the five years the house was empty. Possibly more than once. It's not surprising."

"But you've been here for months. Why are they still broken?"

When the silence stretched, Harry's reaction to her flashed in his mind—and suddenly he knew.

He pulled the car to a stop in front of the house, trying like hell to get ahold of his anger. "No one will come."

"Unfortunately, the second they hear my address or last name, they don't want anything to do with me."

Assholes.

"Come on, I'll walk you in." The words came out harsher than he'd intended, but fuck, he was mad.

He circled the car to her side and touched a hand to her back as they jogged through the rain. The wooden stairs of the porch creaked beneath his feet.

Tilly unlocked her door and turned. "Thank you for driving me home."

"I'm not done here, Matilda. I want to see the boarded-over windows."

"It's Tilly. And you don't need—"

"I do."

For a moment, she looked like she was going to argue, but she must have realized that he wasn't going anywhere, because she sighed and stepped inside. "Okay."

He followed her into the living room, noticing that she turned on the hall light, then the kitchen, avoiding the living room overhead fixture. "Something wrong with the living room light?" His gaze shifted to the bucket on her coffee table.

"There's a leak, and until it's fixed, I don't feel comfortable using it," she said quietly. "I tried to get a better look but had a little...accident."

An accident? "The fall and the injured shoulder..."

It wasn't a question, but if it was, he'd have his answer just by the expression on her face.

Dammit, that had been a week ago.

He moved over to the window, his gut twisting at seeing the flimsy wood that had been nailed over the frame and was barely hanging on.

Tilly's throat cleared behind him. "I'm, uh, not great with that kind of work, but I did my best."

Not only was her house ridiculously easy to break into but it was damn cold, everything outside getting in. "Your heat doesn't work."

Again, it wasn't a question, but she answered. "It doesn't."

Another ripple of anger. He knelt down, noting the wet wood below the window. Suddenly, he wanted to hurt every asshole who'd let her down. Everyone who could have come and made sure her home was sealed and warm and safe but hadn't.

"I want to know the name of every contractor you called." He rose and turned to look at her, only to see her eyes wide.

"Kayden, I—"

"I'm not going to do anything to them, just make sure I don't use them in the future and spread word in town for others to do the same. I'll also call around and find someone to fix these problems."

She was shaking her head before he'd finished speaking. "That's really kind of you, but it's not your problem. It's mine. You've already helped me tonight with driving me home and offering to find someone to fix my car. I can't—"

"You *can*. And you will. I'm not giving you any other option."

Her brows flickered like she didn't understand. And maybe that was his fault, for being an asshole at the beginning. He stepped closer, and like it had a mind of its own, his hand went to her cheek. God, her skin was soft. So soft, it felt like velvet.

He lowered his voice. "Let me help you, Tilly."

Her mouth opened and closed before she whispered, "Why?"

"Because you need help, and because I can."

Something flashed in her eyes. Disappointment, maybe? Had she wanted a different answer?

The emotion cleared quickly. "I don't think anyone will come when they learn who I am."

"Let me deal with that. I always follow through on my promises, and I promise you, I will get the windows, the heat, and the leak fixed. And tonight, I'm also going to get a tarp and sturdier boards to make sure the rain doesn't get in for the rest of the night."

Her breath audibly stuttered, and it took a few beats for him to realize that his hand was still on her cheek. That the heat of her skin was flowing into him. And that he wanted to do more.

To graze his thumb behind her ear. To dip his head and see if her lips were as sweet as her scent.

Fuck.

He stepped away, his hand dropping. "I'll be back in under an hour to seal the window. I'll also let you know about your car and get onto everything else right away."

He turned and left before he did something stupid. Like touch her a second time. Kiss her.

He barely felt the rain beat down on his shoulders as he returned to his truck. The second he was behind the wheel, he leaned his head back and closed his eyes, two images competing in his head—Tilly's sad green eyes as she looked up at him from the driver's seat of the car, like she had the entire world against her…and another image, this time of his father, when he'd told them what Martin had done.

He didn't want to be another asshole who blamed Tilly for her father's wrongdoings, but trust was hard for him, and every so often, the memory beat into him, telling him not to get too close.

CHAPTER 7

"*I*'m sorry to hear about how you were treated by Harry."

Tilly paused in lifting her iced coffee to her mouth, her gaze flicking to Harper, who sat opposite her at Sugar and Spice. "How do you know about that?"

"Word travels fast. I think Harry was complaining to a few people, and Pixie mentioned what she'd stepped into. The story took off from there."

Great. These incidents were becoming newsworthy around town now.

Sugar and Spice always lifted her mood. Mrs. Sandler owned and ran the shop and sold the most delicious cupcakes and sweets. She also served amazing iced coffee. It was exactly what Tilly needed, especially after the look on Kayden's face last night when he'd seen her house.

"It's true. He was an asshole to me, and although Kayden didn't tell me exactly what transpired between them when they stepped out onto the deck, I *do* know it was unfriendly enough for Kayden to ask him to leave."

"Good. I've only met Harry a couple of times when he's come

into the bar, but if he can't be nice to you, he *should* lose business." Harper tilted her head. "How's everything else been?"

Did she really want to know? "Honestly? Not great. Kayden kind of found me in my car crying after work yesterday."

"What? Why? Were you okay?"

"My car wouldn't start, and after Harry and the long day"—long *days*—"I broke down."

"Tilly…you should have called."

"I didn't have a chance because Kayden knocked on my window and offered to both drive me home and make sure my car got fixed. And sure enough, I woke up this morning with a text from him saying the car was out front of my house, ready to drive. And not only that, he said a contractor was coming to look at the leak in my living room, and someone else is coming tomorrow for the heating system." And that was after he'd returned last night and boarded over the broken windows properly.

"You had a leak in your living room and your heat doesn't work?"

"I have quite a few things that need fixing in my house." She sighed before listing off everything that was wrong with her place and explaining her continued problems with contractors.

"I wish you'd said something so I could have tried to help you."

"You've been through so much since arriving in town—"

"That doesn't matter," Harper interrupted. "We're friends, and God knows I've unloaded on you enough. I feel like I've been a terrible friend."

"Oh my gosh, Harper, you've been amazing. You were my first friend and, most days, my only friend. You're probably the only person who's kept me sane. Even on that first night when I came to the bar and was upset about my first day in town, you were so kind when no one else was, and that was everything."

Harper squeezed her hand. "Still, I want you to tell me what's going on with you. We're friends, and I want to hear the good and the bad."

"Deal." Her phone vibrated from the table, and immediately her skin tingled when she saw who it was.

Kayden: Window guys can come tomorrow morning before work to measure. Is that okay?

How on earth had he managed that? Did these window guys know who she was?

Tilly: That works great. Are they local?

Kayden: They are. But they'll be good to you.

For some reason, those simple words calmed her, making it that much easier for her to breathe.

"Is that Kayden?"

She glanced up to see Harper looking at her with a knowing smile on her face. She didn't have a chance to respond though, because the doors to the shop opened and three guys walked in— Theo, Hendrix, and Jake. Jake smiled the second he saw her, while the other two didn't even look her way.

"You know him?" Harper asked, voice hushed.

"I know all three of them. They work on Kayden's SAR team and do tours in the mountains."

Jake crossed to their table. "Hey."

Tilly rose to greet him. "Hey, Jake. How are you?"

"Oh, you know, enjoying a rare day off. Couldn't not give Sugar and Spice a visit. You?"

"Well, I'm always here when I have a spare moment, so if you come often on our days off, you'll likely find me. By the way, this is my friend, Harper."

He dipped his head at Harper. "It's nice to meet you."

"You too."

He looked back at Tilly, one side of his mouth lifting. "So if you're here often, that's more incentive for me to be here."

Okay, *that* was definitely flirting, right? "You should come for the cupcakes and iced coffees. They're amazing. Oh, and try the chocolate chip cookies, you won't regret it. It was nice to see you, Jake." She was about to sit again when he touched her arm.

"Hey, as someone who grew up in this town, I was wondering if you could show me the ropes of the Sunday market?"

Was that a date? No...just a friend showing another friend around, surely. "You want to go to the market together?"

"Yeah, if that's okay?"

She opened and closed her mouth. "I'm not sure, Jake…"

He chuckled. "Come on, one friend helping another friend out. Please, take pity on this poor newcomer."

Friend… "Um…okay, that sounds good."

"Great, you've just made my day. If you give me your phone, I'll put my number in and we can arrange a meet-up time."

She lifted her phone from the table and had just handed it to him as the door to the shop opened and a young girl walked in, closely followed by Kayden.

⅄ ⅄ ⅄

"Uncle Kay, do you think Daddy will get me a snake when I turn nine?"

Kayden smirked at his eight-year-old niece's question. He was taking her to Sugar and Spice to get her favorite cookie before Eastern finished at the sheriff's station. He wasn't a big "kid" person himself; in fact, he didn't see himself wanting kids in the future. But he could never get sick of Avery. She was both cute and smart, two things he liked to joke that his younger sheriff brother was not.

"I don't know. Your father has a bit of a fear of snakes."

She frowned. "I thought he wasn't scared of anything."

Kayden scoffed. "He tell you that?"

"No. But he was a SEAL and everyone at school says SEALs aren't scared of anything."

"Everyone's scared of something, Ave, even the biggest, toughest-looking people. But fear's not always a bad thing."

"I hate being scared."

"Fear can protect us from dangerous situations."

Her nose scrunched like she was thinking about that. "Like when I want to break a rule but I'm too scared, so I don't?"

"Yeah, like that."

She kicked a rock. "Jasmine, a girl at school, said that maybe my mom left because she was scared."

What the fuck?

Avery's mother had skipped town a few months ago without saying goodbye to her daughter or giving anyone, including Eastern, a reason. Even Kayden would like to know why the woman left.

"Regardless of why she isn't here, you'll always have your dad. He isn't going anywhere. And neither am I or Cody."

A small smile stretched her lips. "Jasmine also says I have a cute dad and uncles."

Kayden wasn't sure what he thought about being called *cute* by an eight-year-old girl. "And what did you say?"

"I told her that was disgusting."

He threw his head back and laughed as they reached the door to Sugar and Spice. "Come on, you, let's get that cookie before your dad finishes and tells us no."

The smile disappeared from his face when he stepped inside to see Jake and Tilly across the room. They stood close, and he was handing her a phone.

Avery released his hand and ran around the tables to Harper, giving her a hug. He'd just started moving to follow Avery as Jake returned to Theo and Hendrix, dipping his head at Kayden as he reached the counter.

Avery spoke to Harper at a million miles a minute, while Kayden turned to Tilly, who was still on her feet. "Hey."

The smile she gave him was soft. "Hey. Thank you so much

for getting my car fixed and back to me. And for everything last night. I don't know how you've gotten those contractors to agree to help me, but I'm so grateful. Words can't even say what that means to me."

One look at her tearstained face last night and he would have moved heaven and earth to make sure she was okay.

"It wasn't any trouble." Not true. The second the local mechanic, Ted, had heard who the favor was for, he'd been hesitant. That was until Kayden had pushed that she was a single woman living in a mountainous town and needed a safe car to drive that Ted had conceded.

"Still, thank you." She touched his arm, and goddammit, he felt that touch everywhere. "How much do I owe you for the car repair?"

"I called in a favor. You're fine."

She shook her head. "Kayden, I need to pay for the work."

"When you see Ted around town, just thank him."

She pulled back. "Ted?"

Yeah, everyone knew him. He'd been another victim of her father—exactly why he hadn't wanted to help. Fortunately, his conscience had gotten the better of him.

She wet her lips. "Okay, well, thanks again. And for everything else."

"Your home, at the bare minimum, should be sealed, Tilly."

The relief on her face gutted him. It was so distinct, anyone would think he'd just offered her a kidney. "Thank you."

Harper rose to her feet. "Hey, Kayden. Sorry I can't stick around to chat. I have to get to the bar now."

"I'll walk you," Tilly said quickly.

"Before you go"—Kayden placed a hand on his niece's shoulder—"Tilly, this is my niece, Eastern's daughter, Avery. Avery, this is Tilly, who—"

"Works at the visitors center. I know. I saw her at Linda's retirement party. It's nice to meet you."

Tilly grinned. "Hi, Avery. It's nice to meet you too. What are you getting from Mrs. Sandler today?"

Avery's eyes lit up. "A double chocolate chip cookie. Daddy doesn't let me get them very much because the chocolate keeps me awake, but Uncle Kay said it was a treat."

Yeah, a treat Eastern would kill him for, but hell, sometimes you had to take the risk to be the favorite uncle.

Tilly's brows rose. "What a cool uncle you have. Well, I hope you both have a great day."

As she passed, he got a huge wave of her sweet scent, and it did nothing to ease the tightness of his muscles that only Tilly could elicit.

He cleared his throat. "Come on, Avery, let's order."

As he neared the counter, the guys from work stood a few feet away, their quiet words not quiet enough to slip past Kayden.

"Seriously, Jake? You're going out with her?"

What the hell? Were they talking about Tilly?

"Get off my back," Jake growled. "She's fine."

"Here you go, boys." Mrs. Sandler pushed their drinks across the counter.

Before stepping away, Jake looked up at Kayden. "Hey. See you at work."

He dipped his chin before stepping up to the counter. "Hey, Mrs. Sandler."

"Kayden, darling, it's so good to see you. And you too, Miss Avery. What can I get you both today?"

"Double chocolate chip cookie, please," Avery said quickly, as if by not saying it quickly enough, she wouldn't get her cookie.

Mrs. Sandler laughed. "Great choice. And you, Kayden?"

"Just a coffee, black, thanks."

The older woman nodded and was about to turn when Avery spoke. "Mrs. Sandler?"

"Yes, darling?"

"Have you spoken to Sadie lately?"

Sadie was Mrs. Sandler's granddaughter, and she had also been Avery's nanny, employed by her mother for most of Avery's life.

"Yes. Actually, I'm going to her wedding soon."

Avery's eyes lit up. "Can you tell her I said hi?"

"Of course."

"And maybe I can make her something too. She always liked the pictures I drew her."

Mrs. Sandler's eyes softened. "Whatever you make, I'll pass along and I'm sure she'll love it."

Kayden took Avery's hand. "Come on, let's grab a table."

They were just sitting when the door opened and Eastern walked in.

"Daddy!" Avery jumped to her feet and ran across the room, leaping into her dad's arms.

"Hey, Princess. You been good for Uncle Kay?"

"Yep. So good, he let me get a double chocolate chip cookie!"

Eastern groaned as he reached the table. "Double chocolate chip? Really?"

Kayden lifted a shoulder. "I'm trying to be the favorite. It's not easy with Cody breathing down my neck with his bar pretzels."

"I thought you'd still be a while?" Avery asked.

"Got off early and knew Uncle Kay was bringing you here, so I thought I'd join."

When Mrs. Sandler put the cookie on a plate, Avery ran to the counter.

Kayden took in the dark circles shadowing Eastern's eyes. "You okay, brother?"

"Yeah, I just haven't been sleeping well since we found Macy."

Kayden's hands fisted at the mention of the mountain stabbing. "Still no leads?"

"Nothing. No witnesses. No evidence left at the scene." He ran fingers through his hair, frustration brimming on his face.

"That's not the only thing bothering me, though… I spoke to Jamie last night."

Flickers of rage moved through Kayden at the mention of Avery's mother. "Is she coming back?"

"Nope. When she finally answered one of my calls, she said she'd be back *soon*…and her words were slurred."

Fuck.

Alcohol was a problem Eastern hadn't even realized Jamie had. He'd only learned about it after the woman had left, and Avery had told him how bad it had gotten.

Kayden hated that he hadn't been able to be a bigger part of his niece's life when he'd first returned to town, but Jamie had barely let him see her, and Eastern had still been in the Navy.

"She wanted to speak to Avery, and I told her to call back when she was sober," Eastern continued.

Kayden's back teeth ground together. "Good. Are you worried she'll come back and want Avery?"

"Yes. But everything's documented, included what Avery's said about her drinking and the reports from school, stating she often attended without lunch and in dirty clothes. I'm applying for full custody."

"Anything I can do to help, you let me know." His brother was an amazing father, and if anyone could give the kid everything she needed, it was him.

"Thanks." He scrubbed a hand over his face. "How are you? Doing okay with Matilda Taylor taking over as office manager at work?"

Was he doing okay with it? Hell no. "Yeah. It's fine."

Fine. What an understatement. It didn't even begin to describe how cradling her cheek last night had affected him. How every time he was around her, he felt something he absolutely should not be feeling…and how that scared the hell out of him.

CHAPTER 8

Tilly wrapped her jacket tightly around her waist as she walked down the path. She was late. Late to meet Jake at the Sunday Market because that damn car had thrown rotten eggs on her house *again*, and she'd spent close to an hour cleaning up the mess.

Argh.

And to make matters worse, she hadn't gotten there in time to get the license plate. She'd had enough. She'd even ordered security cameras, but the damn things hadn't arrived yet.

Where did they get off thinking they could harass her like this? What had she done to them? Not her father, *her*? She wanted to know what *she'd* done.

But then, she already knew the answer to that…nothing. Absolutely nothing.

Hurrying, she pulled her phone from her pocket.

Tilly: Sorry. There weren't any parking spots close by, so I ended up parking near the grocery store. Almost there.

She'd already messaged him that she was running late, the parking situation had just made her *more* late.

Her phone dinged with a text.

Jake: That's okay. I'm just out here losing my mind over all the delicious-smelling food. I'm very tempted by the strawberries with melted chocolate in cups.

She grinned. One of the local strawberry growers sold them. They were delicious, not only because the strawberries were super fresh but because the chocolate was such good quality. It made them as addictive as they sounded.

Tilly: Get a cup. They're amazing. I won't be long.

Well, she hoped she wouldn't be long. The market got busy early, so when she'd realized she wouldn't get there on time, she knew her only choice would be to park a bit farther away and walk.

Luckily, she had experience being late to this market because her mother had seldom been on time. But that meant they'd found a hidden parking spot years ago. It was a couple streets away in an alley near the grocery store.

She was about to round a corner when something rustled in the thick hedges beside her. What was that? Slowing her steps, she shifted her gaze to the bush, but there were no more sounds. Not only that, but she didn't see anything either.

Maybe it was the rustle of wind in the leaves.

She sped up her pace. She got about five steps away when it sounded again.

This time she stopped. "Hello? Is someone there?"

Even though silence followed, the fine hairs on her arms stood on end…because she didn't *feel* alone. Was that crazy?

Her gaze moved over not only the hedges but the trees behind them. Her heart had just started to pick up its rhythm when the phone in her hand rang, causing her to jump. She looked down to see a private number.

She touched the cell to her ear. "Hello?"

A buzzing sounded over the line, like there wasn't much signal.

She frowned. "Hello? Is anyone there?"

A deep voice sounded, but the static was so loud and repetitive, she couldn't make out a word they said.

"I'm sorry, I can't…it's a bad line. Maybe call back when it's better."

She hung up and turned—only to screech at the big body in front of her.

She pressed a hand to her chest. "Jake…oh, God, you scared me."

"Sorry. I came to look for you. Are you okay?"

"Yeah, I…" Her gaze lowered to her phone, then the hedges beside her. "I'm okay, just jumpy."

Jake lifted a cup of strawberries and chocolate. "Maybe these will help. I got two forks."

Her mouth watered at the sight of the chocolate-coated fruit. "Oh my gosh, you may have just turned my morning around."

She took a fork and dug it into a strawberry. One bite, and she had to hold in the groan. Christ, it was amazing. Anyone who didn't love chocolate-covered strawberries was crazy. They had to be, right?

"You didn't sound too happy on the phone when you called," Jake said softly as they started walking toward the market. "Everything okay?"

She cringed. She'd called and basically word vomited that she'd be late getting to the market. When he'd asked if everything was all right, she'd given him a firm no without actually telling him why.

"Not really. An hour ago, I was in the middle of a pretty epic breakdown." When he just frowned at her, she lifted a shoulder. "Someone egged my house."

"What the hell?"

She took another bite of the strawberry, the sweetness softening the blow of recalling her morning. "Yep. A pretty crappy thing to do. But it's nothing I can't handle. I got it cleaned up."

"Did you report the incident to the sheriff's office?"

"No, I didn't get the plates, but if they do it again, I will." But even then, what would the officers do? Give the jerks a warning? And if they denied wrongdoing, it would be her word against theirs. Exactly why she needed those security cameras.

"Good," Jake said firmly. "People who do shit things like that need consequences."

"I couldn't agree more." The only thing she was worried about was the possibility of escalation. But this was twice now that they'd egged her house, and she couldn't do *nothing*.

They turned the corner and the market came into view. Immediately, a smile curved her lips. Because this was familiar. This was home.

She looked up at Jake. "Did you explore much without me?"

"A little bit. I felt a bit like a deer in headlights though. This place is huge."

She chuckled. "It is, and everything sold here is great."

"I'm excited for a tour from a local. Have you come here much since getting back to Misty Peak?"

"A couple of times. And pretty much everything is exactly as it was, bar a few new stalls. That's the thing about Misty Peak—not much changes." Even the town's dislike for her. At least the strawberries were still good.

She forked another and took a bite.

"So, what's the best thing here then?" Jake asked.

"Depends on what you like. There are fresh fruit and vegetable stalls from local farmers. Homemade items like knitted clothes and wooden birdhouses and ornaments. There's hot food. Sweets."

"You had me at sweets."

She laughed. "We're obviously cut from the same cloth."

He grinned, then stopped walking when his gaze fell on her cheek. "You have chocolate on your face."

Dammit. She scrubbed at her cheek, but his grin just widened.

"Here, I've got you." He reached out and wiped the chocolate off with the pad of his thumb.

For some reason, the second he touched her, her mind went to someone else. Kayden. Because when Kayden touched her, she felt it everywhere. Her skin, her bones...even the roar of her blood in her veins.

But with Jake, there was nothing.

* * *

KAYDEN'S FINGERS tightened around his coffee cup at the sight of Jake touching Tilly's face. At the way he stood so close to her. And how he looked at her like she was the damn center of his world.

What was it with the guy always being around her?

"Watch out, brother, you're about to wear your coffee."

He forced himself to turn away. Cody had his arm around Harper's waist, and she was watching the way he stared at her friend far too closely.

Shit.

He forced his hold on the coffee to loosen. "I don't know what you're talking about."

"Really?" Eastern mocked. "Because it looked like you were staring at the exchange between Tilly and your fellow team member in a less than favorable way."

Avery tugged on his jeans. "Uncle Kay, do you like Tilly like Uncle Cody likes Harper?"

A few muffled laughs sounded around him.

He forced his features to soften as he looked down at his niece. "No, Ave, she's just a colleague."

"So he says."

The murmured words had barely left Cody's lips when Kayden punched him in the shoulder.

His brother immediately grabbed his arm. "Hey. You'll bruise me."

"That's the point."

He looked back to where Tilly and Jake had been standing, but they were both gone. Why the hell did that annoy him so much? But then, everything seemed to annoy him lately.

He scrubbed a hand over his face. "Come on, let's go find those egg and bacon bagels before I murder one of you guys."

"Why do egg and bacon bagels stop you from murdering people?" Avery asked.

God, it was too early in the morning for logical questions from eight-year-olds.

Harper took her hand. "Because when we're hungry, we don't think properly, and we don't make great decisions."

Kayden was tempted to tell them that killing his brothers might be the best decision he ever made, but maybe that was too much honesty for a Sunday morning.

They were almost at the bagel stand when Theo walked past. He dipped his head, but there was something in the other man's gaze that was less than friendly. The guy had been an ass ever since Kayden had given him a warning for showing up to work hungover. Not in any overly obvious way, because that would just give Kayden cause to fire him. But in little ways. Barely acknowledging directions. Avoiding eye contact, evasive body language.

"Things still tense between you and Theo?" Cody asked as he stepped beside Kayden.

"He's been an immature prick."

Cody raised a brow. "Tell me what you really think."

"I'm just waiting for him to fuck up so I can get rid of him."

Eastern narrowed his eyes on Kayden, no doubt because of the curse.

Shit. Eight-year-old ears listening. "Sorry."

Harper cleared her throat. "I'm glad you and Tilly are getting along a bit better. I think she could use the friendship."

"Yeah, people in this town are ass—" He stopped at the look from Eastern. "Can be unkind." Understatement of the century. Kayden may have his issues with what her father had done, but he'd never be an outright asshole by scaring her or denying her work like others had. "Do you know that contractors have been refusing to help her fix things around her house? She's been living with boarded-over windows."

Cody's brows tugged together. "What the fuck?"

"Cody!"

Cody cringed at Eastern. "Sorry."

Avery lifted a shoulder. "It's okay. I've heard Daddy say it plenty of times."

Harper muffled a laugh while Eastern feigned shock, when what he was probably shocked about was the fact that his daughter had ratted him out.

They reached the bagel line, but Cody's gaze shifted to the stall beside them. "Tacos. I'm sold."

"I could eat a taco," Harper said as she followed him across.

"What do you say, Princess?" Eastern asked. "Egg and bacon bagel, or taco?

She seemed to think about it for a moment. "Taco."

Eastern lifted a shoulder. "You're on your own."

The guys moved to the next line. Kayden was just pulling out his phone when the conversation from the women in front of him pricked his ears.

"You're kidding, right? You really believe Matilda Taylor and her mother didn't know what her father was doing?"

"Well, why would they?"

"Because they were a happy family? Everyone saw them together every weekend. Then he leaves town with hundreds of thousands of dollars that weren't his. They stay for a month and pretend they're just as hurt as we are, before going to join him."

Kayden's muscles tensed.

"I don't—"

"*I* do," the woman pushed, cutting her friend off. "I mean, has she actually told anyone where she went when she skipped town? They supposedly had no money, yet her mother didn't need to sell the house when Matilda's grandmother left it to them, and now Matilda's suddenly back and living in it."

"Why would she come back if she was part of it?"

"I don't know, maybe they blew through the money, but trust me, evil is in a person's blood. Her father had it, and so does she."

CHAPTER 9

*E*xhaustion pulled at Kayden's limbs as he completed his set of pull-ups.

Fuck, he was tired today. He'd slept like shit last night and he had no idea why. It *was not* because images of Jake grazing Tilly's cheek continued to flash through his mind. And it definitely wasn't because of those busybody older women at the market who'd been gossiping about Tilly.

Was it because he'd been having more and more thoughts of his father lately? He closed his eyes and still his dad was there, front and center.

"I lost the house, son."

Kayden frowned. "What do you mean, you lost it?"

Pain laced his dad's features. "Business has been down, and since Martin left with my savings, I had to sell."

"Doesn't mean you have to sell. You have six kids—we'll all help you."

"No. I knew you'd say that. I'm not taking money from my children. It's already done."

Kayden growled and dropped to the ground to complete a set

of push-ups in the outside workout area beside the visitors center deck.

He didn't want to be another person who blamed Tilly for her father's wrongdoings. But then why was it that every day he spent around her, his head battled with his heart?

"You're out here nice and early."

Kayden's jaw locked at the sight of Jake stepping off the deck. "Not really. It's almost nine."

"Yeah, but on a Monday, nine feels like seven." He dropped his bag and pulled off his sweatshirt. "Man, the fresh air in these mountains is so good at this time of morning. I don't know how you left for so many years."

"Wasn't that hard when I was always planning on coming home once I'd served."

"You have two other brothers who also served, right?"

"Four. Two are still on active duty, while Cody and Eastern are out, but we all have different specialties."

Jake whistled. "Impressive family."

Kayden packed up his bag, not meeting Jake's gaze. "Not really. Our father served and we all looked up to him."

There was a beat of pause before Jake spoke. "Hey. Did I do something to upset you?"

Kayden froze, muscles tensing before he rose and faced the guy. "Why would you ask that?"

"I don't know, just the feeling I get. I know things are tense between you and Theo, but I swear, I would never turn up to work hungover like him. Plus, you're the team leader, and I don't want to be on your bad side."

"You're fine."

"Okay, but, um…there's nothing going on between you and Tilly, is there?"

His eyes narrowed. "Why?"

"Because she's cute and funny, and I've been enjoying getting to know her, but I want to make sure I'm not stepping on any toes before I make the next move."

The next move? Why the hell did that make Kayden feel like ramming his fist into the guy's face?

"There's nothing going on between her and me." The words tasted like acid in his mouth and made the exhaustion that had been pulling at his limbs all morning tug that much deeper.

He stepped onto the deck. Every part of him felt tense and on edge, like a single shove could send him over.

He pushed inside the building to find Pixie smiling up at him. "Hey, Kay, everything all right?"

Did he look as shitty as he felt? "Yeah, just need to get a new shirt before I shower. Is Tilly in there?"

"Nope. She just stepped out to get a coffee."

"Thanks."

He entered her office and was pulling a shirt out when his phone rang, Eastern's name flashing on the screen. "Hey."

"Kayden, you got a sec?"

"Yeah, what do you need?"

"I just wanted to let you know there was a break-in at the hardware store down the road from the visitors center last night."

Kayden's brows slashed together. "A break-in?"

"Yep. Money was stolen from the till, also some spray paint, gloves, and a beanie."

"What the hell? So they rob the place and steal stuff to help them commit more crimes?"

"Looks that way. And the door was jimmied the same way the visitors center's was the night Macy was killed."

Something hard and uncomfortable lodged in Kayden's gut. "So it might be the same person."

"It's possible." There was a heavy silence before Eastern spoke. "I need to ask you something."

"What?"

"How was Tilly when she came into work today?"

"Tilly? I haven't seen her yet. Why?"

"Because there's a witness who says they saw someone leaving the crime scene this morning at about three a.m....and they fit Tilly's description. Even mentioned her name. Now, I know she's not popular in this town, and they didn't give me much to go on other than an approximate height and wearing a black sweatshirt with the hood pulled up. That's why I need to tread carefully here."

Kayden ran his fingers through his hair. Jesus. He wanted to tell his brother there was no way in hell Tilly would break and enter, much less kill anyone. But did he really know Tilly well enough to say that? And the women at the market yesterday had been right...they didn't know where she'd been all these years.

He scrunched his eyes, feeling like the ass he was for saying this. "If you think Tilly might be responsible for the break-in, you should question her. I don't know her well enough to say she wouldn't."

A shuffling noise sounded behind him, and he turned to see Tilly staring straight at him from the doorway.

* * *

"Here you go, one steaming cup of double-shot latte."

Tilly smiled at the other woman behind the counter. "Thank you, Elle. You're saving my life with these morning coffees."

"That's good to hear. Mrs. Sandler keeps me on my toes with her phenomenal drink menu, so she's the one to beat."

"You're both amazing."

The other woman grinned. "You're too kind. I hope you have a great day."

"You too."

She stepped out of the café and crossed the deck toward her office. She was actually in a great mood today, and it had everything to do with yesterday. Not only had Jake been good company, but he'd made her laugh and smile more times than she could count. It was probably the most she'd smiled since arriving in Misty Peak.

She didn't feel anything for him more than friendship, something she'd tried to make clear yesterday in the way she'd brushed off any touches and kept everything affable, but even having another friend improved her outlook.

And not only that, but the windows supplier Kayden had scheduled arrived this morning, and a flooring guy to get rid of the damp boards below the windows. When she got home, she should finally have a sealed home.

In the office, Pixie sat behind the desk, talking on the phone. She gave Tilly a small smile as she passed. She stepped into her office only to stop at the sight of Kayden with his back to her near the cabinet, phone to his ear. She was about to step back out when he spoke.

"Tilly? I haven't seen her yet. Why?"

She saw his knuckles whiten around his phone as he listened to whatever the other person said.

"If you think Tilly might be responsible for the break-in, you should question her. I don't know her well enough to say she wouldn't."

The blood left her face. There'd been a break-in? And Kayden was telling whoever he was speaking to—more than likely his sheriff brother—to question her.

Kayden turned and their gazes collided.

Hurt swamped her. So few people in this town had been kind to her, but she'd thought Kayden at least trusted her.

He didn't. Maybe he never would. Maybe no local ever would, and she was just fooling herself by returning here.

She was moving before she could stop herself, turning and walking—basically running—out the back door and onto the deck. Her feet aimed for the mountains of their own accord, knowing that was where she'd find peace. Some calm in this moment to take away the anger and frustration that had been sitting inside her since returning to this town.

She'd come here to do what her mother hadn't been able to… return home. Show the community who she was and prove to them she was different than her father, even though she didn't feel like she should have to prove anything.

But it was never going to happen, was it? She'd always just be Martin Taylor's daughter. The daughter of a thief.

She scrubbed a tear from her face, hating that she was crying. She didn't want to cry, she wanted to be angry. She wanted to let the fury block out the pain and hurt and the voice in her head that told her this was *her* fault. Her fault for thinking people could be better. That her father's sins didn't have to dictate her life here.

Footsteps sounded behind her, propelling her forward. She didn't know if it was Kayden or someone else. It didn't matter. She didn't want to see *anyone*. She just wanted to get lost in these mountains and forget. Forget what her father had done. Forget that five years ago, he'd taken more from her than anyone could ever imagine. He'd taken her home. Her safe place.

"Tilly." Kayden's voice made the rage ripple in her chest, and she forced herself to move faster. "Stop!"

She didn't. She couldn't.

A curse sounded behind her, then strong fingers wrapped around her upper arm. "Matilda—"

She spun on him. "It's Tilly! For the last goddamn time, it's Tilly! *Do not* call me Matilda. I don't like the name Matilda, and I don't want you to use it."

Kayden's frown was deep as he took her in. "I'm sorry."

"If you were sorry, you'd stop using it."

"No. I'm sorry that what I said to my brother hurt you."

So he *had* been talking to Eastern, the Sheriff of Misty Peak.

She swallowed the lump in her throat. *Do not cry in front of him, Tilly.* "That's the thing, I'm not sure you *are* sorry, Kayden. I think you want to be better than all the closed-minded people in this town, but at the same time, you genuinely believe I could rob someone, just like my father."

His jaw visibly clenched, and it was all the confirmation she needed.

She turned and kept moving deeper into the forest, not caring about the branches that scraped across her arms or the way her shoes sank into the damp ground, shoes that were not designed for trekking.

The footsteps once again sounded behind her, and she turned her head to see Kayden close. Too close. "Stop following me."

"I can't do that, Tilly. You've gone off-trail and there was a stabbing in these mountains not too long ago. Not to mention some steep mountain edges."

"I can look after myself."

"You need to go back."

"Tell me, if you really believe I'm as bad as my dad, why did you help me with my car and house? Because you felt sorry for me? Or because you wanted to get close to me so that when I found out it was all a farce, it would hurt that much more?" She tripped over a tree root, and he cursed again and grabbed her arm, but she yanked it back.

"Nothing was a farce. I wanted to help you."

"You wanted to help me even though you think I might be responsible for a break-in?"

"Eastern said someone saw you leaving the scene of the crime. I simply said if he thought it was you, he should question you."

The pain that shot through her chest was so distinct, she almost stopped. She should be used to it, right? The locals setting out to hurt her. She wasn't. And they just *kept* hurting her.

"But you didn't defend me either," she said, with not nearly as much conviction as she'd meant. "You didn't tell your brother you didn't think I could have done it. I don't know why I should have expected you to." But she had.

There was a short pause. "I didn't." He almost sounded like he felt guilty.

She spun on him. "So tell me, what did I do exactly to make you and everyone else in this town hate and mistrust me? Is it that I left with my mother so quickly after my father robbed people?"

"Tilly—"

"I left *for* my mother. Because she needed to for her mental health. People were awful to her. People were awful to *both of us*. They keyed our cars. They cursed at us in the streets. One man spat at my mother in the grocery store—and no one did or said a thing to defend her." Tears burned her eyes at the memory.

"I would have said something," Kayden said softly.

She wanted to believe him. "I don't believe you. You were just as angry at me about what my father did as others in this town."

A muscle ticked in his jaw.

"You know he took money from us too?" she said. "All of his and my mother's savings. Her jewelry. Everything that we had that was worth anything."

But that had paled in comparison to what he'd done to them on a deeper level. Deserting them. Tarnishing them.

"I came back because there's a reason she never sold her home," Tilly continued. "She wanted to return here. To make amends even though they weren't her wrongdoings. But she never did. So I'm doing what she couldn't. Or at least trying to. And to answer the question you've never asked but always wondered, *neither of us* knew what my dad was planning. And I haven't seen him since the day he left. So imagine for a second, the hurt you felt knowing your father's friend stole from him, then times that by a thousand—and that's exactly how it felt for me."

CHAPTER 10

*K*ayden felt like an asshole. Why couldn't he say the right goddamn thing?

Tilly turned and started walking again, but she almost immediately tripped for the second time. Kayden caught her arm to steady her before stepping closer, his mouth moving to her ear and his voice lowering.

"I'm sorry. I don't think you broke into the hardware store, something I should have told my brother."

When she went completely still, he continued.

"I struggle to trust people, and I can be an ass. But my flaws shouldn't flow onto you."

For one whole heartbeat, there was quiet. He didn't even hear their breaths. When she finally turned, there was a glimmer of tears in her eyes.

"I don't have many friends in this town. But out of the few I do have, I thought you were one of them."

The words stabbed through his chest like a knife. He inched closer. "I am. I want to be."

When a tear fell down her cheek, he reached up and grazed it away with the pad of his thumb. He was almost certain she leaned in, like she needed his touch as much as he needed to touch her.

Almost of their own volition, his feet inched forward. His hand on her arm grazed down to her wrist, so that the thumps of her pulse beat beneath his finger.

"I don't like seeing you upset," he whispered, the drops of truth falling from his lips.

Her gaze shifted between his eyes. "Kayden, I—"

The radio on his waist sounded, Jake's voice on the other end.

"Guys, is anyone close to the location where they found the Hodgkin girl's body?"

Fuck. He didn't want to be interrupted. Not here, not now. Kayden pulled out his radio. "I'm not far. Why?"

"I found something a bit south of there. I don't want to touch it in case there are prints, but I don't have gloves."

"What did you find?"

"It's—"

Suddenly, a loud bang cut off his words. It was so loud, he didn't just hear it on the radio. It cracked throughout the mountains, loud and violent.

Tilly gasped. "Was that—"

"A gunshot." His fingers tightened around Tilly's wrist. Shit, he wasn't carrying, but he couldn't *not* go to Jake. "Jake? Jake, can you hear me?"

Nothing.

"Tilly, you need to go back to the office and lock the doors." He lifted his radio again. "Theo, Hendrix, you there?"

"I'm here." It was Hendrix. "Was that a fucking gunshot?"

"I'm going to find Jake. Lock down the visitors center and call the sheriff's office and an ambulance."

But dammit, he didn't want to leave Tilly alone in these mountains when there was a shooter somewhere out there.

"I'm coming with you," she said, as if reading his mind.

"Tilly—"

"I can help give first aid to Jake if he needs it. And even if I couldn't, I'm safer with you than on my own."

She was right. The shooter could be anywhere. He needed to get his damn head on straight.

He reached for her hand and slipped his fingers through hers. "Stay close."

They jogged through the mountains, and the entire time Kayden studied his surroundings. The trees. The bushes. Searching for any movement that was out of place. There was nothing. But that didn't stop the anxious pit from digging into his gut.

Who the hell was this shooter? Was it the same person who'd stabbed Macy? And if so, had they shot Jake because they'd seen him with a piece of evidence that linked them to the crime? How did they even know Jake had *found* evidence?

He sped up, hearing the gasp from Tilly before spotting the body.

Jake lay on his stomach, a bullet wound on the right side of his middle back, crimson blood soaking through the material of his top.

Goddammit. He dropped down beside Jake and lifted his wrist to feel his pulse. Faint, but there.

Quickly, he removed his sweatshirt and pressed it to Jake's back. "Tilly, I need you to hold this on the wound."

Her face was pale, but she nodded, dropping to Jake's side and pressing her hands over the sweatshirt.

He kept his hands over hers for a moment, pressing them down to demonstrate. "I need you to apply a lot of pressure to stem the bleeding. Are you okay with that?"

She nodded again, some of the shock leaving her eyes, replaced with determination.

Kayden scanned the woods. Empty. By the looks of it, whoever had done this was gone.

He pulled out the radio. "Hendrix, you there?"

"Yeah, I'm here, Kay. The center's locked down—everyone here's safe. You find Jake?"

"Yeah, he has a bullet wound to the right side of his middle back."

"Shit. Pulse?"

"Yes, but we need to get him out of here now. I need you to bring a stretcher."

"I'm on it. Theo's here too. We won't be long."

"Kayden..." Tilly's quiet voice sounded, and Kayden lowered beside her.

"What is it?"

"He has a wound on his head too."

Kayden moved around his body and inspected Jake's head. Damn, she was right. His gaze shifted to the log beside Jake's body, narrowing on the blood and bark disturbance. He'd hit his head when he'd fallen.

"Help's on the way. They won't be long." When she didn't reply, Kayden looked at her. "Tilly."

She was slow to look up, and when she did, worry glazed her eyes.

"Are you okay?"

"Someone shot him," she whispered.

"They did."

"Someone shot Jake while we were out here in the mountains, not far away."

Kayden cupped her cheek. "My brother will be here soon. It will be his job to find the asshole who did this. Right now, we're gonna make sure he gets to the hospital alive."

She swallowed and nodded. He wanted to say more. Hell, he wanted to promise her things he had no right promising. Like that Jake would make a full recovery. That Eastern would find the person who'd shot him and arrest him before he struck again. But he had no idea if any of that would be true.

It didn't take long for Theo and Hendrix to arrive, and when they did, they were all business. The three of them carefully lay Jake on the stretcher while Tilly kept the top pressed to his wound, then they jogged him out of the woods. They'd just reached the parking lot when the paramedics arrived, closely followed by Eastern and a few other officers.

Once Jake was in the ambulance, Eastern moved over to him. "What happened?"

"He found something to do with Macy's murder."

Eastern straightened. "What did he find?"

"I don't know. He radioed to tell us, but before he could say what it was, the gunshot fired. Whatever it was, he said he was scared to touch it in case there were already prints on it. I had a quick look around his body but didn't see anything."

"So it's the same location as Macy's body was found?"

Kayden nodded. "Almost, just a bit closer to the highway."

Eastern scrubbed a hand over his face. "This is getting out of fucking hand." He turned to his deputies and relayed the information, giving them instructions on where the shooting took place before turning back to Kayden. "I'm shutting down the visitors center until further notice. And I want to interview everyone who was here."

Kayden nodded, not surprised by his brother's call. "Okay. Tilly was with me at the time of the shooting."

"She was?"

"Yeah. We were together up the hill."

Eastern nodded slowly. "Okay. Well, that takes her off the list of possible suspects. We'll still need to interview her though."

"Yeah, I get it. But she might be a bit rattled." He turned to look at her, his gut clenching at the pale color of her skin.

* * *

TILLY TOOK a right turn as she headed home. The sun was just starting to set, but she felt like she'd been awake for so much longer than she had.

Shot. Jake had been *shot* right there in the mountains beyond the visitors center.

Her fingers tightened around the wheel. After what had felt like hours of questioning from an officer who clearly didn't like her, Tilly had been ready to go home and collapse. Particularly because the questions hadn't just revolved around Jake's shooting, but also her whereabouts from the previous evening.

Even though she'd wanted to go straight home, she hadn't. She hadn't been able to, not knowing Jake was on his own in the hospital. He had no family here in Misty Peak, and no part of her had wanted him to be alone.

It had taken a while to find out which room he was in, and she understood why. She wasn't family. She'd waited, though. And when a shift change had come and a nicer nurse came on, she'd finally found out what room Jake was in.

Just about every nurse and doctor who'd walked into the room had looked at her like she was a pariah. She didn't care.

God, he'd been so pale.

She'd sat with him for hours, waiting for him to wake up. But he hadn't. The entire time, the same question had been flickering through her mind…what had he found in those mountains? What had been so incriminating that it had almost cost him his life? Because surely that was why he was shot?

She didn't have answers. No one would know until he woke up and told them.

She turned down her driveway. The second her house came into view, her heart slammed against her ribs.

Because there, sitting on the steps by her front door, was Kayden.

What was he doing here, and how long had he been waiting?

She parked the car in front of the house and climbed out. He rose, and like every other time her gaze fell on him, her breath stuttered at just how big he was—wide shoulders, thick chest, tall…

"What are you doing here?"

He waited until she was at the top of the steps to answer. "I needed to check that you were okay."

Her pulse picked up speed, her belly warming at his easy admission. No one really checked on her anymore, not since her mom had died.

Her gaze lowered to the paper bags in his hand. "What's in there?"

"Takeout. I guessed you hadn't eaten and thought we could eat together."

Another rippling of her heart. Because he was right—she hadn't thought about food all day. And she probably wouldn't have made herself anything tonight. "You didn't have to do that."

"I wanted to. It's been a long day for everyone…especially you. And I didn't want you to be alone."

This time, it wasn't just her pulse that sped up, it was her thoughts.

She wanted to let him in and allow his gesture to wipe away the horrible day. But… "I can't just forget about our argument this morning, Kayden."

She'd felt betrayed. Worse than that, she felt stupid and embarrassed that she'd trusted him after such a short amount of time.

He inched closer. "I told you, I'm an ass. But I'm an ass who's trying to be better. Let me be better."

Christ, how was she supposed to say no to that? And the argument did feel kind of trivial after seeing Jake bleeding out on the ground.

"So…are you gonna let me in?" he asked when she hadn't said anything.

"Depends. What did you bring?"

"Burgers, sweet potato fries, and cupcakes from Sugar and Spice."

Did he somehow know those were her favorites? Even that she always chose sweet potato fries over normal fries?

"I even got one of each sauce for the fries," he added.

"The selection of sauces kind of makes it impossible to say no." She stepped up to the door and unlocked it.

"So you're not sending me away?" he asked.

"Well, I don't like my chances of wrestling the takeout bags from your hand, so I guess inviting you in is my only choice."

One side of his mouth lifted. "Guess it is."

He stepped inside, and just like the last time, it felt like he took up all the space in her small hallway.

When he entered the living room, his gaze moved to the windows. "They look good."

"They do, don't they?" But then, anything would look better than boarded-over windows. "They installed them while I was at work today. Thank you for organizing it."

"It was nothing."

But it wasn't, and they both knew it.

When his gaze held hers a beat too long, she cleared her throat and closed the door before heading to the kitchen, where she opened the fridge. "Drink? There's soda, juice, water…"

When he didn't respond, she closed the door—only to gasp at how close he was. He was there…like *right* there, behind where the door had been. How had he moved without making a sound?

"Kayden—"

"I'm sorry I didn't catch you before I left today. When I was finally finished with the officers on the scene, you were gone."

"After they questioned me, I visited Jake."

"You went to see him at the hospital?"

"Yeah, a nurse took pity on me and gave me his room number."

"How was he?"

She lifted a shoulder. "I don't know. He didn't wake up. But he was breathing." Which was good. Today could have gone a lot differently.

There was a short pause, and Tilly could almost see Kayden's mind working. She squirmed before finally asking, "What is it?"

"Are you two…"

Her brows shot up. "Dating? No. We're just friends."

He nodded slowly. "Good."

Good? Why was it good? She wanted to ask, but a part of her was scared of the answer. Or maybe she was just scared that she'd like it.

CHAPTER 11

illy snuck a peak at Kayden from beneath her lashes. They sat on the couch in front of the TV, but if someone asked her what they were watching, she'd have no idea. A movie with a wooden cabin and a woman who looked worried? Yeah, didn't really say a lot.

She dunked another sweet potato fry into the sweet and sour sauce. She'd gotten about two thirds of the way through her burger before moving on to these fries. Not that she was concentrating on the food any more than she was the movie.

Good. That had been Kayden's response to her not dating Jake. Why did that single word give her more questions than answers?

Of course, instead of asking those questions, she'd just about run out of the room like it was on fire to take a shower, and it was only after changing into the comfiest clothes she owned—yoga pants and a loose sweater—that she'd returned to find Kayden had set up their meal on the coffee table and turned the TV on.

It felt oddly intimate to see him so comfortable in the same space she'd grown up in.

She nibbled the end of the fry, almost jumping when Kayden broke the silence.

"I don't understand why you eat your fries with sweet and sour sauce."

She frowned. "Lots of people eat fries with sweet and sour sauce."

"You're the first person I've met who does. Most people eat their fries with ketchup."

She wrinkled her nose. "I don't like ketchup."

He looked like she'd just admitted to hating baby animals. "You don't like ketchup? Everyone loves ketchup."

"Guess I'm not everyone."

She expected more banter, but his blue eyes held hers, turning to an almost navy. "No, I'm starting to realize that."

Her heart gave a little twist, and for some reason she had to look away. Quickly, she shoved the rest of the fry into her mouth.

"Why did you spend so long with Jake at the hospital today if he didn't wake up?" Kayden asked quietly.

She dipped another fry into the sauce. "Because he's new in Misty Peak and doesn't have many friends here. I didn't want him to wake up alone. Not that he'd woken up at all, but I know what being alone feels like, and it sucks."

Something she couldn't place flashed through his expression. "I'm sorry you've felt so alone in this town."

"It was expected. I couldn't have chosen a worse time to return though, could I? With what happened with Macy, the break-in at the hardware store, and now Jake."

Kayden's brows slashed together. "Did Eastern question you about the hardware store break-in?"

"No, one of his deputies did. They were *very* interested in my whereabouts last night, actually. And I'm afraid I didn't have a lot to tell them other than I was here, by myself, with no one to corroborate my story." Just like the night of Macy's murder. Was she a suspect in that too?

Her skin chilled, but she forced herself not to concentrate on that.

"I'm sorry."

She lifted a shoulder. "It's not your fault. If someone told police they saw me leaving the hardware store at the time of the break-in, they had to question me. I have nothing to hide though. It wasn't me, and they won't find any evidence at the scene suggesting it was."

"People can be assholes."

She laughed. "Oh, I've realized that. My mother always taught me to find the good in people, because there's good in everyone, but man, it's hard sometimes."

"Your mother sounds like she was a good person. I'm sorry I didn't get to know her while she was here."

"She was the best. Kind. Nurturing. And I hate that she was pushed out of here. It was her home, and she loved it so much. Maybe she thought she was doing *me* a favor by leaving, because she knew I'd only leave if she did."

"Sacrifice doesn't feel like sacrifice when it comes to protecting those we love."

She glanced up. "You sound like you have experience."

"After my mom died, I always felt responsible for my family. Dad was hurting, and so were my five younger siblings, so I did what I could to keep us in one piece."

"But were *you* in one piece?"

He gave her a half smile, and it told her everything. He hadn't been, but he'd kept his pain to himself to help his family.

"Do you regret it?" he finally asked.

"Regret what?"

"Coming back."

That was a loaded question. "Sometimes. The hard times. But I also don't. After Mom died, Cleveland didn't feel like home anymore. I kind of just felt lost. Then I crossed the border into Misty Peak, and despite everything, it felt like I was home again."

For some reason, tears started to gather in her eyes. "She's here. I can feel her. In this house. In the mountains. And anytime I think about leaving, a part of me feels like I'd be leaving *her*, so I just... don't."

Kayden shifted closer and reached out a hand. She wasn't sure what he was doing until he swiped a tear from her cheek. "You feel like you have her back when you're here."

"Yeah. I know it sounds crazy. But she was my best friend, and this was her home for most of her life. Coming back here would have meant the world to her. I just wish we could have done it together."

She expected Kayden's hand to drop. Instead, it curved around her cheek, cupping her face. He'd done that before, and each time it felt so incredibly intimate.

"It would have taken courage."

It took everything in her not to lean into that touch. "It didn't, actually. Because I had this naive belief that people would see the good in me and be kind. What takes courage is staying every time something makes me feel like running."

His hand curved around her neck, and when he spoke, his words were almost a whisper. "I don't know if this is the right or wrong thing to say, but I'm glad you've stayed."

Her belly tingled, not only at his words but the way his touch made her skin sensitive. It was deep inside her, from her neck right down to her toes.

"Kayden..." His name was a whisper on her lips, and she wasn't even sure why she'd said it.

"Tell me not to kiss you, Tilly."

Little flickers of awareness came to life inside her.

"Tell me to back away," he pushed. "To take my hand off you and go home."

She opened her mouth, not sure what words were going to come out...and in the end, nothing did. Not a single sound. Because no part of her felt capable of telling Kayden Walker to leave. Even the thought of his hand dropping brought an uncomfortable twist to her stomach.

So instead, she lowered her gaze to his mouth. Traced those full, thick lips with her eyes. Lips she craved to feel on her own.

A growl reverberated from his chest, then his head lowered, his mouth crashing to hers.

The second their lips sealed together, she was breathless. And tingly and hot and lost. God, so lost.

The fries and sauce slipped out of her fingers, and suddenly she was free to touch him. To slide her fingers up his chest and neck, then into his hair. It was softer than she'd thought. Smooth and kind of silky.

When he nibbled on her bottom lip, she gasped, and his tongue slipped into her mouth, melding with hers.

She groaned, a deep, primal sound that fell into the quiet of the room.

He leaned her back and suddenly he was on top of her, the soft couch at her back in complete contrast to the hard chest at her front. His weight was heavy and intoxicating and made her want to grind against him.

At the feel of his hand moving up her side, her heartbeat stumbled over itself. Because even though the material of her sweater separated his fingers from her skin, it felt like there was nothing between them.

His hand kept moving, sliding over her ribs, only stopping at her breast, then he was cupping her, palming her breast as she moaned.

God, his touch on her was like nothing else, and she wanted more.

When he found the bud of her nipple through her bra and swiped with his thumb, a whimper tore from her throat, and she lifted a leg around his hip, tugging him closer. Grinding against him.

His mouth had just started moving down her cheek and neck

when something sounded from the front of the house. A car engine followed by…small thuds against the door.

Oh no…

* * *

KAYDEN WANTED to devour this woman. To touch and kiss and taste every inch of her velvet skin. To spend hours getting lost in her.

She was so damn sweet, just like her scent. And those soft curves against him…God, they did something to him.

He moved his mouth from hers and kissed her cheek, then her neck. Every part of this woman deserved to be loved. He was about to lower his mouth to her breast when a car engine sounded from the drive.

He froze. Then he heard something hitting her front door.

The fuck?

He lifted his head. "What is that?"

Without meeting his gaze, she quickly shimmied out from beneath him and ran to the window, where she peeked her head around the closed curtain. "Oh my God…they actually got out of the car this time. I need to write down the plate numbers!"

What the hell was she talking about?

He rose from the couch and looked out the window to see two teenage boys throwing eggs at her front door and windows. Not just any boys…the local electrician, Harry Jacobs' kids.

Motherfuckers.

Rage rushed through his blood as he stormed to the front door and yanked it open. The second the boys saw him, the color left their faces.

Good. They knew they were in deep fucking shit.

One of them managed to scramble into the car before Kayden reached him, but not the other. Kayden grabbed the kid by the back of his shirt and shoved him against the Honda.

"What the fuck is wrong with you?" Kayden growled.

Footsteps sounded behind him, but he ignored them.

The kid opened and closed his mouth twice before getting words out. "I'm…we're…egging Matilda Taylor's house."

"I can see that," Kayden said through gritted teeth. "*Why?*"

"Because, well, my father says she's a thief and she stole from us. That she cost him a job…"

"Does Harry know what you're doing?"

The slight widening of the kid's eyes gave him away. Harry knew.

Kayden lowered his head. "You have thirty minutes to clean the egg off the house. If you don't, I call the sheriff, and you can both experience what a night behind bars feels like."

The teenager spluttered, the color not returning to his face.

"*Okay?*" The word from Kayden was somewhere between a shout and a growl.

The kid nodded. "Okay! We'll clean the house."

"Good. I'll get you a bucket. I want the house sparkling fucking clean. And if I ever hear about either of you pulling a stunt like this again, you'll spend more than a night in a prison cell. Do you understand?"

He nodded quickly, and Kayden reached inside the car and grabbed the keys before shoving the kid back into the car. No way did he trust them not to leave the second Kayden turned his back.

When he turned back toward the house, it was to see Tilly standing on the stairs of the porch, her arms wrapped around her ribs, and her eyes…not angry, more disappointed as she looked at the kids. He jogged up the steps, then slipped an arm around her waist and led her inside.

He waited until the door was closed before speaking. "They've done this before?" He already knew the answer, but he needed her confirmation.

"Yes." That was all she said. Then she walked down the hall.

He followed. "Why didn't you say anything?"

"Who was I going to say something *to*? You?" She stopped in the laundry room, grabbed a bucket, and began filling it with water. "You didn't even like me for a while. No one did. I had one friend—Harper."

A vein throbbed in Kayden's temple, because it was fucking true. He'd been an asshole, and so had just about everyone else. "You could have told Eastern."

She scoffed as she squirted cleaning liquid into the water. "I didn't get their plates, and some of the officers at the station hate me."

"So, what was your plan, to let them throw rotten fucking eggs at your house every other week?" Shit, he needed to calm down.

"No, I've ordered security cameras and they would have gotten their plate numbers. I was going to report them as soon as possible, even though I'm not sure the officers would have done anything." The last part was said more to herself than to him.

She lifted the bucket, and he immediately slipped it from her hands. "The next time they pull a stunt like that...hell the next time *anyone* does any shit like that to you, tell me."

"Kayden, it's not your—"

"I'm not joking, Tilly. Promise you'll tell me."

She frowned. "Why do you care so much?"

Wasn't that obvious? He'd been fighting his attraction to her like crazy, but that kiss...there was no fighting *that*.

He stepped closer. "You know why." She swallowed, her gaze lowering to the floor. He touched a hand to her chin and tilted her face up. "Tilly, please...I need to know you're okay. That you're being treated with respect."

One deep inhale, and she nodded. "Okay. I'll tell you."

CHAPTER 12

"*H*e kissed you?"

Tilly gasped at the volume of Harper's voice, the knife she was using to chop chocolate almost slipping. "Shh! Cody's just in the other room."

Harper rolled her eyes. "They're brothers, and Kayden's always at the bar talking to him. Trust me when I say that Cody would have been the first to know."

Was that true? Had Kayden told his brother about the kiss? And if he had, how had he described it? Nice? Hot? Something that under no circumstances would ever happen again?

After not calling or texting in the last few days, she was leaning toward the latter. Hell, with the visitors center being closed for the last four days, she hadn't even seen him.

"So…" Harper said, this time in a quieter tone. "He kissed you."

They stood in the kitchen of Harper and Cody's new house. The place was ridiculously cute with its white picket fence and Hamptons-style decor.

"Honestly, I don't really know if he kissed me or I kissed him," she finally said, her gaze on the flour Harper was measuring into

90

a mixing bowl. "It's a bit of a blur. We were just on the couch in my living room, and we kissed."

"Two people never *just kiss*. Set the scene. What happened before the kiss?"

That was a good question. Everything before the kiss just kind of felt…insignificant. "We were eating dinner on the couch with a movie on, although I wasn't watching the movie. We talked a bit about my mom and why I moved back." She wrinkled her nose. "I may have gotten a bit teary, and he swiped the tear away with his thumb."

Harper lowered the measuring cup. "Oh, Till, I'm sorry."

"It's strange that I feel so comfortable talking to him about my mom and how hard it's been since she died. I don't usually talk to anyone about that stuff."

"I always told Cody his big brother was a softy at heart." She leaned closer and lowered her voice once again. "Was it good?"

"Was what good?"

"The kiss!"

A warm tingle danced over her skin, and she almost touched her lips as though they somehow held the memory. "It wasn't just good… I don't even know how to describe it. It was hot and addictive and…easy."

"Easy?"

"Not in a take-it-or-leave-it kind of way. In an I-could-do-this-over-and-over-again kind of way."

Harper sighed, her hand going to her chest.

Tilly lifted a shoulder. "If people hadn't egged my house, I honestly don't know if I'd have had the willpower to stop it."

"I love that. I love everything about you two being together. You know, that would kind of make us sisters."

"Let's not get ahead of ourselves. The man hasn't so much as texted me since." She pushed the board of chocolate forward. "All chopped."

Harper frowned as she took the chocolate. "He hasn't made contact at all?"

"Nope. Well, unless you consider formal responses to work emails 'contact.'"

"Not exactly the contact I was talking about."

"Didn't think so." She watched as Harper melted the chocolate over the stove. "So this is a new recipe?"

"Yeah, and to be honest, I'm not sure how it's going to go. The shop was all out of white flour, so I have to use whole wheat."

"Well, that makes it a semi-healthy chocolate cake, right?"

Harper laughed. "Hmm, maybe." She glanced up at Tilly. "You're coming to his birthday dinner, right?"

"Me?"

"Yeah. It's Monday night because that's when the bar's closed, and we're going to the local Chinese restaurant. Please come."

"But I don't really know Cody that well. He probably doesn't want me there."

"I would love you there." At the deep, masculine voice, they both turned to see Cody walk into the room. He moved straight behind Harper, slipped his arms around her waist, and kissed her neck.

An ache formed in Tilly's chest. What did it feel like to have someone love you so openly and fiercely? She'd only ever felt that easy, unhesitant kind of love from one person before...her mother.

Harper turned to face him and pressed her hands to her chest. "You cannot be in here. I'm making your cake."

"I'm not here for the cake, but I could do with something sweet..."

Okay, way too much love in the room for her. She was about to excuse herself to go to the bathroom—either that or just hide in a bedroom until they were done—when the front door opened. There was no knock or ringing of the doorbell. That meant it had to be Eastern or—

Cody grinned toward the door. "Kayden!"

"Shit, what did I walk into?" His deep, raspy voice slid through her, making her blood rush faster throughout her body.

Harper pushed at Cody's chest again. "Stop, we have people here. You'll make them uncomfortable."

"Uncomfortable watching me love my woman? Not possible."

"Possible," Kayden cut in. "Very possible."

He stopped beside Tilly. Like, *right* beside her. So close she could feel the heat of his body radiating onto her own.

As Cody continued to ignore them and nuzzle Harper's neck, while Harper laughed, Kayden looked down at Tilly. Even though she wasn't directly looking at him, she could feel his eyes like hot beams. "Hey. I didn't know you'd be here."

Finally, she mustered up the courage to look at him. And yep, it only took that one glance at his beautiful blue eyes to make her heart go off in a gallop.

She cleared her throat. "Harper asked for my help with Cody's cake, although I'm not much help."

"Not a baker?"

"Oh, I can bake. Cupcakes. Cookies. Never cakes. They always sink in the middle."

One side of his mouth lifted. "It's the taste that counts."

Why did those seemingly innocent words slide into her belly, making her want to squirm on her stool?

"All right, I guess we should go work on that broken fence," Cody said, finally stepping away from Harper.

"I'll see you around." Kayden bumped her shoulder, and that small touch did so much more than it should have.

Yep, she was screwed.

* * *

"WHAT'S GOING on with you and Tilly?"

Kayden paused from nailing a part of the broken fence back into place. "Nothing. We're friends and colleagues."

A damn lie. He hadn't been able to sleep these last few nights because memories of touching her, kissing her, had haunted him.

"Really?" Cody asked with an annoying, shit-eating grin on his face. "Do you always kiss friends slash colleagues?"

What the fuck? "Who told you that?"

"No one. I'm a nosy prick and heard the women talking when I was in the study."

"So you were eavesdropping." He scrubbed a hand over his face. "Yeah, we kissed."

"So why haven't you texted or called or visited since?"

"Tilly told Harper that?"

"She did." Cody drove a nail into the wood. Some of the humor left his features as he gave Kayden a pointed look.

"You got something to say about that?"

Cody turned. "She's already got a lot going on with moving back to this town and dealing with narrow-minded locals."

"I know she does. What does that have to do with me?"

"You don't date."

Kayden shot his brother a frown. It was true, he didn't date. But Tilly was starting to make him reconsider.

"You also don't trust," Cody added.

This time, he straightened. "I trust *you*."

"Because we're family and you've known me since the day I was born. Can you really tell me you've let everything with her father go?"

A muscle in his jaw ticked. He wanted to lie, but what would that do? "I'm trying to."

Cody nodded slowly, like he'd already known the answer. "Just...try not to hurt her. She's become good friends with Harper."

He would never set out to hurt Tilly. Fuck, even the thought of it made him want to kick his own ass. But people rarely planned to hurt those they cared about. So instead of giving his brother an answer, he nodded.

They worked on fixing the fence for another half hour before his phone rang, Jake's number on the screen.

"I'm gonna take this." He stepped away from his brother to answer the call. "Jake, how you doing?"

The other man had woken up the day after he'd been shot, and Kayden had visited him a couple of time since then. Tilly's words had been running through his head...about Jake having no family here. About him being alone.

"I'm okay. Stronger every day. I just wanted to call and say thanks for the supplies. They were from you, right? The food and drinks and puzzles that were left and signed 'boss.'"

Kayden raked his fingers through his hair. "Yeah, they were from me. The nurses told me you were asking for puzzles."

Jake laughed. "I like to keep busy. And I loved the snacks and drinks. Hospital food sucks."

"I'll bring you lunch today. What do you want?"

"No, you don't have to do that."

"I want to. And trust me, you'll be helping me. I've been going batshit crazy with no work." He wasn't joking. He was also a man who liked to keep busy, exactly why he was here at Cody's place, searching for things to do.

"Well, if you're offering, I'd love a burger."

"Done. I'll see you soon."

When he hung up, Cody raised his brows. "You're taking him lunch?"

"I am."

"Who?" Harper asked, as she and Tilly stepped out into the yard.

"Jake."

Tilly's eyes widened. "Do you mind if I join? I visited yesterday but would like to see him again."

It shouldn't bother him, but fuck, he didn't like that Tilly wanted to visit Jake every day. That probably made him an asshole, what with Jake being shot and all.

"Sure."

Once the fence was fixed and in place, he and Tilly said goodbye to Cody and Harper and took separate cars to the hospital. Even though Kayden stopped to grab the burger, they arrived at the hospital at the same time, her car pulling up next to his truck.

Kayden raised a brow at the milkshakes in her hands as she climbed out.

"What?" she asked defensively. "He told me he likes Sugar and Spice milkshakes, so I got him one." She reached into the car and pulled out a coffee cup. "I also got you a coffee."

One side of his mouth lifted. "Really?"

"Mm-hmm."

"That's funny. Because I got you a burger."

A grin curved her lips. "You did? I mean, I wanted to ask but held off because this isn't about me."

"No need to ask."

The smile widened, and it was so damn radiant that it took him too long to get his eyes off her. When they finally made it into Jake's hospital room, that smile appeared again, but this time for the other man.

"Hey. How are you doing?"

"Better now," Jake replied with a grin. "I didn't know you were coming."

"I was with Kayden when he said he was coming here."

Jake's gaze shifted between them, like he was trying to work something out.

Tilly lifted the drink. "I brought you a milkshake."

"It's like you're an angel." He slipped the drink from her fingers and put the straw to his mouth.

Tilly lowered into the seat beside the bed. "You haven't regained any memories from the day you were shot?"

Frustration twisted Jake's features. "No. The doctor said it's normal with how hard I hit my head. They may come back. They may not."

Tilly nodded. "You know what? If they don't come back, then that's your brain saying you're better off without them."

When the two smiled at each other, Kayden couldn't help the tug of jealousy that skittered through his chest. Not because of their closeness, or the way he looked at her like she was *his*...but because every smile she gave Jake, he wanted for himself.

CHAPTER 13

$\mathcal{T}$illy parked her car in the restaurant's lot. She was running late for Cody's birthday dinner. Man, she was always running late these days, but tonight, she had no one to blame but herself. She'd gotten so caught up in painting the new window frames that she hadn't realized the time, then it had been a mad dash to shower, change, and get out of the house.

Quickly, she grabbed her purse from the passenger seat and rushed out of the car. She was almost to the door when her heel hit a rock and she half fell to the ground, grazing her knee.

Ouch!

Good God, she was a mess.

She pushed back to her feet, cringing at the small graze on her knee before moving inside the Chinese restaurant. Despite it being a Monday night, the place was busy. Not a surprise—this restaurant was a favorite in Misty Peak. She spotted Harper and the others immediately. They sat at a large round table near the front.

Of course, Kayden was the first to glance up at her. His gaze collided with hers before lazily roaming over her body like he was taking in every part of her figure-hugging short black dress.

An involuntary shudder rolled down her spine, and she forced her feet to move forward. It took effort...certainly a lot more than it should have.

When Harper saw her, her friend rose and gave her a hug. "You made it."

She pulled back. "Sorry I'm late."

"You don't need to apologize. I'm just glad you're here."

Cody stood next and gave her a brief hug. She handed him a bottle of wine. "I know you own and run a bar, but I don't think you sell this one."

He read the label, a small whistle sounding from his lips. "A Shiraz Grenache all the way from Paxton Winery, South Australia."

"It's a good one."

"I can't wait to try it."

She smiled and greeted both Eastern and his daughter, Avery. It was only when Kayden rose to his feet that she noticed the one remaining empty seat was between Harper and him.

Kayden leaned in and pressed a light kiss to her cheek. "It's good to see you, Tilly."

That touch, those lips...they felt like fire. Was she red? Because she felt red. "You too, Kayden."

He held her seat out for her, and she lowered into it. He settled beside her and she was suddenly all too aware of how close the seats were. So close, she was basically grazing Kayden's shoulder. Not unusual for Chinese restaurants.

She was just laying her napkin onto her lap when he leaned over, his mouth almost touching her ear as he whispered, "Is your knee okay?"

He'd seen the scrape? "Depends. Is a person okay when they fall to the ground in an empty parking lot?"

Instead of appearing amused, he looked worried. "Do you want me to look at it?"

Would it be pathetic of her to say yes, just so he touched her? Yeah, it probably would be. "I'm okay."

"Guess what I'm eating, Tilly."

Thank God for Avery. She shifted her attention to the eight-year-old, who was leaning over the table. "Noodles?"

"Yes. And honey chicken and fried rice."

"Oh my gosh, what a delicious combination."

"And Daddy said I could get fried ice cream for dessert *and* have a piece of Cody's cake."

Tilly's jaw dropped. "They serve fried ice cream here?"

"Yep! It's my favorite."

She grinned at the girl. "Mine too."

Over the next hour, the group talked and ate and drank. Kayden was more relaxed than she'd ever seen him, while she *was not*. How was she supposed to relax when the man was so close that every time his arm moved, it grazed hers? Every time he passed her food, their fingers touched. And when he spoke to her, he leaned into her space, lowered his voice, and whispered so that his warm breath brushed her skin.

It was torture.

But he didn't affect her appetite. She was well and truly full when her phone rang. She pulled it out, relieved for the distraction, only to frown at the private number. Was it the same person who'd called her at the market? Whoever it was, they'd called a couple of times in the last week, but she'd missed the other calls. Not once had they left a message.

"Who's that?"

She jumped at Kayden's voice. She'd been so caught up in the call, she hadn't seen him angle closer to read the screen.

She lowered her phone to her lap. "I'm not sure. But if they have something to say, they can leave a message."

Kayden was still watching her closely when the phone stopped ringing. She was just turning her attention back to the table when her phone vibrated.

They'd left a message.

Something kicked in her chest…a little bout of unease.

"I'll be back in a sec," she said to no one in particular, but she knew at least Kayden heard because he was still watching her.

After rising from the table, she waited until she was alone in the hall at the back of the restaurant before pressing the phone to her ear to listen to the message.

"Matilda, baby, it's Dad."

Every part of her froze—her muscles, her breath, even her gaze stilled on a small black dot on the wall.

That voice…it was like a bucket of ice water over her head. She hadn't heard her father's voice in over five years.

"I need to talk to you. Next time I call, please answer."

The message ended, but for a moment, she didn't move. She couldn't. She felt stuck.

Why? Why was he calling her now? Did he want something from her? She wanted nothing from *him*. Absolutely nothing.

Eventually, she forced her legs to engage, but she was so deep in her own head that she didn't see the waitress until it was too late. She crashed right into the woman, and the plate of food in the lady's hand fell, half onto Tilly and half onto the man sitting at the table beside them.

"Oh my God," Tilly gasped. "I'm so sorry!"

The man at the table shot to his feet, noodles falling off his white shirt, and the blood drained from Tilly's face.

Harry…the electrician who'd towered over her that day at the visitors center. And sitting at the table with him were the two teenagers who'd egged her house.

* * *

Everyone was talking around Kayden, but his attention remained fixed on Tilly across the room. Her face was too pale as she left the hallway, her eyes glazed, almost like she wasn't seeing what was in front of her.

Who the hell had left her that message?

He stood, clocking the potential disaster before it took place, but he was too far away to do anything.

He cursed when the two women collided, and the food tipped on both Tilly and the man sitting at the table. Not just any man. Harry. He'd seen the electrician at the back of the restaurant but had been hoping the two of them wouldn't cross paths.

Shit.

He hurried as Harry loomed over her.

"What the fuck is wrong with you? It's not enough you come back to my damn town, you have to cause me to wear my damn dinner?"

Fury burned through Kayden's veins. The guy went to grab her arm when Kayden pushed between them, shoving Harry's wrist away.

"What the hell are you doing trying to touch her?"

"Did you see what she did?" Harry growled.

"Yeah, it was an accident."

"An accident?" Harry spluttered. "Are you kidding me? She walked straight into the fucking waitress while she was holding food over my chair."

"I'm sorry," Tilly said quietly from behind him. "I wasn't watching where I was going."

"No, you fucking weren't."

Harry tried to step forward again, and Kayden shoved him in the chest. "Back...the hell...off."

Harry's eyes narrowed. "And *you*...you think I don't know what you said to my boys? You've made it clear whose side you're on here."

"First of all, your boys threw *rotten eggs* at her house. More than once. If their own goddamn father isn't going to condemn their behavior and tell them it's wrong, then I will." He inched closer. "Secondly, there are no sides. She's a local. She's one of us. And she deserves to be treated as such."

The anger in the man's eyes darkened, glittering with the threat of violence. Kayden reached behind him and pushed Tilly farther back in case the guy threw a punch. He almost hoped he did so Kayden had reason to throw one back.

But Eastern stepped between them before either of them could act. "Okay, I think we all need to walk away and cool down."

Kayden didn't. Not immediately. Instead, he lowered his voice to a hard line. "You make her feel threatened again, you'll have me to answer to."

He turned before the asshole could respond, placed a hand on the small of Tilly's back, and led her to their table at the front of the restaurant.

Harper was on her feet. "Tilly, are you okay?"

Tilly nodded quickly. "Yeah. But, um, I think I should go."

"No, please! We haven't had cake yet."

Tilly reached into her purse and pulled out some money, leaving it on the table. "Thank you so much for having me. I'm sorry I caused a scene on Cody's birthday. And God, I'm *so* sorry that Avery saw."

Harper leaned forward to hug her. "It's not your fault. Do you want me to walk you out?"

"I'll do it," Kayden interrupted before Tilly could respond.

Tilly shook her head. "You don't need—"

"I'm walking you out." There wasn't any leeway in his tone. He needed to make sure she was okay, so that was exactly what he was going to do.

A beat passed and finally she nodded.

When they stepped out of the restaurant, Kayden didn't take his hand from her back. He couldn't. His concern for her warred with the rage that still filled his lungs at the way Harry had towered over her.

What had he been planning? To grab her? Hurt her?

When they stopped at her car, Tilly reached into her bag and pulled out her keys, but her fingers trembled so badly they dropped from her fingers.

"Dammit!"

Her whispered word just reached his ears as he leaned down and lifted the keys for her. But he didn't give them back. Instead, he looked into her beautiful green eyes, searching for…what, exactly, he wasn't sure. Some sort of reassurance that he could let her leave like this.

Needing to touch her, he cupped her neck. "Are you okay?"

She opened her mouth, but no words came out. Then, instead, she nodded, like words were too hard.

Kayden frowned. "I wouldn't have let him hurt you."

"I know."

Then what had her so rattled? Was this about Harry? Or was it about the voice message? "Everything okay with the private number?"

The change in her was instant. Fear flashed back into her eyes, and something else. Uncertainty?

It *was* the message… Who'd left it and what had they said?

"It's fine," she whispered.

Did she realize that her body gave her lie away? In the way she barely met his gaze and the tensing of her muscles. "If it wasn't fine, you can tell me. You can trust me to help you."

Her frown deepened and she opened her mouth. For a second, he thought she might tell him something important. Let him in on whatever had her so scared.

But maybe that was just a wild hope inside him, because then she blinked, her gaze turning down, and she shook her head. "I don't need help. But thank you for tonight."

Slowly, she reached up to her toes, slipped her hand into his hair, and tugged his head down before lightly kissing his cheek.

Then she whispered, "Really, thank you, Kayden. For saving me yet again."

He wanted to take her lips. Kiss her until she opened up to him. Until he had every one of her secrets. But instead, he let her slip away from him, and he watched with a new tightness in his chest as she drove away.

CHAPTER 14

*H*er father had called her last night. Her father had *freaking called her*. After five long years and just when she'd returned to Misty Peak, he'd made contact.

Why? What on earth could he want after all this time?

She pulled up in front of the visitors center, her heart beating too fast in her chest. Her pulse had been far too fast since she'd heard his voice at the restaurant. It taunted her. Replaying in her mind over and over again.

Matilda, baby, it's Dad.

She turned off the engine and closed her eyes.

Baby…it's what he'd always called her. That and Matilda. And wasn't that why she hated people using her full first name, because every time they did, it reminded her of him? Of his betrayal? The way he'd hurt her and her mom and about a million other people, then run?

It was her mother who'd called her Tilly.

When Kayden had looked at her last night and asked her to trust him with her secrets, she'd wanted to. God, she'd wanted to, so badly. But he wasn't her boyfriend. He wasn't even really her friend. She didn't know *what* he was. And he'd already admitted to having trust issues. Would he trust that last night had been her father's first contact with her? That she wanted nothing to do with him? Or would he revert back to the old Kayden? The one who'd looked at her with hatred and distrust in his eyes?

No. She'd tell him, but not right now. She couldn't lose one of the few people she had in this town, and certainly not Kayden, when their relationship was so fragile. Maybe if they grew to the point she felt like she could confide in him, then she would.

The person she had told was Eastern. That's why she was running late to work this morning, because she'd stopped at the sheriff's office to make a report. She'd had to. Her father was a wanted man...felony grand larceny. He'd stolen a lot of money. So not notifying authorities was like aiding and abetting a criminal, right?

She'd asked Eastern not to tell anyone, and technically Eastern was bound by law not to tell Kayden, so that made her feel safe in what she'd done.

With a sharp inhale, she climbed out of the car and moved toward the visitors center. They'd received confirmation from Eastern that they could reopen in a week, and a few of the SAR guys had said they'd be here today, so she'd come to get some work done. Work was also resuming on the skywalk, which was a relief because it meant they might not fall too far behind from their opening date.

She was about to step inside the building when her phone vibrated with a message. Her body locked, and she was slow to look at the screen because a part of her was scared it would be her father again.

His words repeated in her head...

Next time I call, please answer.

That was worse than if he'd left a contact number, because now all she could do was wait, knowing he'd call again. Eastern had asked her to let him know the second her father called.

She tugged her phone from her pocket and sighed when she saw it wasn't him.

Harper: Hey. I just need to check that you're okay after last night. I'm so sorry about what happened. Harry was a jerk.

Tilly: He was a jerk, but nothing I can't handle. Although, I was glad Kayden was there to help.

Harper: Yeah, he's a good guy. But if he hadn't stepped in, you know Cody or Eastern would have. Still, I'm sorry.

Tilly: You shouldn't be apologizing, I should. I hope I didn't ruin Cody's birthday.

Harper: You definitely didn't. And I have a piece of cake saved for you. I had to hide it from Avery so she didn't devour it.

She chuckled.

Tilly: You're amazing. I was looking forward to trying that chocolate cake we made. I'll drop by later today.

Harper: Sounds great.

She was still smiling as she slotted her key into the door... only to frown when she discovered it was already unlocked. Strange. Had one of the SAR guys gone through the visitors center when they arrived?

It was dark inside the foyer, so...empty? Maybe whoever had come in just hadn't turned the lights on.

Before she could talk herself out of it, she lifted her phone and texted Kayden.

Tilly: Hey. Did you unlock the front door to the visitors center?

The three dots immediately appeared.

Kayden: Yeah, I did. I'm on the trail. Why? Is everything okay?

She blew out a breath. It was just Kayden.

Way to overreact, Tilly.

Was it because of her father's voice message? Had he made her paranoid? Probably.

She walked toward her office, head down, typing out a response to Kayden. She was halfway through the text when she pushed open the door to her office. The room was almost pitch black, thanks to closed blinds and the lights off. It was only the sound of movement that had her looking up.

The person was a flash of black, racing toward her and shoving her hard as they ran past.

She cried out and fell sideways, her temple hitting the wooden doorframe as she fell to the floor.

* * *

KAYDEN FROWNED AT HIS PHONE. The three dots had appeared from Tilly a few moments ago, but so far she hadn't responded.

He quickened his steps as he turned back toward the visitors center. He'd been completing a run and checking that the paths were clear as he went. As he jogged, he lifted his phone to his ear and called Tilly.

It went to voice mail. What the hell? What was she doing?

He needed her to answer. He didn't like her being inside the building alone, not when there was still a shooter on the loose. Fuck, he wanted to curse his brother for telling staff they could return to work this week. No one should be returning until the damn perpetrator had been found.

He knew that wasn't the most reasonable request; it might take months. Hell, they might never find them, but closing the center felt safest.

When he reached the deck, his feet pounded against the wood. He'd just stepped inside when he stopped. The lights were off.

"Tilly?"

A soft sound reached his ears. A small moan near her office.

He shot across the room, only to stop dead at the sight of Tilly on the floor, groaning as she pushed up to a sitting position, hand to her head.

"Tilly!" He dropped beside her, helping her sit with hands at her elbows. He cursed at the sight of blood seeping from a wound on her forehead. "What happened?" The question came out as more of a growl, but he couldn't fucking soften his voice.

"I don't know. I…" She started to hyperventilate, puffs of air whipping out of her chest.

He forced his voice to gentle. "Tilly—look at me." It took her a moment, but when she did, her eyes were wide with vulnerability. "Breathe."

He sucked in a long, exaggerated breath, and she followed, breathing in deeply before releasing it. They did that three times before she finally spoke, this time with less of a tremble in her voice. "Someone was in my office. My head was down because I was looking at my phone, so I barely saw them. They were wearing black and they ran past me, shoving me against the doorframe."

Shit.

He pulled out his phone and hit his brother's number. Eastern answered on the first ring. "Kayden—"

"Someone was in Tilly's office. They shoved her and ran."

"I'll be there in ten."

The second he hung up, he helped Tilly to her feet and onto a chair before grabbing a first aid kit. As he dabbed the wound, he noticed she wasn't looking at him. She glanced over his shoulder, but he was almost certain she wasn't seeing anything.

"Does it hurt?" he asked.

"A little, but I think it was more the shock than anything else. I don't understand what they were doing in my office or why they ran."

Who the hell knew. If this was the same person who'd stabbed Macy, opened the safe, and shot Jake, then what the hell were they doing in her office? And if it wasn't the same person, then who was it?

"I'm sorry I left the door unlocked," he said quietly.

She glanced back at him again. "It's not your fault. I'm the one who came in because I'm a workaholic and I don't know how *not* to work."

"I'm the same. Guess it's something we have in common."

Several minutes later, the door behind him opened and his brother walked in, closely followed by three deputies.

Over the next twenty minutes, Eastern both got his and Tilly's version of events while his deputies checked the building. When they were done, Tilly searched her office to see if anything was missing, but when she came back out to the foyer, she shook her head.

"I didn't see anything gone."

Eastern nodded, and by the expression on his face, Kayden knew he wouldn't like what was coming next. "We've taken some prints, but unfortunately, the door was left unlocked, so the perp didn't break in. Because you didn't get a good look at the attacker, and we don't even know if they were male or female, there isn't a whole lot we can do."

"You can keep the goddamn visitors center shut until we know who's behind these attacks," Kayden growled, more force than he'd intended behind his words.

"Kayden, we don't know if the same person's responsible for Macy, Jake, and today. It could have just been a crime of opportunity. And I can't keep the center closed. We don't know how long this investigation's going to take."

Kayden damn well knew that. But he also knew there shouldn't be a risk to the safety of staff or the visitors.

Eastern sighed. "I can put some guys on the center."

"That's not enough!"

A smooth, warm hand touched his arm, then Tilly's soft voice said, "Kayden…it's okay."

But it wasn't. It didn't feel anywhere close to okay.

Eastern looked at her. "You should get that cut checked out in case you need stitches."

"I'm fine."

She went to move past him into her office, but Kayden grabbed her arm and stepped close. "I don't want you working here until the place is back up and running and there's a full staff."

"Kayden—"

"And even then, I don't want you leaving late. If you need to do that, you call me, and I'll accompany you."

She swallowed, and when their silence stretched, he stepped forward, eliminating the last of the space between them before grazing her hip with his thumb. "Please."

"Okay."

CHAPTER 15

*T*illy leaned her head back against the hospital wall. She'd been in the waiting room for hours. What was the time? Three? Four in the afternoon? She wasn't sure, but she hadn't eaten or drunk anything since breakfast, so not only was she hungry, she was exhausted. A bone-deep exhaustion that tugged at her limbs and was doing nothing for her aching head.

The waiting room was busy, and she knew people with higher needs would be put ahead of her, but it seemed everyone was coming and going and she was just…waiting.

There'd been a changeover in staff at the front desk about an hour ago, and when the first, older nurse had left, she'd whispered something into the younger woman's ear, then they'd both looked her way. Because they were intentionally making sure no one saw her?

Kayden had wanted to drive her here, but he'd been busy talking to Eastern, so she'd accepted a ride from one of the deputies with the thought that the sooner she arrived, the sooner she'd be seen. Well, that had not been accurate.

Screw it. She rose from her seat for what had to be the twentieth time since arriving.

The woman behind the desk huffed. "Miss Taylor, I've told you, you need to wait."

"I've been here all day. All I need is a doctor to check if I need stitches and make sure I don't have a concussion."

"There's nothing I can do. The doctor's busy." She said the words slowly, as if Tilly was an idiot and wouldn't understand otherwise.

On another day, Tilly might have let it slide, but today…today she was angry and tired and completely over this entire town treating her like a pariah. "I know what you're doing. You're punishing me for being my father's daughter by denying me medical care. You know you could lose your job over this, right? Is that a risk you're willing to take?"

"Oh, trust me, Matilda, this town has already learned not to take *risks* when it comes to members of your family. It certainly didn't bode well for mine. But if you have a problem with the service you're receiving, you're welcome to put in a complaint."

She shoved a form over the counter. A form Tilly was sure if she filled out, would swiftly be placed in the trash.

She wouldn't be seeing a doctor today. And suddenly, she had no fight left. The headache was pounding in her temple, and all she wanted to do was go home.

Ignoring the form, Tilly turned and headed for the door, blinking back tears of frustration. She'd just stepped outside when her phone beeped with a text.

Kayden: Just checking in? What did the doctor say? I hate that I didn't go with you.

For some reason, she considered lying to him. Telling him she'd been seen and all was fine. Maybe because she didn't want his pity. But honestly, she didn't even have the energy for that.

Tilly: I was never seen.

That's all she wrote. Because how was she supposed to express in a text the reason behind not being seen?

Immediately, her phone rang.

"Kayden—"

"What do you mean, you were never seen? Why?" He sounded angry.

"They've been telling me all day that I need to wait my turn, but…"

"But what?"

She almost laughed as she massaged her temple. "But this town hates me. So it's clear my turn will never come."

There was a heavy beat of silence, and when Kayden spoke again, his voice held barely concealed rage. "Don't leave. I'm coming down there."

"No. Kayden, I don't want you to keep fighting my battles. I'm fine. I'm pretty sure I just need rest. I'm just going to go home and—"

"I'm coming. Don't. Go." They were his last words before the line cut off.

Maybe she *should* have just told him everything was fine. Because what was his plan? To come here, threaten someone and demand she be seen?

She didn't have to wait long. Five minutes later, Kayden stepped into the waiting room. His eyes were almost black with anger and his hands were fisted.

He stopped in front of her, his gaze running over her face. "Are you okay?"

She nodded, then cringed, because even that hurt her head.

His anger deepened, and he slipped a surprisingly gentle hand to the small of her back before leading her toward the desk. The woman looked up. When she saw Kayden, her eyes widened, maybe because of the fury on his face. Either that, or the way he marched toward the desk.

She rose from her seat. "Kayden—"

"Why hasn't she been seen?"

Tilly almost flinched at the fury in Kayden's tone. It was so deep and dark, it almost didn't sound like him.

The woman's mouth opened and closed a couple of times. "Well...I mean...it's been busy."

"She's been here for *hours.*"

"I'm sorry. I...there was a shift change and...I'll get a doctor to see her right away."

"Yes, you will—if you want to keep your damn job."

The woman scurried off.

Tilly glanced up at Kayden. He kept saving her from this town, and a part of her wanted to object. She wanted to be able to save herself, or better yet, not need saving. But every time he did it, all she could feel was gratitude...and maybe a hint of relief that there was at least one person here who wanted her to be okay.

* * *

KAYDEN COULD BARELY KEEP his outrage in check. First, Tilly had been shoved into a goddamn doorframe. Then she was made to wait in the hospital all day just to have her wound seen. Would they *ever* have let her see a doctor if Kayden hadn't come?

His fingers clenched.

He should have trusted his gut and gone in with her, but dammit, he kept expecting more from this town. For people to treat her with some respect. Denying her medical attention was the last goddamn straw.

"All right, Miss Taylor, the wound is all taken care of. Like I said, no need for stitches and no concussion."

Tilly nodded from where she sat on the edge of the hospital bed, new bandaging on her forehead. "Thank you."

"I'm sorry you had to wait so long. Jadie said your form got missed?"

When Tilly didn't answer, Kayden did. "It wasn't missed. They intentionally didn't allow her to see anyone."

The doctor's white brows pulled together. "What are you talking about, son?"

"People in this town don't like me very much," Tilly said, straightening her spine.

The doctor shook his head. "Oh, no, they wouldn't—"

"They did," Kayden interrupted.

The doctor huffed out a breath. "If that's true, that you were intentionally denied medical care, I'll personally make sure those responsible are reprimanded."

"It *is* true," Kayden pushed, his hand going to Tilly's back. "And we appreciate you doing something about it."

Frustration brimmed on the doctor's face as he nodded and left the room.

"Kayden, I didn't need you to speak for me," Tilly said quietly.

He stepped in front of her, not missing the shadows under her eyes. "You're tired. Let me take care of you, even if it's just to let a doctor know what the staff at this hospital did."

Her brows flickered, and when she didn't respond, he knew how right he was…she was exhausted.

"Are you okay?" he asked.

"Better after the doctor got me some water and painkillers. Now I'm just hungry. I haven't eaten since breakfast."

Since breakfast? Fuck, he was going to kick his own ass for not coming here with her. "Come on. Let's get you home and fed before I murder someone." It wasn't even a joke.

On the way to her house, they grabbed pizza. He wanted to talk to her on the drive. Ask her how she was feeling. So many emotions flickered across her face. Was she scared after today's incident? Was she angry at the way she'd been treated? Sad? Frustrated? Or was it a medley of everything?

He barely stopped himself from asking because he knew she needed rest.

When they pulled up at her place, he carried the pizza inside. Even while they ate, the conversation was minimal. Mostly about little, insignificant things, like the week ahead. Kayden spoke about the work he'd done on the mountain, of clearing the walking trails, and Tilly filled him in on the skywalk progress.

After they were finished eating, Kayden wanted to stay. To look after her, make sure she was okay. But once the table was clear, Tilly looked longingly toward her bedroom. "Thank you for everything today, Kayden. I feel like I'm a broken record, thanking you all the time."

"I could stay a bit longer if you need?" Hell, he'd stay all night if she asked.

"I'm actually really tired. I might just shower and go to bed."

"Are you sure?" The last thing he wanted to do was leave her alone.

"Yeah, I'm not in pain or anything anymore, but I need to wash this day away." Before he could respond, she leaned in and kissed his cheek. "Thank you for being you."

She started to turn, but before she could walk away, he wrapped his fingers around her wrist and tugged her back to him.

One hand went to her hip and the other to her cheek, as he said quietly, "Call if you need anything, Tilly. *Anything.*"

Her gaze flickered between his eyes, maybe searching for something? Maybe studying him. Finally, she nodded. "Okay."

Then, because he couldn't stop himself, he lowered his head and touched his mouth to hers. The kiss was merely a graze—lips against lips. But it was also everything he needed before he could leave her. "Promise?"

"I promise," she whispered.

"Good." One more kiss, and he finally released her and headed out. Just as he slid behind the wheel of his truck, a text came through on his phone.

Cody: Eastern came in, said there was an incident at the visitors center. Everything okay?

Kayden: No, not even close. Some asshole was in Tilly's office but we don't know who it was or what they wanted. To make the day even fucking worse, she went to the hospital and the women at the desk wouldn't let her be seen.

Cody: Shit. I don't know what to say, other than I'm sorry. Anything I can do?

Kayden: Not right now. But thanks for checking in. Watch your back. I have a feeling this is the same person who stabbed Macy and shot Jake.

Cody: Will do. You watch your back too.

Kayden: Always.

He shoved his phone into his pocket, but instead of driving away, he looked up at the house, wishing like hell things were different. That she'd let him stay. That she'd lean on him.

Maybe he wasn't the only one with trust issues.

Tilly was exhausted. Not just from the long wait at the hospital or the head wound that had come before that. Exhausted from this town and their treatment of her. Exhausted from always being on guard and being treated as an unwelcome guest.

She turned her head up toward the water and let it fall over her face and chest, mindful of her bandage. Today had been something else. And not something good. First the person in her office, then the mess that was her hospital visit. Never when she'd considered coming back here had she thought it might be this bad. Sure, a bad month or two, some hostile looks here and there, but the denial of medical care?

A mix of anger and frustration and exhaustion coursed throughout her limbs. It was never-ending.

She turned the water off and grabbed her towel. In the bedroom, she pulled on an oversized tee and some fresh panties before stepping into the living area—only to jump when a knock sounded at the door.

Someone was here? Who?

Slowly, she moved over to the door and looked through the peephole, gasping at the sight of Kayden.

Why hadn't he left?

Without thinking about the fact that she wasn't wearing pants, she tugged the door open. The second his eyes fell on her, they roamed down her T-shirt and bare legs, darkening another shade with each inch of body he traced with his gaze. She hadn't pulled on a bra, and the shirt barely covered her ass.

"What are you doing here?" she asked.

His gaze rose back to her face, an expression she couldn't read on his own. "I never left. I couldn't. Not without being certain you were all right."

She wasn't. Not five minutes ago when she'd been in the shower, and not now.

"Sometimes I feel like I'm drowning in this town. Like every person who threatens me, towers over me, looks at me with hate, or denies me some kind of service or care pushes me that much deeper under the surface. And I don't know how much longer I can hold my breath."

The muscles in his arms flexed and he stepped closer, that familiar, strong hand once again cupping her cheek. "I won't let you drown."

"I don't want to need you. I want to stand on my own two feet."

He seemed to consider her words for a moment. Then his head lowered, his warm breath brushing the skin beside her ear. "You will. But for now, let me help you. Let me keep tugging you back to the surface."

Her eyes shuttered, those soothing words breathing air into her lungs.

For a fraction of a second, they remained so still that she wasn't even sure either of them took a breath. Then his head lowered that tiny bit, and his mouth whispered over the back of her ear. It was the second time his lips had touched her that night, and each time was more powerful.

A shudder rolled down her spine, and he did it again.

She grabbed onto his shirt, as if she needed to hold him to keep herself upright.

Those soft lips nipped at her jawbone, then her cheek.

"Is this okay?" His question whispered across her skin.

One more kiss, this time right beside her mouth, before she answered, "Yes. Kiss me, Kayden."

A noise that barely registered cut from his chest—maybe a growl, maybe a groan—then his mouth collided with hers. It wasn't a light or glancing kiss. It was a full, mouth-against-mouth, tongue-tangling consumption.

He tugged her body against his, and she felt all of him. Every hard ridge. Every flicker of movement.

She groaned as his tongue teased hers, her fingers sweeping into his hair, pulling and tugging. She was just losing herself when he growled and lifted her off her feet before turning and pressing her to a wall. There was the soft thud of the door closing as she wrapped her legs around his waist, her core pressing against him.

God, it was heaven. It was a thousand flutters of her belly. A million degrees of heat on her skin.

His day-old scruff swept over her cheek, the hand on her hip dipping beneath the shirt, which had risen to her waist. When that hand slipped up her side, her heart began to beat faster. Every inch it moved closer to her breast had her breaths short-ening further. Then he cupped her, and as the weight of her bare breast lifted in his hand, all rational thought left her as she threw her head back and moaned.

His mouth slid down her neck, sucking as he palmed her breast, his thumb finding her nipple and rolling it back and forth.

The air moving in her lungs became short pants as her hips ground against him of their own accord.

"Where are we taking this, Tilly?"

She barely heard his words through the buzzing between her ears.

He lifted his head, and she wanted to groan and tug him back. "Tilly, I need to know how far you want to take this."

How was she even supposed to answer that while he had his hand on her breast and her core was pressed against his rock-hard belly? "I want you to carry me to the bedroom, and I want you to make me forget anyone who came before you."

Something dark and dangerous flashed through his eyes. Then his mouth crashed to hers once more, and he was moving, the air whipping around them until he stopped in her bedroom and tugged at her shirt. In one fell swoop it was gone, and all she wore were black panties. But she didn't have time to think about that because his head dipped, his lips wrapping around her pebbled nipple.

The cry that tore from her lips was loud in the otherwise quiet room, her fingers impatient as they latched onto his hair. Every swipe of his tongue sent her deeper into the spiral of desire swirling through her.

He lowered her so she lay flat on the bed, his body coming over hers as he switched to her other breast. She whimpered and writhed as he sucked and licked her nipple like it was candy. Like he wanted to devour her as much as she wanted to be devoured.

She dug her fingers into his shoulders, wrapping a leg around his waist and tugging him closer.

God, he was so hard.

His hand moved down her side, and when it slipped inside her panties and found her clit, her entire body jolted. He swiped again and again. Her nails dug into him, almost breaking skin. His lips were just trailing back up to her mouth when a finger slipped inside her.

She cried out, but the sound was muffled by his mouth against hers. As he continued to thrust in and out of her. Her fingers went to the hem of his shirt, almost desperate as she tugged it over his head. The second it was gone, his hand returned to her core.

When she felt his bare chest against hers, a million sensations rolled through her. She grabbed for the waistband of his jeans and undid the button, then the zipper. When she reached inside his briefs and wrapped her fingers around his cock, he froze... stopped thrusting his finger inside her, stopping sucking her neck.

She moved her hand from his tip to base, then back again, exploring. He was big and thick and hot, everything she knew he would be. His muscles were hard and tense as he burrowed his face into her neck, breathing hard.

It was strangely empowering, knowing she could bring such a powerful man to a standstill. Knowing that her touch could elicit such a strong reaction.

His breaths came faster as they brushed across her neck, the muscles in his shoulders tightening until they were so thick, they seemed twice the normal size.

She was still touching him, still grazing and exploring every inch, when suddenly he growled, his finger slipping out of her as he rose and shoved down his jeans and briefs.

Her mouth went dry. God, if she thought he *felt* huge, that was nothing compared to seeing him. Every part of him was big and hard, like he was carved from stone. He grabbed his wallet from his jeans and pulled out a foil square, then opened it before slipping the condom over his cock. Then he leaned over and gently slipped her panties down her thighs.

His eyes heated when he looked at her, and she realized she liked his gaze on her. Liked that when he looked at her, she felt claimed. Owned.

He leaned over, kissing her hip bone, then her belly. When he reached her chest, his lips once again wrapped around her nipple and sucked, before releasing it with a pop. Then he was between her thighs, his cock pressing against her core, his eyes on her. Just her. He looked at her like she was the most beautiful woman he'd ever seen.

No one had ever stared at her like that before.

He brushed a lock of hair from her face. "You're so fucking gorgeous, Tilly."

"You make me feel like I am."

He lowered his head and kissed her, then slowly, inch by inch, he eased inside, stretching her walls, causing her back to arch. She groaned against his lips, the pinch of tightness competing with the desire thrumming through her lower belly.

His tongue slipped inside her mouth, tangling with hers as he teased her nipple with his fingers.

"Relax," he whispered, his hips perfectly still as he sat inside her.

She did, and he slid a bit deeper. So deep, a noise released from the back of her throat that even she didn't recognize. For a few thick seconds, he just kissed and teased her lips, then his hips rose and he thrust back in.

She cried out as he hit a spot deep inside her that made her wild. And she wanted him to do it again.

He did. He continued to rock into her until she started to lift her hips, meeting him thrust for thrust, needing him with such a ferocity that it almost scared her.

* * *

Tilly's walls were tight, hugging his cock and wiping any and every rational thought from his head until she was all that existed...all he could see and feel and think about. She tormented his every thought.

With his fingers, he continued to tease and tug at her nipple. Her breasts were so fucking beautiful, he could play with them for hours. But then, *all* of her was beautiful. Every inch of her body. Every graceful movement.

He made love to her mouth as he lifted and lowered himself, nipping her bottom lip, swirling her tongue with his own.

When he lifted his head, it was to see her eyes closed, her chest moving up and down in fast pants.

He rolled them so she was on top. She didn't miss a beat, groaning deep in her throat as she sank deeper before pressing her hands to his chest and riding him. He watched, transfixed, as her breasts bounced with each movement. As she completely lost herself in him and them and what they were doing.

Fuck. Where had this woman been his whole life?

The air in his lungs shortened, his heart beating so hard it felt like it was about to burst out of his goddamn chest. He was close. So close he couldn't hold on much longer, but he needed her to fall first. To watch her tumble over the edge.

Reaching up, he cupped her breasts and pinched her nipples.

She screamed and quickened her thrusts.

He lowered one hand between her thighs to stroke her clit. Her body tightened around him, her movements becoming harder. Faster. He did it again, using his thumb to draw circles around her bud.

"Kayden...I can't..."

He rolled her nipple between his thumb and finger, desperate to see her lose herself.

One more stroke of her clit, and she screamed and shattered, her walls hugging his cock so fucking hard that it was almost torture as she broke. His hips started moving of their own accord, thrusting into her at a new speed, a new force, prolonging her orgasm as she continued to cry and shake, her hands steadying herself on his chest.

Then he lost all sense of time and space as his body broke, and he fell along with her. But he didn't stop thrusting. His hips kept lifting, trying to get deeper, losing a part of himself as his world narrowed to just Tilly.

Until, finally, there was stillness as she toppled onto his chest.

Long beats of silence passed as she just lay on him, their breathing ragged while he was still seated deep inside her. He wrapped an arm around her back and his other hand cupped her head.

This woman…this damn woman…what did she do to him?

He'd had his share of women before, but nothing had ever felt like *that*. Nothing like her.

"Kayden…"

Her whispered voice pricked through the haze, and he brushed some hair from her face as he looked at her. "Yeah, honey?"

"That was so much more than I ever thought it could be."

That was the thing, though—he'd known *exactly* what it would be like if they got together, right from the first time they'd met. He'd just been running from it. Because he'd known the second he had her, the second she became his, there'd be no shifting back.

CHAPTER 17

illy's lips were curved up as she typed out the email. The visitors center had been open for a couple of days, but that wasn't what had her smiling—it was everything that came before today, and all of it involved Kayden.

Since their first night together, he'd come to her house every evening. Spent every night in her bed. And God, those nights… they were memories that were cemented into her head, never to be erased. Every time he touched her, held her, she felt this thing she'd never felt with anyone else before. It was a mixture of safety and security and something else…something deeper that she didn't want to name just yet.

She cursed under her breath when she realized she'd made three spelling errors in one sentence. Dammit. She was trying to concentrate, but Kayden had gotten so deep into her head that she couldn't even spell.

They certainly hadn't told anyone at work. Sometimes, when she walked past him and got a wink or a small smile, she felt like his dirty secret. But she didn't really have the right to feel that way, did she? Because she hadn't initiated a conversation about what they were doing either, or said she wanted to let people at work know they were dating.

She'd just finished reading over the email and correcting a million little errors when a knock came at the door. She swiveled around to see Harper standing there.

Crap, was it lunchtime already? She lifted her phone. Yep, twelve.

Harper grinned. "Ready to eat? I'm starving."

"I am always ready to eat." Even when she forgot the time, her stomach eventually reminded her. Rising from her desk, she grabbed her purse and moved to the door.

Harper pulled her into a hug. "It's so good to see you. I'm sorry this lunch couldn't come sooner."

They'd struggled to find time together, with her working days and Harper evenings. "But we got here eventually."

"Yes, we did."

They headed out of the office, and Pixie smiled at them from behind the desk. "Off to lunch?"

"Yes, looking forward to Elle feeding us. Would you like me to bring you anything?"

She shook her head. "No, I'm good, thanks. I'll take my break when you get back. Have fun."

"Wow, it's so beautiful here," Harper said almost wistfully as they crossed the deck toward the café. "You must love getting to look at these mountains every day."

"It's the best part of my job, but I'm almost jealous of the guys who get to actually be *in* the mountains all day. Even Elle has a great view from her café. I didn't get so lucky with my office." No, her office overlooked the parking lot, unfortunately.

Harper bumped her shoulder. "More reason to take extra-long lunch breaks."

Inside the café, a couple of tables were taken, but the place wasn't too busy. Elle stood by the counter and a new barista was working at the coffee machine. Elle had admitted that she was finally ready to hire someone to replace Macy, so they'd gone through applications and the interview process together. The girl was young but had experience working in cafés, which was what they wanted.

Elle grinned at her as soon as she looked up. "Hey. Here for lunch?"

"Yes," Tilly sighed. "I'm dying for one of those salmon and cream cheese focaccias."

Elle chuckled. "I actually had one of them for lunch too."

"Have you met Harper?" Tilly asked, turning toward her friend.

"No, but I've heard about you, what with this being a small town and all. It's nice to finally put a name to a face."

Harper cringed. "Good things, I hope."

"Well, depends if you think 'can make a mean cocktail' is a good thing."

"In that case, the town can talk away." Harper glanced up at the menu on the board. "Is there anything you recommend?"

"The salmon focaccia's always a crowd-pleaser, but my personal favorite?" Elle leaned forward. "The Reuben."

"Oh, I love corned beef. Yes, please. And an iced coffee would be great."

"Make that two," Tilly said.

Elle nodded. "Done."

They paid and chose a table by the window.

"So, tell me how the bar's doing," Tilly said once they were seated.

"Really well, actually. Cody's hired a couple more people, who have been great, and we're finally able to take nights off every so often."

"Oh, Harper, that's amazing." Since Tilly had arrived back in town, it had been just Harper, Cody, and an older guy named Barry working at the bar. They'd always needed more people, but in the small town of Misty Peak, that wasn't so easy to find.

"It's a huge weight off our shoulders, especially Cody's. Everything's been so great that I'm almost scared to blink in case when I open my eyes, we're back to danger around every corner and having no help at the bar."

Tilly reached across the table. "I think you've been through so much that your hard times are over."

"I'm praying on that being the case."

Elle set their drinks onto the table. "There you go. Food won't be long."

She'd just walked away when Harper tilted her head. "So...I haven't seen Kayden at the bar the last few evenings."

Did she know? She couldn't, right? Tilly certainly hadn't said anything to her friend yet, she'd wanted to wait and tell her in person. Had Kayden told Cody?

Tilly took a big sip of her iced coffee before speaking. "We've sort of been seeing each other."

"*What?*"

"Shh!" God, had everyone in the café heard Harper?

"Sorry." Harper lowered her voice. "Wait, back up, what does 'seeing each other' entail, because I know you kissed, but did something else happen?"

"After Kayden took me home from the hospital last week, we kind of had sex."

Harper's eyes bugged so far out of her head that it was almost comical. "Last *week*? And you didn't tell me?"

"Shh!" She glanced around. Yep, people were definitely staring. "I wanted to tell you in person."

"Well, yeah, having sex with Kayden Walker is kind of big news that *should* be dropped in person." Harper leaned forward. "Tell me he hasn't been at the bar because he's been with you each night."

"He hasn't been at the bar because he's been with me each night."

"Oh my Lord." Harper leaned back and massaged her temple like she needed help digesting the information. "This is huge."

"It *is* huge. I mean, it feels huge to me. We haven't spoken about where it's going or anything but…it feels good."

"I am so happy for you, Tilly."

"Thank you." She nibbled her bottom lip. "The thing is…I like him. Like, *really* like him. And I think I'm a bit scared to ask questions about the future in case I get answers I don't like."

"Till…if he's spending every night with you, then I don't think that will happen."

"It might. All of this might just be temporary for him, and I'm scared of what that might do to me."

"Has he said anything to make you think it's temporary?"

She ran a finger over the edge of her glass. "No. But he hasn't said anything to the contrary."

"Maybe you should ask him."

She could…it was just working the "I'm scared" out of her first. "We haven't spoken about whether we'll tell anyone at work. On the first day, he just smiled at me, and we sort of slipped into this secret relationship."

Harper tilted her head. "That doesn't necessarily mean anything."

Maybe not. Or maybe it meant he didn't want his colleagues knowing he was dating Martin Taylor's daughter.

Argh. She hated feeling so insecure.

When her phone rang from the table, she looked down, thinking—hoping—it might be Kayden. Her skin chilled at the private number that flashed on the screen. This was the first time he'd called since Cody's birthday dinner.

Did she want to talk to him? Absolutely not. Did she want to know why he was contacting her though? Yes. A million times yes.

She was about to excuse herself to take the call when the door opened, and Kayden walked in. His gaze moved straight to her, as if he could find her in any crowd, amongst any number of people. For a moment, she couldn't breathe, and that was what he did to her with one single look.

This time, instead of smiling, his eyes darkened before he nodded. It wasn't until he looked away that she sank deeper into her seat.

Harper leaned forward and whispered, "That look he just gave you was not a 'this is temporary' look."

No…it didn't feel that way to her either.

Her phone stopped ringing, and she realized she'd missed her father's call. One look from Kayden and she'd forgotten all about it.

* * *

"Hey, Kayden, how's your morning been?" Elle asked as she made his coffee. He noticed the new worker serving food at the other end of the counter.

"One tour done and no missing people yet, so that's a success."

She chuckled. "It's always nice when you come back with the same group size as you left with."

"How's the café?"

"It's okay. Back to its normal bustling self. It's just *me* who feels different. I miss Macy." She gave him a sad smile that made the familiar anger pulse through his veins that Macy had been killed right here in these mountains.

"Eastern will find the asshole who killed her," Kayden said quietly. He believed that wholeheartedly. It was taking him longer than Kayden would have thought, but he'd get there.

Elle just nodded, and he wasn't sure if that meant she believed him or not.

When she popped the lid onto the Styrofoam cup and pushed it across the counter, he cleared his throat. "I spoke to Jace last night."

The small smile that had been on her face slipped just a fraction, and to anyone else, it probably wouldn't have been noticeable.

Fuck, he'd thought hearing about his brother would pick up her mood. Jace and Elle had been friends in high school. Good friends, to the point they'd stayed at each other's houses regularly and been in contact with each other every day. They hadn't dated, something Kayden never really understood, because he'd always thought they were great for each other. But they'd been close.

"Really?" she finally asked, voice unnaturally high and bright. "How's he doing? Still chasing adventure?"

Like Kayden, Jace was in Air Force Special Warfare, but a different spec ops group. Combat controller.

"Always. Don't think that will ever change."

"No," she said almost sadly. "I don't suppose it will."

He frowned. "Do you still keep in touch?"

"No. We did for a while, when he first left, but…you know, we live different lives. He's off saving the world and I'm here, in this small town, serving coffee."

"Every job, big or small, is important. In fact, I would argue caffeinating and feeding us SAR guys is top of the importance list here in Misty Peak."

The small smile returned to her face. "Thanks, Kay." She seemed to think about her next words for a moment before adding, "Tell him I say hi."

"I will."

Lifting his coffee, he turned to see Tilly still sitting opposite Harper, the two women talking in hushed tones. When Tilly's eyes flashed up at him for the second time, he winked before heading out of the café.

The last week with her had been…fuck, he didn't even have words. He craved their evenings together. Touching her. Talking and hearing her voice. The way she looked at him with her deep green eyes. He was addicted.

Back in the visitors center, Jake was leaning over the desk, talking to Pixie. He looked up, a smile curving his mouth. "Kayden, hey."

"You're back."

"Well, I'm out of the hospital." He straightened. "Not back to work just yet but hoping it won't be long."

Kayden stopped in front of the other man. "How are you feeling?"

He lifted a shoulder. "Not too bad, considering I was shot in the back." He shook his head. "Sorry, dark humor."

"Still no memory of what you found?"

"Actually, I've been getting small flashes of picking something up. A piece of jewelry, maybe?"

"Jewelry?"

"Yeah, I don't know. I see something silver in my hand but it's a blur." He frowned, then shook his head. "I'm hoping more comes back to me."

"I'm sure it won't be long."

Jake gripped Kayden's shoulder. "Thanks again for your support while I was recovering, both the food deliveries and the visits. Really appreciate it."

"Just glad to see you on your feet again."

Kayden went into the office and grabbed the details for his next tour. Tilly had created cubes for each of them, and in Kayden's was his printed tour information. Another reason to be hooked on the woman—she was damn organized.

Before leaving, he jumped on her computer and logged into his emails, something Tilly had already said he was welcome to do whenever he needed. When he read a message he needed to take notes on, he opened a drawer and searched for something to write with. There was nothing in the top or second drawer.

In the third, he pushed aside a watch and a few sticky notes before grabbing a pad of paper and a pen. After scribbling the information down, he logged off and headed back outside.

He'd just stepped onto the deck when he almost collided with Tilly.

"Kayden!" She almost sounded out of breath. And damn, but that incited memories of other times she'd been out of breath recently.

"Hey, Till."

She wet her lips, and immediately, his gaze lowered to those luscious lips. "You shouldn't do that."

"Do what?" she almost whispered.

He lowered his mouth to her ear. "Wet your lips like that while we're at work…it makes me want to taste them."

She made a small choking sound. "Kayden!" Her breaths became choppy before adding, "But I wouldn't mind, you know… if you tasted my lips at work."

His cock hardened. "That's a dangerous thing to say to me, honey." His lips grazed her neck, and she shuddered.

"Maybe I like living on the edge."

Fuck it. He lifted his head and crushed his lips to hers. The kiss was warm and intimate and familiar. So much more fucking familiar than it should have been considering how long they'd been seeing each other.

She leaned into him, a soft hum slipping from her lips. And when her mouth opened, he dove in, caressing her tongue with his.

Jesus, she was sweet. And those soft little moans that were escaping from her throat made him want to drag her back to the office, bend her over the desk, and take her.

He was tempted to do just that when a throat cleared behind him. They both froze before turning to see Hendrix and Theo looking at him in shock…and Jake beside them, appearing less than impressed.

CHAPTER 18

"Are you going to do it?"

Tilly cringed at Harper's question. They stood at a tall table while Harper took a break from working behind the bar to have a drink. This morning had been another perfect day of waking in Kayden's arms, having out-of-this-world shower sex… and another morning of not talking about what they were doing or where the relationship was heading.

Was it just sex? Or were they in a relationship? And if they *were* in a relationship, was it long term?

A week ago, when the guys in Kayden's SAR team had caught them kissing, it had been Hendrix who'd asked what they were doing, and Kayden had told them it was none of their business. But he'd kissed her so openly…that surely meant something, right?

Tilly dropped her head into her hands. "I don't know."

"What don't you know?"

"If I can do it." If she could ask a simple question without fear rendering her completely silent.

Argh.

Harper wrapped her fingers around Tilly's wrists and tugged her hands away. "You can do it."

"I'm scared." Understatement of the freaking century.

"What are you scared about?"

"That he'll tell me we're a fling. That he'll look at me like I've just asked him for a ring. Or even that he'll run. The few relationships I've been in, I've never cared if a guy walked away, but with Kayden, I do."

Harper tilted her head. "Tilly...the way he looks at you reminds me of how Cody looks at me."

Tilly laughed. "That is not true. You are all Cody sees. The center of his world. He told you he started falling in love with you the first time he saw you. The first time Kayden saw me was when I returned to this town, and trust me when I say, love was the *last* thing on his mind."

"Everyone's story has a different beginning," Harper said quietly. "But love is love."

"He definitely doesn't love me."

Harper simply raised a brow.

"Don't."

"Don't what?" Harper asked innocently.

"Don't make me want something I may never have."

"Don't you already want it?"

Dammit, she was right. And that was all the more reason to be scared.

The door to the bar opened and even though the room was packed, Tilly easily spotted him through the crowd. Kayden's shirt was steel gray, and it was so tight it hugged the thickness of his arms and wide chest. And his eyes, those intense blues, were her downfall. They could break many hearts...starting with hers.

"Why does he have to be so beautiful?" Tilly asked, more to herself than to anyone else.

"To torture you."

Oh, he definitely did that. When his eyes met hers, they

beamed right into her, stealing her breath and her very ability to think.

"Remember," Harper whispered, leaning forward. "Talk to him. You'll feel better after."

Unless she didn't.

Her friend squeezed her hand before moving away.

Tilly wasn't even sure if she responded to Harper. All she could do was watch as Kayden moved toward her, so big and fierce it was like nothing and no one could get in his way.

The second he was by her side, he touched the small of her back before leaning his head down and whispering in her ear, "You look too sexy, Tilly. I don't know if I like all these guys staring at you."

A shiver rolled down her spine, but that was less about his words and more about the brush of his breath on her ear. She wore high-waisted jeans and a strapless top that showed off a couple inches of her bare waist.

"I think I should be the one worried about women looking at *you*," she finally whispered.

"Doesn't matter if they look. I've only got eyes for one woman." His lips grazed her cheek. "I missed you today."

She laughed. "We woke up together, then both worked at the visitors center all day."

"And I barely saw you." Finally, he straightened, and she had to crane her neck back to look at him.

She lifted a shoulder. "We were busy."

"Dance with me."

She turned her head to look at the empty dance floor. "We'd be the only ones out there."

"I don't care. I want to hold you."

Lava pooled in her belly, making her want to both run and lean into him at the same time. "I want you to hold me too."

Gently, he took her hand and pulled her to the dance floor. She wasn't sure what she expected, but it certainly wasn't for

Kayden to wrap his arms tightly around her waist and tug her into his chest.

There was no space between them, not a single whisper of it. She could feel every hard ridge of his body. Every breath he took.

His mouth lowered and he nuzzled her neck. "Mmm, you smell good." Coming from the guy who was like a walking forest, fresh pine and all man. "Why didn't you wait for me?" he asked, lifting his head. "We could have come together."

"I wanted to talk to Harper for a bit first."

Her friend's words of advice came back to her. She wanted to be brave and ask him what she needed to know. Get some clarity on what this thing was between them. But the fear was alive and kicking in her bones.

Come on, Tilly. You can do it. One question, and whatever he answers with, you can take it.

It took another ten minutes of swaying in his arms before she finally took her head off his chest and looked at him. "Can I ask you a question?"

There was the slightest pinching of his brows before he answered. "Sure."

"Where do you see this thing between us leading?" Her heart thumped the second the words were out.

"This thing?"

Shit. Had she worded it wrong? "You know what I mean. Are we dating? Are we friends with benefits? Do you see us as long-term or short-term?"

At his hesitation, the thumping of her heart turned into a full-blown gallop. It was so loud she swore she could hear it over the beat of the music in the bar.

Kayden's hold on her loosened, and the smallest bit of space appeared between them.

That was bad, right? The hesitation, the physical distance, it was all in preparation to give her an answer she wouldn't like.

"I'm not sure."

His softly spoken words pricked at the bubble of her carefully held composure.

He wasn't sure. That was his answer. He wasn't sure what they were doing, what he wanted out of this, or whether they were long-term.

She'd been scared she wouldn't like his answer. But maybe she should have feared this more. That he wouldn't actually *have* an answer. That even after spending every night together for over a week, he wouldn't know what he wanted…or whether he wanted her for anything lasting.

The silence was so thick it almost got stuck in her throat. It was only the ringing of her phone that finally allowed her to step away as she tugged her cell from her back pocket.

Her throat tightened at the private number.

"Who's that?"

Her gaze shot up at Kayden's question. And suddenly she wondered if his inability to commit to her had something to do with who her father was…and his old distrust of her.

And if it was, and she told him that her father was in contact with her again, what would he do?

The fear was like a bolt of lightning down her spine.

Ignoring his question, she took a step toward the hallway. "I'm just going to take the call. I'll be back."

She waited until she stood in the hall near the bathrooms and checked to make sure it was clear before pressing the cell to her ear.

"Dad?"

At the sound of something behind her, she turned her head, only to see the women's bathroom door closing. She frowned. Had someone been about to step out?

"Matilda…baby, I'm so glad you answered my call."

Just like when she'd listened to her father's voice message, a chill swept over her skin. "What do you want?"

"I want to see you. I miss you."

Bullshit. She didn't believe that for a second. "It's been five years since you robbed half of Misty Peak and deserted me and Mom, and now you want to talk? I can't imagine what you could possibly want to talk about."

"Baby—"

"Stop calling me that! I'm not your baby. I'm your *nothing*. As far as I'm concerned, you're dead to me. So leave me the hell alone."

She hung up before he could get another word in, the anger so thick inside her, she could barely breathe. It took her a moment to pull herself together enough to turn—and when she did, it was to find Jake standing behind her.

* * *

"I NEED A WHISKEY, STAT." Kayden dropped to the barstool opposite his brother.

Cody raised a brow. "What happened?"

"Nothing." Lie. Huge. Damn. Lie.

Cody pulled out a shot glass and set it in front of Kayden. As his brother poured the whiskey, Kayden's eyes went to the hall. He couldn't see Tilly, but he knew she was there.

"Tell me what happened."

Kayden lifted the glass and shot the liquor back, welcoming the burn to his throat before finally looking at Cody. "Tilly asked what we were doing."

Cody raised a brow. "And?"

"And I told her I didn't know."

The expression his brother pulled was something between a wince and a "what the fuck?" Both were fair. "Why exactly don't you know?"

Kayden dropped his elbow to the bar and ran his fingers through his hair. "If I knew the answer to that, I wouldn't be sitting here shooting whiskey."

Cody leaned over the bar. "Want my two cents?"

"I'm sure I'll get it anyway."

"All six of us experienced losing our parents, but it shaped us all differently. Jace became an adrenaline junkie. Lock joined one of the most dangerous ghost ops teams in the world. And you've never been able to trust people. Not really, and not completely."

"Mom died of cancer." It was devastating, but he failed to see how that affected how he trusted people.

"Yeah, and you stopped trusting people and letting them in, in case you lost them. Then everything that happened with Dad just cemented it."

Fuck, his brother was right. It all came back to trust, and honestly, he wasn't sure if he was capable of it. Not the complete, make-himself-vulnerable kind that was required to have a real fucking relationship. "So what do I do?"

Cody lifted a shoulder. "That's a question only you can answer. How much do you care about her, and how would you feel at the prospect of losing her?"

A band wrapped around his chest at the thought, and his gaze once again shifted to the hallway. Fuck, where was she? She'd been in there for too damn long.

"I'm gonna go find her." He rose, no damn idea what he'd say to her, but he needed to be close. He'd just stepped into the hall when he heard a male voice...

Jake's voice.

"It's just that...since I saw you and Kayden together, I've been concerned."

"About me?" Tilly asked.

"Yeah. This is none of my business, so feel free to tell me to go away, but I'd hate myself if I didn't say anything. You and Kayden are just so different. You're light, and he's...I don't know. He was great to me while I was in the hospital, but a lot of the time it feels like he has a chip on his shoulder. I don't want you getting hurt."

The *fuck?*

Kayden stepped forward. "What the hell are you doing, Jake?"

The man spun around, shock widening his eyes "Kayden…"

"Are you telling her to leave me?"

He shook his head. "I'm just telling her to be careful."

"You think I'll hurt her?"

Jake swallowed.

"This isn't about me," Kayden said, taking a small step forward. "This is about *you* wanting *her.*" He'd seen it in Jake's eyes when the other man had caught them in an embrace at work the other day.

A muscle ticked in Jake's jaw. "I haven't made my interest in her a secret. It doesn't affect what I said though."

Like hell it didn't.

Kayden stepped forward again, but then Tilly was there between them, touching his arm. "Kayden, it's okay. I can handle this."

Her touch was the only thing that kept him where he was.

She looked at Jake. "I appreciate you looking out for me, but I'm doing okay. You don't need to worry."

Then she turned back to Kayden, grabbed his hand, and tugged him out of the hall. She walked straight through the crowd and didn't stop until they stood outside the bar.

"Are you okay?"

He scrubbed a hand over his face. "Yeah, just pissed off." Pissed didn't even do justice to how he felt.

Tilly inched closer, her hands moving up his chest. "I don't know if this is the wrong thing to say, or maybe the right thing at the wrong time, but even though you don't know what we're doing, *I* do. I like you. Like, *really* like you. And I want a relationship with you, Kayden. One where we commit to each other. Let the world know that you're mine and I'm yours."

Her words pierced his chest, making it hard for him to breathe or speak. "Tilly—"

She touched a finger to his lips. "You don't need to respond to that right now. But I need you to know that I'm in. I am all in. And I'll give you the time you need in the hopes that you get to where I am." She leaned up on her toes and touched a light kiss to his mouth. "Good night, Kayden."

Then she was gone, unlocking her car and slipping inside before driving away. While all he could do was stare and wonder what the hell was wrong with him that he hadn't been able to give her the answer she'd needed tonight.

CHAPTER 19

It was crazy that she was happy, right? Last night, her father had made contact with her again, and she'd had to notify Eastern of the contact.

Not only that, but Kayden had told her that he didn't know what they were doing. Didn't know if he saw them as long-term or even in a relationship. Yet she wasn't upset about it, because instead of pulling away from him, *she'd* told *him* how she felt. She'd put it out there, and now, the ball was in his court.

Of course, the way he'd responded to Jake had given her some confidence...like she was his.

Sure, there was a tinge of nerves that he wouldn't feel the same way, but for some reason, she'd woken with this unwavering faith that Kayden would choose her over whatever block he had going on. Maybe because their physical connection was so strong. Maybe because when she was with him, everything felt right. Whatever it was, it had everything to do with this intrinsic gut feeling she had.

Okay, maybe it came less from her gut and more from her heart.

With a shake of her head, she turned off the shower and grabbed her towel.

How would he act at work today?

In her bedroom, she dropped the towel and changed into work slacks and a crisp white shirt.

Her phone vibrated from the dresser, and her heart thudded at the possibility it could be Kayden. Last night had been the first night they'd slept apart in nearly two weeks. Was he checking in?

She glanced at the screen. Not Kayden.

Harper: How'd the chat with Kayden go? You left so quickly last night I didn't get a chance to ask you.

Tilly: Not so great. He doesn't know what we're doing.

Harper: Oh, Tilly, I'm sorry.

Tilly: I'm choosing to feel optimistic about it today. I told him how I feel and now the ball's in his court.

Harper: I love that. Let me know if you want to get lunch or something and chat about it.

God, she was lucky to have Harper as a friend. Who would have thought that first night she'd returned home, when the small town of Misty Peak had felt like it was stomping on her, that Harper would serve her a drink and become her closest friend.

Tilly: I'd love that. I'll let you know.

She hadn't even set the phone down before something sounded from the other side of her closed bedroom door.

What the hell? It almost sounded like the front door opening. But that wasn't possible. She'd locked her front door. She *always* locked her front door.

Quickly, she shoved her phone into her pocket, then, with slow steps, moved toward the bedroom door and opened it quietly.

Her heart stopped, one single word slipping from her lips. "Dad..."

His green eyes swung to her. He stood in her living room, a framed photo of her and her mother in his hand. "Matilda—"

"How did you get in?"

He set the photo back onto the mantel before turning to face her. He looked older. More gray to his hair and new lines beside his eyes.

He held up a key. "Under the potted plant to the left of the porch. Your mother used to hide the spare key in the same place in case she locked herself out."

An irrational part of her wanted to leap across the room and grab it.

Her father was in her home? And it *was* her home because her mother had left it to *her*, not her father. "You shouldn't be in here. This is my house."

He pocketed the key. "Yeah. Frustrating that this house was still in your grandmother's name when your mother and I separated. If it had been in your mother's, it would be half mine."

"Didn't you take enough from her?"

He took slow steps toward her. "Baby, I loved your mother."

"You're a goddamn liar. If you loved her *or* me, you wouldn't have done what you did. I don't even think you know what love is, unless it's a love for money."

Her father had always holed himself up in his office to work. As a kid, she'd told herself that he was working hard for the family. But that wasn't true. It was all for him. And when the opportunity arose to acquire money that wasn't his, he'd taken it.

"Sometimes we have to make hard decisions," he said quietly.

She laughed, but the sound was almost manic. "Hard decisions? You mean like robbing eighty-year-old Harvey Clinter of his entire life's savings so he had no retirement? Or maybe you're talking about stealing Toby Walker's money, a man who was supposed to be your friend, which forced him to sell his family home and mortgage his bar. Or perhaps you're talking about deserting me and Mom with nothing but the roof over our heads!"

He scrubbed a hand over his face. "I didn't enjoy doing any of that. But I'd made some bad investment calls, and I needed money."

"And that made it okay?"

"No. It made it necessary. It was all about survival." He stopped in front of her. "Matilda—"

"It's Tilly."

"I need your help, baby."

He was shitting her, right? He wasn't actually standing here, in her home, years after what he'd done, asking her for something? "Get out."

"I can't do that. This house should be half mine. We both know that. Your mother and I had lived in it since before you were born."

He wanted her *house*?

"I'm in a bad position, baby. I need money, and with the sale of this house—"

"*Get out!*" The words were almost screamed, so loud her voice bounced off the walls.

"No."

"Fine. I'm going outside and calling the sheriff. You're a wanted man and he already knows you've made contact." She grabbed her phone and key and started toward the door, but strong fingers wrapped around her wrist and tugged her back.

"No. You need to help me."

"Let go!"

He didn't. He tightened his hold until it was bruising before shoving her against a wall. "Just *listen* to me."

The panic and wild need to get away overrode every other thought. She brought up a knee, nailing her father between the legs. He groaned, and the second he released her arm, she shoved him away, ran out the door, and got into her car.

She didn't even slow to put her seat belt on, just started the engine and drove. Tears pressed at her eyes while her wrist throbbed from where he'd grabbed her, but she ignored it all, only thinking of one thing. Only needing one thing. Her new sense of safety…Kayden.

* * *

KAYDEN LIFTED pieces of chopped wood and carried it toward the visitors center. A tree had fallen in the high winds last night, and all the guys had been working overtime to get it off the path. Jake was helping with the small bits where he could, while Kayden was trying like hell to ignore the asshole.

His words from the previous night still played over in his mind. Fuck, every time he thought about it, it made him angry as hell. The guy had *warned* Tilly against him, like he had the right to involve himself in his and Tilly's relationship.

Theo dropped the wood in his arms onto the pile before rubbing his temple.

Kayden eyed him suspiciously. "You doing okay, Theo?"

The guy's eyes shot up. "I'm fine. Just a headache."

Hendrix came down the path and dropped the next handful of wood, his gaze shooting between them. "Everything good here?"

"What did you do last night?" Kayden asked, almost feeling like he was picking a fight but not caring. He'd woken angry, and that anger wasn't going anywhere.

Theo's eyes narrowed. "I wasn't drinking, if that's what you're asking."

"It is."

Anger reddened the other guy's cheeks, and he stepped forward. "You're our leader, but that doesn't give you the right to harass me."

Kayden stepped forward too. "Only it does, because you've done the wrong fucking thing before."

Hendrix pressed a hand to Theo's chest. "Hey. Let's chill out, okay." He turned to look at Kayden. "I was with Theo last night.

We hung out, watched some football, and that was it. No drinking."

"Good," Kayden growled. "It better stay that way."

He knew he was being a damn hypocrite. He'd been at his brother's bar last night drinking, but the difference was, he never drank to excess, particularly not on a work night.

Theo's eyes grew colder, but he let Hendrix pull him back down the path toward the pile of wood as Jake came to stand beside Kayden. "Hey, uh, is everything all right?"

Not even close. "It's fine."

He started to turn, but Jake grabbed his arm. "Before you go, I just wanted to apologize for last night. I'm sorry. It was none of my business, and if I was dating a woman and someone said to her what I said to Tilly, I'd be pissed as well. I let my feelings for her cloud my judgment."

Kayden scrubbed a hand over his face. The apology sounded authentic, but it didn't change what Jake had done, and right now he didn't feel all that forgiving. "I'm taking a break."

Before Jake could respond, Kayden was moving, getting the hell out of there before he did or said something he'd regret. He'd just stepped onto the deck when his phone rang, Cody's name on the screen.

"Cody. Everything okay?"

"Actually, I need to tell you something, and you won't like it."

Kayden wrapped his fingers around the railing. Maybe he should have just stayed in bed today. "What?"

"You know how Flint Matthews bought our family house when Dad couldn't afford to keep it?"

The guy had owned the land beside their father's and bought it to expand his farm. "Yeah."

"He's knocking the house down."

Kayden's blood ran cold. To most, it would just be a house. Walls and floors and lights. To him, it was where all his memories still lived. Of his mom. His dad. Their family gatherings, before loss and devastation had hit. "You're shitting me?"

"I wish I was. Barry heard it from Mrs. Sandler. I called Flint, and he confirmed it."

Kayden hung his head, something dark and dangerous building in his chest.

Flint couldn't knock down the house. In Kayden's eyes, it was still their home. "I'll buy it back from him."

"We've tried that before," Cody said softly. "He's not willing to sell. The house was just a bonus for him. What he really wanted was the land so he could increase his livestock."

Kayden rubbed his temple, the beginnings of a headache forming as his father's words repeated in his head.

"I've sold the family house, son. I'm sorry. I had no other choice."

Not just his words…the pain behind them. The guilt, as if his father had somehow let Kayden and his siblings down. He hadn't. Martin fucking Taylor had.

"Kay…you all right?"

No. He was far from all right. "I need to go."

He hung up and moved into the visitors center.

Pixie stepped out of the eco room, brows shooting up, probably from the expression on his face. "Hey."

He nodded but that was about all he could manage before walking into Tilly's office. He stopped at the door…empty. Where was she? She was usually here by now. He turned back to Pixie as she lowered into her desk chair. "Tilly's not here?"

"No. She must be running late, which is unusual."

He pulled out his phone, about to call her, when Pixie spoke again.

"Hey. I'm actually glad I caught you before she got here. I'm not sure if I should tell you this, but I heard that you and Tilly are dating, so…"

Kayden lowered his phone, wanting to tell the woman he

didn't have the capacity to deal with anything else right now, but she was already speaking.

"Last night, I was at Meridian and about to leave the bathroom when I heard Tilly on the phone…she was talking to her father."

Kayden's entire body locked, only a pulse beating at his temple. "What are you talking about? She doesn't have anything to do with her father." She'd told him that herself, and he believed her.

Pixie lifted a shoulder. "I just know what I heard. The phone was pressed to her ear, and she called the person on the line 'Dad.'"

That couldn't be true. It just fucking couldn't. She wouldn't lie to him. Not about this.

"I'm sorry," Pixie whispered. "I just…I thought you should know."

Kayden swung around, heading back out onto the deck and toward the mountains, hoping they could somehow give him the peace that felt so fucking out of reach, he was drowning.

CHAPTER 20

Tilly's hands shook and she couldn't suck in a single deep breath.

Almost there. She was almost at the visitors center. Her need for safety and comfort overrode everything else. She knew she needed to call Eastern, but rational thought had completely left her, and all she could concentrate on was her need to see Kayden. Because at some point, he'd become her safety.

Her father had never touched her like that before. Never hurt her or stared at her with that manic, desperate look in his eyes.

She'd had to pull over halfway here because of the panic. It had gripped her like a fist around her heart, squeezing. Tugging. Taking.

She pulled into the visitors center parking lot but didn't get out of the car right away. She needed to breathe. To get herself together at least so that if she ran into other people, she didn't look as completely wrecked as she felt.

She tilted the rearview mirror, hating the ghost-white of her skin and the red that rimmed her eyes. Over the years, her father had become a monster in her head. A man who could destroy lives without a backward glance.

And today…today she'd seen that monster with her own eyes.

Screw it. She wasn't going to look any better from a few deep breaths in the car. She took out her phone and called Kayden.

On the fifth ring, she realized he wasn't going to answer.

When Pixie glanced up as she entered the visitors center, her eyes widened. "Tilly…are you okay?"

"Do you know where Kayden is? I really need to speak to him."

"He's out on the trail."

There were miles of trails. "Do you know where, exactly?"

"No, I don't, sorry. But there was a tree that fell across the north walking path. He might still be there."

She nodded. Good. Surely, that's where he'd be.

She'd just stepped off the deck when Jake's gaze collided with hers. His brows slashed together as he took her in, clearly seeing what Tilly had seen in the mirror…a mess.

He moved over to her. "Tilly, are you okay?"

"Not really. I need Kayden. Do you know where he is?"

"Uh, yeah, he's just down that path, moving wood. The rest of the guys and I are taking a break. Do you want me to come with you?"

"No. I'm okay to find him. Thank you." Her words came out in a rush.

She felt Jake's eyes on her as she moved down the path, but she didn't look back.

Her father was back. Had been in her home. Touched her. Demanded her help. Wanted her *house*! It was all she could think about.

The panic was just rising in her chest again, tightening, when she saw him. Kayden's head was down as he lifted pieces of wood from the ground.

She quickened her steps, almost jogging toward him. "Kayden."

His back was to her, and for a moment, he froze. Went so still, his back didn't even move with a breath.

"What do you want, Tilly?"

She frowned. Why didn't he turn to look at her while he spoke? And why was his voice so hard? "I need to talk to you about something."

He dumped the pile of wood in his arms into a wheelbarrow. When he turned back around, he still didn't look at her.

What the hell was going on?

She stepped in front of him, blocking his way to the woodpile. "Kayden?"

"What is it?"

The panic that had set in at the first sight of her father rippled and expanded in her chest, making it hard for her to breathe. "Will you look at me?"

It took three beats, then, finally, his gaze rose. But his eyes… they were a mix of anger and…something else. Something she couldn't name, but she knew she didn't like. "What's wrong?"

"Are you here to tell me about your father?"

She flinched. How did he—

"Are you back in contact with him?" Kayden asked before she could get a word in. "Was he the one you were speaking with on the phone last night at the bar?"

She opened and closed her mouth, suddenly unsure what was going on. "Yes, but—"

"*Jesus*, Tilly!" He stepped back, running his fingers through his hair as frustration flashed across his features. "And you didn't feel the need to tell me? Was it *him* who left you a message at Cody's birthday dinner too?"

"Yes. But Kay—"

"This entire time, you've been lying to me."

"No! Well, yes, I didn't tell you, but I told Eastern—"

"You told my brother but not me?" If possible, his eyes darkened further.

"He's the sheriff."

"Were you ever planning to tell me?"

"That's why I came here. He came to my house this morning."

"He's *here?*" Kayden asked, his eyes turning almost black. "In Misty Peak?"

"Yes, but Kayden—"

"I can't do this, Matilda."

She flinched at his use of her full name. At the way he stepped around her and walked away like he couldn't stand to be around her.

"You can't do what?" she asked, words almost a whisper.

"I should have listened to my gut," he said, almost to himself. "I knew you were a Taylor, and yet I *still* allowed myself to believe that you could cut him out after what he did. I allowed myself to believe you were different."

"I *am* different."

"How?" He spun on her, but there was no softness in his expression. "How can you be different when you talk to him, have him in your home, knowing what he did to my father? What he did to so many goddamn people in this town?"

He stepped closer to her again, but she couldn't move. She felt numb. Like she wasn't here, this wasn't real, and his words weren't really what she was hearing.

"I have so many memories of what your father's theft did to my dad," he continued. "Of what losing his house, our family home, did to him. We'd already lost so much and were in the midst of his sickness, then *your* family just stepped in and took even more."

If she wasn't so numb, his words might have felt like blows to her midsection.

Tears gathered in her eyes, and she wanted to defend herself. He stood there, *waiting* for her to respond. But what was the point? After everything they'd been through together, all the progress they'd made, after what she'd said to him last night, he still didn't trust her.

He probably never would.

"It was always going to end like this, wasn't it?" she whispered, a tear falling down her cheek.

He turned his head, like the sight of her crying was too much to bear. "You should go."

Go? Where was she supposed to go? She'd come back to Misty Peak looking for that sense of home, and for a fleeting moment, she'd thought she'd found it.

Forcing her feet to move, she turned and walked toward the visitors center. Getting to her car was a blur, and so was the drive. She didn't even realize where she was going until she pulled up in front of Harper's house.

Still numb, she climbed out and walked to the front door, but it wasn't Harper who opened it…it was Cody. The smile on his face dropped the second he saw her. She hadn't checked herself in the mirror this time, but if she looked anything like she felt, it wasn't good.

"Tilly? Are you okay?"

She opened her mouth to say no, to ask if Harper was home, because she needed one person, just one, who trusted her. Cared about her. But before she could utter a word, Harper appeared behind him.

Her friend gasped. "Tilly!"

That was all it took. Her name being spoken by a friend, and she fell apart. Let all the tears flow as she fell into Harper's arms.

* * *

KAYDEN'S SKIN crawled as he transferred the wood from the wheelbarrow to his truck, Tilly's expression playing over in his head again and again. Her tears. The sadness in her green eyes.

He'd done that to her. He'd put that sadness there.

Fuck.

He dropped another handful of wood into the bed of the truck. There weren't any tours today, and he needed to move. To exhaust his body and get her out of his head.

Was he wrong in saying what he had? Her father was in contact with her, yet she'd said *nothing*. Oh, she'd told his brother but kept it a secret from him even after everything they'd done together.

The hurt in his chest rippled, not only at her deceit but at the fact that he'd allowed himself to date the daughter of the man who'd hurt his deceased father.

The two images, one of his father and the other of Tilly, competed in his head, plaguing and tormenting him.

He grabbed another handful of wood from the wheelbarrow.

Even though every fiber of his being screamed at him that family took priority, he cared about her, dammit. He cared about Tilly regardless of who her father was or what he'd done or whether she'd forgiven him and let him back into her life. And maybe that was the reason there was this niggle at the back of his head, this whisper, telling him she wasn't that person.

Had that phone call about their family home being knocked down affected his judgment? Jesus, had he even let her speak?

A wild panic suddenly clawed at his chest. And her tears— fuck, her tears were all he could see. That and her pain. Pain that he'd caused before she'd walked away, because he'd told her to go.

He'd just dropped the last of the wood into the truck when a car entered the parking lot, pulling in beside him. Cody's eyes were narrowed as he climbed out, his mouth a thin line. His brother rarely got angry, but right now…right now, he looked furious.

"What the hell is wrong with you?" he growled.

Kayden faced his brother. "What are you talking about?"

"I told you not to hurt her. I gave you simple fucking instructions."

The band around Kayden's chest tightened, making each breath a battle. "How do you know I hurt her?"

"She came to our house. She was a mess, Kayden. Told Harper that her father just showed up *inside* her house this morning. That he grabbed her. She has *bruises* in the shape of fingerprints on her arm. I sat with her while she called Eastern, and she shook the entire time."

What the *fuck*? "He hurt her?"

"You didn't know? Is that because you didn't listen to her when she tried to tell you?"

Goddammit! He ran frustrated fingers through his hair. "I was a mess, Cody! I wasn't thinking straight." Jesus, he *still* wasn't thinking straight.

"I came here to tell you that I know my call this morning about Matthews selling our family home rocked you," Cody said, a bit more calm in his voice. "But you hurt her. *Really* hurt her. And that's not okay."

A million emotions pummeled through Kayden. Anger at her father. Frustration at himself. And guilt. So much damn guilt.

Cody rubbed the back of his neck. "Look...I know you didn't set out to hurt her. But if you care about her at all, you need to make this right. Give her some time, get your head on straight, and decide if you care about her enough to work on yourself. And if you do...fight like hell to get her back."

CHAPTER 21

A light knocking sounded, pricking at Tilly's sleep. She groaned and rolled to her side, pulling the pillow over her head. She'd been awake for hours last night, sleep completely evading her while her mind was in overdrive. Sometimes because of her father, sometimes because of Kayden. Then, even when she *had* gotten to sleep, the two men had bombarded her dreams as well, leading to her waking up feeling completely unrested.

The knock sounded again, this time accompanied by her friend's voice. "Tilly? Are you awake? Can I come in?"

She tugged the pillow down. As much as she wanted to just stay under the covers and ignore the world all day, that was not a good long-term plan. And Harper had been a wonderful friend yesterday, welcoming her into her home. Feeding her. Sitting with her as she'd told Eastern what had happened. She and Cody had even driven Tilly to her house to grab some stuff. They'd stayed by her side the entire time in case her father returned…he hadn't.

"Yes, you can come in."

The door opened and Harper stepped into the bedroom, a tray in her hands. "Sorry if I woke you, but Cody and I are getting to the bar early today to do some restocking, and I wanted to talk to you before I left." She sat on the edge of the bed and lay the tray on the sheets. "I've brought you a delicious, gourmet breakfast."

Tilly glanced at the cereal, milk, and coffee.

"Okay," Harper rushed out. "We're out of a lot of groceries and this is all we had, but it's the thought that counts, right?"

She gave her friend a small smile. "Thank you. I really appreciate it. And thank you for letting me stay last night."

"Not just last night, you can stay for as long as you need." She pushed some hair behind Tilly's ear. "How are you feeling this morning?"

"Like crap." She ran her finger over a crease in the sheets. "There's this sickly pit in my belly because my father's in town. Because he took a key to my house...a house that he wants and obviously feels entitled to."

"So, we'll change the locks. And if he ever catches you alone, you speed-dial me or Cody or Eastern and we'll be there."

She was so lucky to have this woman as a friend. "Thank you."

"What about Kayden?"

Her heart clenched at the mention of his name...how stupid was that? "Honestly, I feel like an idiot. I asked him that night at the bar what we were doing, and he basically told me that he didn't know, yet I still woke up the next morning trusting he'd come back to me with the answer I wanted to hear. That he'd choose me, not for a fling or just to share my bed, but because he cared about *me* and maybe...maybe one day...love me."

Harper squeezed her thigh. "That doesn't make you an idiot. It makes *him* an idiot for not treating you right."

"I trusted someone I had no business trusting."

"Because you care about him."

Love...she was falling in love with him. And that made all of this so much worse.

She scrubbed a hand over her eyes, not wanting to shed any more tears. She'd already cried enough.

"Has he texted you?" Harper asked.

"I'm not sure. I turned my phone off last night, and I haven't turned it back on yet." Maybe because a part of her was afraid Kayden *hadn't* texted or called and her father had.

Harper glanced at the phone on the bedside table, then back at Tilly. "Want me to be here while you turn it on?"

She shook her head. "No. I can do it." She was an adult, so she should be able to do that alone. Keyword—should.

"All right, but before I go, I need to tell you something."

Why did her gut tighten at those words? "Okay."

"After you came over so upset yesterday, Cody kind of went and spoke to Kayden."

Her belly twisted. "What did he say?"

"Not much...but Cody thinks Kay knows he screwed up. He has trust issues."

Tilly dropped her head into her hands. "Harper—"

"I know! It wasn't his place, but that's Cody. He needs to act when the people in his circle are hurting, and you're in his circle." Tilly looked up to see Harper nibbling her bottom lip. "What do you think you'll do if he says he's sorry and wants you back?"

A million emotions ran throughout her body, but she instantly squashed almost all of them.

"I can't take him back," she whispered, the words hurting more out loud than in her head. "I can't leave myself open to that kind of hurt again. I deserve someone who trusts and protects me. Who can be there on my hardest days. I needed him yesterday. I needed him more than I've ever needed another person... and he let me down."

"He did," Harper said softly. "You deserved more."

"I can't change what my father did. All I can do is be myself and show those around me who I am. Kayden and I shared so much together, but it wasn't enough to convince him I'm different to my dad, and I don't think anything ever will be."

Harper's eyes saddened, then she tugged Tilly into a hug. "Well, you'll always have me. And Cody, because we're kind of a package deal these days."

Tilly hugged her friend back, not realizing how much she needed it until this moment. "Thank you."

"You sure you're going to be okay today?"

"Yeah." She pulled back. "I'm going to spend a few hours at work but get there late and leave early. I'll do everything else I need to do here."

"Okay. Call if you need anything."

When Harper left, she didn't get right up. She didn't eat the cereal either. She had no appetite, just took a few sips of the coffee before finally lifting her phone and turning it on. No voice messages, but one text. It took her a few breaths of courage to click into it.

Kayden: I'm sorry. Can we talk?

She clicked out of the text and dropped the cell onto the bed as if it had burned her. *Jesus.* She scrubbed her hands over her face, a part of her wishing she could not go to work today, but the other part of her not willing to hide. She'd done nothing wrong. There was no reason she had to stop living her life.

She'd get through today and each day after, and hopefully soon, working in the same place as him would get easier.

Over the next half hour, she changed, did her hair, and applied enough makeup so that her face didn't look so red and puffy. Well, mostly not red and puffy.

When she got to the visitors center, she had to work up the courage to get out of the car. It took more time than it should have. Yesterday, she'd come here looking for refuge. Today... today she'd be okay if she just got through it without running into Kayden.

Inside, she gave Pixie a small nod before moving to her office and closing the door. That's when she took her first full breath. This was good. She was at work. She wasn't having a meltdown. Now she just needed to get through the next seven hours.

* * *

"We had a break on Jake's shooting."

Kayden's gaze scanned the parking lot from where he stood on a rise, barely able to concentrate on the phone call from Eastern. He'd stuck close to this part of the trail all morning, just because it had a great view of the parking lot. He needed to know when Tilly got here. He needed to know she was okay.

"What's the break, Eastern?"

He was still pissed at his brother for not telling him about Tilly's father. Of course, the rational part of him understood that he hadn't been allowed to, but the irrational part of him…that was angry as hell.

"Jake remembered what he saw before he was shot."

At the beat of silence, Kayden blew out a breath. "You gonna make me guess what it was?"

"A watch…and it was covered in blood."

"A watch?"

"Yep. He said it was unisex so could belong to a male or female. We must have missed it because it was under a patch of dirt. Maybe it fell off the person as they were leaving the scene."

"It's gone though, right?"

"Yeah, but it's something." His brother paused. "You still pissed at me for not telling you about Martin Taylor?"

"Yes." The word was instant and he didn't care how fucking immature it was.

Eastern sighed. "Technically, it was an ongoing case and I wasn't supposed to share it."

"Screw ongoing cases. I'm your bother."

"Kayden."

Kayden's back teeth ground together. "It's not your fault. And it's not hers either. If I'd done more to trust her, she might have told me." He straightened when he saw Tilly's car pull up in the parking lot.

"Well, if you see her father, call me," Eastern continued. "He has a lot to answer for in this town."

"If I see the asshole, I'll be doing more than calling you."

"Kayden—"

"I've got to go."

He hung up before his brother could get another word in, watching as Tilly climbed out of the car. Blood pumped faster in his veins, his heart taking off in his chest. She was so damn beautiful. Even while her eyes were sad and her lips downcast, she was still the most beautiful woman he'd ever seen. He'd taken that for granted. Then let the insecure parts of him screw everything up and hurt her.

He didn't move right away, instead taking a moment to breathe. Run over the words he had to say to her in his head. Until, finally, he felt capable of going to her.

Every step felt harder than the last because he knew the chance of her forgiving him, the chance of her taking him back, was slim. And God, that hurt.

In the building, Pixie looked up from behind the desk. "Hey, Kayden."

He dipped his head, not trusting his voice to work. Not yet. When he reached her office, he didn't knock, and he wasn't sure if that was a smart decision or not, just knew that he couldn't risk her not allowing him in.

He stepped inside and closed the door behind him.

Tilly was on her feet by the printer. When she turned, her mouth opened, but no words came out. For a second, they both just stood there, and he almost felt frozen in the moment of uncertainty.

But he forced the two words out of his mouth. Words he'd

already texted her. Words he needed her to hear in person...to know that he meant. "I'm sorry."

Her brows flickered, but still she remained silent. Just continued to stare at him like she didn't know what to do. He didn't either.

He took a chance and stepped toward her. "There's no reason you should listen to anything I have to say. I didn't listen to you when you needed me to. But I *am* sorry. I messed up. I was in a bad headspace. I'd just found out the guy who bought my dad's house has plans to knock it down, and I just...I built a story in my head where you were the villain, because in that moment I needed someone to blame, and that someone became you."

Another step toward her. Another beat of silence.

"I can't take back what I did," he continued, so quietly he wasn't even sure his words crossed the distance. "But I *can* tell you that I'll do better next time. That I'll work harder to be the man you deserve. To be your protector and your greatest advocate."

One more step forward before he stopped. He was just reaching out a hand when she stepped back, and that small distance she put between them felt like a mile.

"Kayden..." Her voice was a pained whisper. "I can't do this. Not now. Not today."

Her words slashed at his skin like a blade. "Do what?"

"Us." The word was spoken quietly, but it may as well have been a shout, it rang so loudly throughout the room. "I appreciate your apology, and maybe I even believe that you *want* to trust me, but I don't think you ever can...not completely. Not in the way I need. And I'll always be waiting for the next thing to pop up to give you reason to question me."

How was he supposed to argue that when everything she said was something *he'd* made her feel? "I'll prove it to you."

This time when he stepped forward and reached for her hand, she didn't pull away. He grazed the back of it with his thumb before lowering his head so his mouth almost touched her ear. Then he whispered, "I will earn your trust back. That's a promise I'm making to you here and now."

He was almost certain he felt a small shudder work its way down her body.

He wanted to kiss her. To let his lips touch her cheek just one time. But she needed to know she could trust him...trust that this thing between them wasn't just physical. So instead, he straightened and stepped back.

He held her gaze for one more beat before forcing himself to turn and leave the room, maintaining the firm belief that he would get her back.

CHAPTER 22

"These might be a bit strong, but I thought, what the hell, we both have the night off. Let's go crazy."

Tilly eyed the four cocktails on the tray suspiciously. Yes, four...for the two of them. "I don't know if alcohol and my current mood are a good combination."

"See, that's where you're wrong. Cocktails are great for broken hearts. But if you don't want them, I'm happy to take them all." To prove her point, Harper lifted a glass and took a big sip.

They were at the bar, and Tilly was taking a well-deserved night off from worrying about everything. Her father. Kayden. She'd been thinking about both of them far too much this last week. Especially Kayden. It was kind of unavoidable when the guy worked with her and seemed to have every reason under the sun to visit her office ten times a day. It was like in the week since the incident with her dad, he suddenly had a million work questions, and they were all directed her way.

"You're right." Tilly lifted the first cocktail and cringed at the heavy taste of rum. "Okay, I think this is supposed to be a Mai Tai but you seem to have forgotten some of the juice and grenadine."

"Nope. Didn't forget." Harper lifted the stick with the cherry and slid it into her mouth. "We're having a night off, remember?"

Tilly smiled as her gaze inadvertently moved around the bar. "You're sure he's not coming here tonight?"

"I have it under good authority that Kayden is looking after Avery tonight, and I'm sure even after Eastern gets home, Kayden will stay and have a drink with his brother."

She should be happy about that, right? Because there was no way she wanted to see him. Not after they'd ended things and she'd told him she knew he'd never trust her.

"So…" Harper started slowly, "is he still coming into your office every day?"

"Every. Day. Multiple times a day. About tour schedules and rosters and progress on the skywalk." She sipped her cocktail, slowly getting used to the rum. "I tell myself I hate it, but every time I see him, a small part of me wants to just say to hell with everything and fall into his arms. Is that sad?"

Harper's features softened. "Definitely not sad. You care about him. Those feelings don't just go away because he hurt you."

"Feelings suck."

"I'm interested to see how hard he intends to work to get you back."

She gulped down some more Mai Tai. She needed a change in subject. "You still haven't told me what I owe you for arranging the change of locks on my house."

Cody and Harper had offered to organize everything, and even though she'd initially said no, they'd pushed, and she'd caved. Thank God she had, because not only had she not wanted to return to the house with her father still having access, but she wasn't even sure the local locksmith would do the job for her.

Harper cringed. "About that…"

Oh, Jesus, what now?

"Kayden did everything," Harper rushed out.

"What?"

"Cody was going to do it all and the morning he went over there, Kayden called him and got out of him what he was doing. Kayden just took over after that. He put the best locks on every door and window and refused the payment Cody and I offered."

"So now I owe Kayden money and a thank-you?"

"I doubt he'll accept money, and after what he did, the thank-you is probably optional."

She barely tasted the next gulp of Mai Tai. She was well aware that she was drinking the thing far too quickly now but couldn't seem to care. "This is not good."

"I thought it was kind of sweet," Harper said quietly.

Yeah, it was. That was the problem. How was she supposed to get over the guy when he did things like that?

"You know," Harper started, "Cody said he's never seen his brother like this before."

"Like what?"

"Lovesick and lost."

Tilly gave her friend a pointed look. "He did not say that."

"He absolutely did."

Kayden *had* been different over the last week. Every time he'd spoken to her, his voice had been soft and there'd been this kind of yearning in his eyes. There'd also been accidental touches here and there, all so incredibly gentle.

But he hadn't brought up forgiveness or getting back together again. Because he was giving her space?

She shook her head. "Let's talk about something else. Tell me about how you and Cody are doing."

Harper's eyes lit up, and when she talked about her relationship with Cody and the home they'd moved into together, it was like every bit of stress on her face eased.

Harper was happy. Good. She deserved to be happy after everything she'd been through.

Tilly smiled as she listened to all the little things Cody did that made him perfect. The breakfasts in bed. The constant checking on her. The hard work to make the house everything Harper had always dreamed.

"That's amazing, Harper," Tilly said after listening to her friend for a solid twenty minutes while drinking way too much rum. She was already almost finished with her second cocktail and feeling the effects. "Like really amazing. You deserve all the good things."

"Thank you. I feel so lucky to have him and be here. Maybe that's why a part of me has this reckless trust in you and Kayden."

"Really? We're back to Kayden?"

"I just want you to be happy. I mean, you could always just text him and ask him how he's been."

"Why would I do that?"

Her friend lifted a shoulder. "It's like an olive branch for the friendship."

"Kayden and I have never been friends." She finished off her second drink.

"Finished! Time for more cocktails."

Tilly shook her head. "No, Harper, I think—"

"This is for me too, Tilly. And I need some rum punch!"

Before Tilly could stop her, Harper was grabbing the empty glasses and moving back behind the bar.

Her gaze shifted to her phone on the table. Would it hurt to text him? She *did* miss him. God, she missed him so much. And he'd been so sweet for the last week…

She lifted her phone and clicked into his name, her fingers hovering over the keys.

She shouldn't, right? It would be crazy after what he'd assumed of her and the things he'd said. She was about to set the phone down when a text came through.

Kayden: I miss you.

* * *

"How was Avery tonight?"

Kayden gave his cell one more glance before looking up. He sat on Eastern's couch as his brother carried a beer over to him from the kitchen. He'd just gotten home and changed out of his sheriff's uniform.

"Same as usual, amazing," Kayden said, taking the beer from his brother. "You have a good kid."

Eastern sat opposite him. "She is, isn't she? God, I love her." He looked down the hall like he wanted to go into her room and wake her up.

"You heard from her mother recently?" Kayden asked.

A muscle tightened in Eastern's jaw. "She called last week. Said she's met someone. That she still doesn't know when she'll be back."

Anger roared through Kayden's veins on behalf of his brother. That the woman could just up and leave her daughter like it was the easiest thing in the world. Some people would give anything for a kid like Avery.

"Does Avery ask about her?"

"That's the thing. She doesn't. She asks about Sadie more."

Sadie was her former nanny and also Mrs. Sandler's granddaughter. She'd left town right around the time Kayden had returned home because her fiancé had gotten a job in Atlanta.

Kayden glanced down at his phone screen before looking back at his brother. "Maybe she'll come back and visit."

"I hope so. I didn't know her well, I just knew *of* her. I think in recent years, she'd looked after Avery a bit less though…probably Jamie's way of hiding this drinking problem she'd developed."

Kayden's back teeth ground together. Another thing that had come out once Eastern got home. Avery's mother had been drinking far too much on a daily basis, to the point where Avery was being sent to school in dirty clothes and without lunch. If Kayden had known, if the woman had let him have access to his niece, he would have done something about it. He and Cody both.

Eastern's fingers tightened around his beer. "Every so often, Avery will mention something about the last year, and each incident makes me angrier."

"But you're recording everything she tells you, right?"

"Every damn thing. And it all brings me one step closer to gaining full custody of her."

"Good." Another glance at his screen. Still nothing.

"Why do you keep looking at your phone?"

For a moment, Kayden considered lying, but what was the point? "I texted Tilly. It's the first text I've sent her all week. I've been trying to give her space, but after so many days of barely touching or talking to her, I'm going crazy."

"She hasn't texted back?"

"Not yet." He sucked in a long breath. "And I understand why. Hell, I wouldn't trust me either. But if this last week has shown me anything, it's that I need to be better, because I need her. I need to be close to her. To hear her voice."

"Jesus, Kayden, that almost sounds like love."

The word should have scared him. It didn't.

When his phone dinged, his eyes shot straight down.

Tilly: I think I miss you too.

He frowned. Think?

Before he could respond, another text came through.

Tilly: That might be the cocktails talking. I'm not sure. I wish you'd trusted me.

Kayden: I wish I'd trusted you too. Next time I'm tested, I promise you, I will.

Tilly: That would require us getting back together.

Kayden: We are going to get back together.

The three dots popped up, then disappeared.

Kayden: Where are you?

Tilly: Oh, no. No, no, no. I cannot see you while I'm under the influence of alcohol. You'll take advantage of my poor judgment.

Kayden: I'd never do that. I'll look after you. Where are you?

"They're at the bar."

Kayden's gaze shot to his brother. "How do you know?"

"Cody mentioned Harper was taking the night off to have some drinks with Tilly." He tilted his head toward the door. "Go. Fix what you broke."

"Thank you, brother."

"Thank you for looking after my daughter."

Kayden drove too fast to the bar, all the while wrapping his fingers far too tightly around the wheel. Even though the drive was short, it felt endless. The moment he stepped into the bar, he spotted her. The place wasn't too busy, and she was just shuffling out of a booth, Harper opposite her, a half dozen empty glasses on the table.

He walked straight over to her. When she got to her feet, she wobbled, and he held her arm to steady her.

"Hey, I don't—" She stopped when she saw it was him. "Kayden...how did you—"

"Eastern told me you were here."

"The snitch." Her eyes were glazed, and she seemed so unsteady that he didn't want to release her in case she toppled over.

Harper cleared her throat. "Tilly, I know Cody was going to drive you home, but I think it's a bit busy. Would you mind—"

"I'll take her," Kayden cut in.

Tilly glared at her friend, a suspicious gleam to her eyes. "There's no one here, Harper."

"Sure there is." Harper pulled Tilly into a hug and whispered something into her ear that Kayden didn't catch, before stepping back and looking up at Kayden. "Get her home, safely, okay?"

"Of course."

He slid an arm around her waist, not sure if she'd pull away from him. She didn't. In fact, she leaned into his side, and it was the first time he'd felt good in the last week.

When they reached his car, he helped her in before climbing behind the wheel.

He expected Tilly to glance out the window. Maybe sleep a bit. Instead, she leaned her head back and watched him. He waited for her to say something. It was a good couple minutes into the drive before he broke.

"Why are you staring at me, Till?"

"Anyone else and I would have written them off after what happened, but with you, I can't. And I'm not sure why."

Fear buzzed in his ears at the thought of her writing him off. "Because you know that there's a lot more to our story still to be told."

When she was silent, he glanced over to see her frowning at him before she asked, "Why didn't you trust me?"

"Because I'm an idiot." He didn't even need to think about that answer. "Because I didn't realize what I had. Or maybe I did realize, but I was stupid and let it slip away."

She shook her head. "But you're not stupid, that's the thing."

"I am. When it comes to you, I'm the biggest fucking idiot on the planet. But I'm trying to be better."

When they pulled up in front of her house, he didn't miss the immediate tension in her body. The way her gaze skirted around the area like she was searching for her father.

He climbed out, muscles tense as he took in the woods. The dark shadows and easy hiding spots. Nothing. Nothing that he could see, anyway.

Carefully, he helped her out, and yet again she gave him her weight. Fuck, she felt right in his arms.

When they stepped inside, she went straight to her room while Kayden locked the doors and checked the house. When he finally returned to her, it was to see she'd slipped on a T-shirt…*his* T-shirt.

Something rippled in his chest. It was fierce and territorial.

His. She was *his*. He just needed to work out how to make her realize that.

"I'm sorry, Tilly."

Her eyes beamed into him. "You've said that already."

"And I'll keep saying it until you believe me."

She slid beneath the covers. "I do believe you. But I don't believe it won't happen again."

He crossed the space between them and perched on the side of the bed. Like his hand had a mind of its own, he reached for her cheek and cupped it. "How can I prove it to you?"

She leaned into him. "I don't know."

That was the problem. Neither of them knew. He lowered and touched a light kiss to her forehead. He wanted to stay, to keep his lips on her skin. To taste more of her.

Instead, he started to rise, but before he could step away, she grabbed his arm.

"Kayden, will you stay with me? As a friend."

Something akin to fear flashed in her eyes. Even with the new locks on her doors, she was afraid to be alone.

"Yeah, honey, I'll stay. I'll sleep on the couch."

"You could. Or you could sleep with me. The bed's big. We wouldn't have to touch."

He almost laughed. He could barely be in the same room with this woman without touching her. And now she wanted them to be in the same *bed*?

"Please," she whispered when he still hadn't replied. "I don't like being here on my own at the moment. And having you close will help."

There was no saying no to that. He turned off the light, then removed all his clothes except his briefs. When he slid into bed, he was fucking tense. Because all he wanted to do was tug her into his arms.

He heard her roll to her side. Felt her breath on his shoulder. Then her hand was on his chest. "Thank you."

And that was enough to allow the air to slip into his chest with a bit more ease...her simple touch.

CHAPTER 23

*T*illy scrunched her eyes closed, willing the nausea in her belly to fade and the dull throbbing in her temple to ease.

God, why had she drunk so many cocktails last night? Harper had been smart, just sipping hers, while Tilly had acted like a woman dying of thirst, downing everything that was put in front of her.

Dumb. So dumb.

She tried to move but stopped at the weight around her waist. Not just stopped, completely froze. Because it wasn't just any weight…it was an arm. It curved right around her while a hand sat on her bare hip. Yes, bare hip, because the damn shirt she'd worn to bed had ridden up.

Then she started to notice other things…the thick, muscled thigh beneath her leg. The warmth under her cheek. Warmth she'd originally thought was a pillow, but pillows didn't have heartbeats.

Oh, sweet Jesus…she was sprawled over Kayden's sleeping body. His *near-naked* sleeping body.

Shit. This was not part of her stay-away-from-Kayden plan. It was nowhere near it. Her freaking thigh was wrapped around the man, for God's sake.

It was fine. She just needed to untangle herself and get the heck out of the room without waking him. Easy.

Carefully, she started to lift her leg, only to stop. Did his thumb just graze her hip?

Her heart beat faster, and for a moment she remained perfectly still. So still, she didn't even breathe.

He didn't move. Maybe he wasn't awake, which meant he'd either grazed her hip in his sleep, or he hadn't grazed her hip at all and her hungover, overactive mind was making things up.

She tried to lift her leg again. And she did, a good inch, before that arm on her waist tightened and a deep voice pricked the silence.

"Every time you move, your breasts brush against my chest and it drives me wild, Tilly."

Her jaw dropped.

He was awake. How freaking long had he been awake? By the sound of his voice, possibly longer than her.

She lifted her head to see him looking straight at her. And God, that day-old beard, along with the just-woke-up, mussed hair, sent an entire fleet of butterflies off in her belly.

"Sorry." She wasn't sure if she was apologizing for rubbing her chest against him, waking up sprawled over his body, or just this entire situation. "I should get up."

"Do you *want* to get up?"

Well, her body certainly didn't. But that damn thing was betraying her left, right, and center.

She wet her lips, and Kayden's gaze immediately zoned in on her mouth. God, but did that set off a stampede of need in her belly.

"Don't." One whispered word from her lips.

"Don't what?"

"Look at me like that… We're not together anymore." That

was a very simplistic way of putting it. But she felt simple right now, so it was fitting.

"If that's your only reason…" Before she could comprehend what he was doing, he rolled them over so he hovered above her on the mattress. "I fucked up."

"You did." More whispered words. She pressed her hands to his chest, telling herself she intended to push him away. She didn't. Instead, she let his heart thrum against her fingers. Let the warmth of his chest run down her arms.

His head lowered, and she held her breath as his lips grazed her cheek. "When I lost my mother, something inside me…shifted."

He pressed a kiss to her skin, so light it was just a whisper.

"I became scared to lose another family member, terrified of feeling that kind of pain again," he continued, breath running over her skin. "Of seeing the others so hurt."

A hand trailed up her side, making her itch to arch her back. To press herself into him.

"Then years later, Martin stole from my dad, and not only did it renew my fear of family getting hurt, it instilled a new fear in *me*. A fear of trust…because trust makes us vulnerable. It certainly did for my father."

His mouth moved down to her chest, over her T-shirt.

"I'm sorry…" she whispered, hating that his family had been through so much.

"But I'm learning that trust isn't always bad." His lips suddenly closed over her nipple, sucking through the material of her shirt.

She gasped and bowed off the bed, pushing herself farther into his mouth as his teeth grazed her bud. As his tongue swept the nipple back and forth.

"Trust can let a new person in. And Tilly, I have to let you in… because I need you. I've started to crave you, from the moment I wake up in the morning to the moment I sleep." His mouth switched to her other breast, and she squirmed as a new onslaught began. "I'm sorry for what I did. And I will prove that to you, in everything I do from this point on."

She grabbed his shoulders, trying to steady herself. Could a woman orgasm from just a man's mouth on her breasts? Because it felt like she could.

Suddenly the material was shoved up, and his mouth was on her bare breast, teasing and tugging while his hand moved down her body. She groaned and arched again.

"If you want me to stop, you need to tell me now, Tilly."

His words were almost white noise behind the buzzing in her ears. The throbbing in her lower belly.

"Tilly…"

"Don't," she whispered. "Don't stop!"

He growled and latched back onto her breast as his fingers dipped into her panties and stroked her clit. She cried out, her body jolting at the touch. He did it again and again. Swiping and playing. Swirling and teasing.

When he released her nipple, she wanted to plead with him to return to her, but then his mouth moved down her belly, kissing her hip bone before her panties were tugged down her legs.

"Kayden…" That's all she got out before he widened her thighs, closed his lips over her clit, and sucked.

She screamed, her hips trying to rise off the bed, but Kayden's arms around her thighs kept her exactly where she was. His tongue ran down her core, flicking and sucking.

The heat in her belly grew, until there was a delicious burn in her lower belly. She threaded her fingers through his hair and tugged at the strands.

When fingers went to her entrance, her breath stopped. Then he pushed inside, and she bowed off the bed, a cry falling from her lips.

He thrust in and out of her, his mouth never leaving her clit. She could barely breathe. It felt like a giant fist was squeezing her chest.

He changed the angle of his thrust, hitting that spot deep inside her that made her want to gasp and cry and fall. He sucked her clit hard, and suddenly, she broke. Screamed as her body catapulted over the edge and she shattered into a million pieces.

The scream was cut off by Kayden's mouth on hers, his tongue sweeping between her lips and tangling with her own while his fingers continued to work her, his thumb on her clit.

Her body pulsed as Kayden's kiss softened, slipping into something else, something smoother…gentler.

When his head finally lifted, his eyes were an intense blue, and he looked at her like she was the only thing he saw.

His mouth lowered to her ear, and he nipped her lobe. "You're so fucking sweet." When he finally slipped his fingers out of her, she whimpered. She tried to reach for him, but he gripped her wrist, halting her. "That was just for you, honey."

"Kayden…"

His mouth trailed back to her mouth before he lifted his head. "I'm gonna take a shower, then make you breakfast."

She nibbled her bottom lip. "How am I supposed to stay mad at you when you make me feel so much?"

One more kiss of her lips before he whispered, "You're not."

* * *

Kayden turned down the heat on the eggs. He'd taken the coldest damn shower of his life, but even that hadn't calmed his heated body. Touching Tilly, tasting her…fuck, it made him lose his damn mind with need.

He grabbed the bagels out of the toaster and placed them on the plates.

But he was a patient man. He had to be. Last night she'd asked him to stay with her because he made her feel safe, and this morning she'd let him touch her. Hell, he'd woken with her body slung across his. That was progress, and he just needed to keep building on that and chipping away at the wall that had been constructed because of his doing. Soon, they'd be back to where they'd been before…only better.

He'd just placed the bacon on the plates when Tilly stepped out of the bedroom. Her hair was down and falling over her shoulders, and she wore black pants that hugged the curves of her thighs.

For a moment he couldn't move…couldn't breathe. "You're so damn beautiful."

One side of her mouth lifted. "I'm wearing work slacks and a sweater."

"Gorgeous."

A hint of a smile pulled at her lips as she perched on a stool at the small island. "You made bacon and bagels."

"And eggs and coffee." He slid the eggs onto the plates before finishing the coffees.

When he returned to Tilly, it was to see her brows knitted together as if she was deep in thought.

One side of his mouth tugged up. "What's on your mind, honey?"

"Did you mean what you said? That the reason you struggle to let people in is because of your mom, and you want to be better?"

"Every word." He lowered to the other stool but angled his body toward her. "I'm not good at letting people in, and I kind of knew that, but it was confirmed when I met you. I wanted to let you in so damn bad, and I was terrified. But I want to keep trying. You make me want to be the man you deserve."

Her brows flickered. "I'm scared to let you in again. Relationships are tested all the time."

His heart cracked. "I *will* be better at the next test." When she still didn't look convinced, he reached out and took her hand. "I know it's hard to believe right now, but the next time something happens, I'll be your greatest protector, Tilly. That's a promise I intend to keep."

Hope flickered in her eyes. She wanted to trust him, he could see it. But he'd fractured her belief in him.

He lifted her hand and kissed the back. "Eat, honey."

As they ate, he turned the conversation to work. She spoke about the visits she'd organized for local schools. The progress on the skywalk, which was almost complete. She loved her work. It was obvious in the way she lit up when she talked about it. The excitement in her eyes as she talked about the increase in visitors and exposure. They didn't talk about what had happened with Macy's stabbing or Jake's shooting, instead keeping conversation light.

"I just want everyone to experience what I did as a kid," she said quietly.

"And what's that?"

"The magic of the mountains we get to call our backyard. All my best memories growing up were in those woods, and all with my mom."

"Not your dad?"

Her smile slipped, and her gaze lowered to her almost finished plate of food. "He worked a lot. I barely saw him. I think that's why my mom and I were so close. I was an only child, and she was my best friend."

"I'm sorry you lost her."

"I was lucky I had her to raise me. Others aren't so fortunate. Harper showed me that."

"One person's pain doesn't diminish another's."

For a moment their gazes held, and damn if he didn't want to lower his head and kiss the woman again. But before he could so much as lean forward, she looked away.

"We should get to work."

She rose, grabbed his empty plate and her almost empty one, and took them to the sink.

Ten minutes later, and they were just stepping outside when a car pulled up in her driveway. His eyes narrowed, while Tilly gasped and stepped back...that's when he realized who it was.

Martin Taylor parked in front of the house and stepped out of his car, a frown on his face when he glanced at Kayden. The man looked older, but he also looked exactly the same—like the fucking thief he was.

The guy stopped, seeming to reconsider whatever he was about to do.

"It's gone, son. All of it. Martin took it, and he's not coming back."

The memory of his father's words was like gas on the fire of his rage. Before he could stop himself, he was marching forward.

"Kayden!"

Tilly's panicked voice sounded behind him, but no one could have stopped him. "You have some fucking nerve showing your face in this town again."

He'd taken a few steps off the porch when Martin pulled a gun from a concealed holster.

Tilly gasped, crashing into Kayden's back when he stopped, and he wrapped an arm behind him to keep her shielded.

"I don't want to shoot anyone, son," Martin said, voice steady. "I just want to talk to my daughter about this house and some money owed."

"I don't owe you anything, Dad." Tilly's voice was almost breathless with shock. "This is *my* house. You need to leave."

"I really need the money." His gaze shifted to Kayden, eyes wide, almost wild. "Leave us, and I won't hurt you."

"The fuck I will," Kayden growled. "I am *not* leaving her with you. You'll have to say what you need to say in front of me or shoot me."

Tilly's fingers tightened on Kayden's arm, and she tried to shift in front of him, but he tugged her back, refusing to let her. "Kayden—"

"Stay behind me, Tilly."

She made a sound of protest before speaking to her father.

"Dad, you're not a killer. Just go, before you do something you can't take back."

Taylor's eyes shifted between them, frustration and…something else in his expression. Fear? Yeah, there was definitely a bit of fear there. He didn't want to shoot anyone. Maybe he couldn't even if he wanted—

Martin pulled the trigger, and Tilly screamed.

There was a puff of dirt from the ground in front of Kayden before Martin shouted, "Go!"

"No." Kayden's voice was low and dangerous.

Long seconds of silence passed before Martin finally growled, slipped back into his car, and left.

CHAPTER 24

*H*ours had passed since her father's visit to her house, yet her hands still shook. Even after Eastern and his deputies had come and taken statements, assuring both her and Kayden that they'd scour the town to search for him.

No one had found him in five years, so she wasn't exactly optimistic that they'd find him now, even if he was right here in Misty Peak. At least Kayden had thought to memorize the license plate. Tilly had been too busy losing her mind.

A gun! Her father had pulled a *gun* on them. Did he even know how to shoot? She wouldn't have thought so, but then, she'd probably never known her father at all.

She opened her second drawer to look for sticky notes. When there were none in there, she opened the bottom drawer and shuffled a few things around before pulling out a yellow pad. The second she lifted the notes, she stopped.

There was a watch in her drawer. Where had that come from? It certainly wasn't hers. She didn't even own a watch.

Lifting it, she studied the beige band and the intricate hands. She turned it, only to frown at the specks of red on the silver.

Wait…was that *blood*?

"Sorry to bother you, Tilly, but do you have—"

She looked up to see Jake in her doorway. He stopped, mouth open, eyes on the watch.

"Jake? Are you okay?"

His eyes shot back up to hers, and it took a moment before he answered. "Y-yes. I'm fine. I just…I remembered I'm supposed to be somewhere."

What? Then why had he come to her office? "Jake—"

But he was already gone before she could finish. What the hell was going on?

She followed Jake to the front room, but he was nowhere to be seen. Pixie sat at her desk, eyes on the screen of her computer.

"Pixie."

She glanced up, a small smile on her face. Kayden had told her that it was Pixie who'd informed him about the phone call. When Tilly had approached her about it, the other woman had apologized for involving herself in the matter. Tilly had been annoyed. If Pixie had really wanted to protect Kayden, she could have asked Tilly about the circumstances first, to be certain she had her details correct.

But at the end of the day, what was done was done. There was nothing that could change what had happened.

"Do you know if Jake's okay?" Tilly asked, leaning against the desk.

Pixie glanced up at the doors, then back at Tilly. "He didn't say anything before he left. Why? Is something wrong?"

"I'm not sure." She glanced down at the watch still in her hand before holding it out to show Pixie. "Have you seen this before?"

Pixie shook her head. "No. Should I have?"

"I don't know. It was in my bottom drawer. I guess it could have been Linda's. She left quite a few items in the office, and I didn't clear everything out of the drawers. But I would have thought I'd have seen it before now." She shook her head. "Anyway, it's not your problem."

She went back to her office and set the watch onto the desk, making a note to contact Linda about it when she got back from her cruise. But that wouldn't be anytime soon. The woman would be gone for months and quite often had no signal.

Okay, time to concentrate, Tilly. You have a million things to do today, and you cannot afford to be distracted.

Forcing her eyes to the screen, she made herself work. She got through half a dozen emails, two bookings, and paid some invoices for the skywalk construction before a loud commotion in the other room had her attention drawing toward the door.

What the heck was that? There were a couple of tours this afternoon, but they'd already left.

She rose to her feet as the door to her office was pushed open —and Eastern was there. He wore his sheriff's uniform, but there was no smile on his face. Jake stood beside him, and a few officers followed.

Tilly's heart clenched. Had something happened? Did it involve her father? "What's going on?"

"That's the watch," Jake said quietly to Eastern, as he pointed to the watch on Tilly's desk.

Eastern's expression turned almost confused before his gaze returned to Tilly. "Tilly, we need to take you into the station for questioning."

What on earth? "Questioning about what?"

"About why a watch that was previously covered in blood and found by Jake right before he was shot is currently in your possession."

* * *

"You're very lucky to work in these mountains, young man."

Kayden looked down at the older woman as they neared the visitors center. His tour group was small, with three men and two women, all in their sixties. It had been a slow hike but also a nice, easy one.

"I remind myself that every day, ma'am."

"Oh, please. I've told you, call me Beatrice. Ma'am makes me feel old."

Kayden dipped his head. "Well, that brings us to the end of our tour. Thank you all for visiting, and I hope you come again."

The second woman touched his arm…she'd been touching his biceps all tour. "Oh, we will."

One of the men scoffed. "Come on, Betty, the young man's probably had enough of us."

Kayden bit back a grin as he watched the group walk the few remaining yards to the visitors center. It had been good to have several tours come through today. It took his mind off what had happened this morning with Tilly's father.

The muscles in his arms contracted at the memory. He'd pulled a fucking *pistol*. Why had he been carrying that to visit Tilly? Was it just precautionary? Or had the man had other intentions?

Theo and Hendrix rounded the building, laughing at something between them. Theo, in particular, looked pleased.

"Something funny?" Kayden asked as they neared him.

Both men turned their attention to him, the smiles wiping clean from their faces.

Hendrix cleared his throat. "You hear the news?"

"What news?"

There was a subtle smirk on Theo's face. "We were talking to Pixie at the desk, and she told us your brother came in with a few other officers."

Kayden frowned. What the fuck? Eastern hadn't told him he was coming. "What did they want?"

"Apparently," Theo started, "our boy Jake called them after spotting a watch in Tilly's hands. The same watch that he found covered in blood just before he was shot."

Kayden's throat closed. "That's not fucking possible."

"It is," Hendrix said quietly. "I'm sorry, Kayden."

What the hell?

Kayden ran toward his truck, the need to get to Tilly, protect her, so fucking strong he couldn't feel anything else. He tugged his phone from his pocket and called his brother. When Eastern didn't answer, he cursed and got behind the wheel.

Had Jake spoken to anyone before calling the fucking sheriff's office? Or had he just assumed the worst?

He got to the station in half the time it should have taken him. He'd just stepped inside when he saw Jake coming down the hallway. Kayden was moving before he could stop himself, grabbing Jake by the collar of his shirt and pushing him against the wall before shouting, "What the hell did you do?"

Jake lifted his hands as an officer shouted at Kayden from behind.

He ignored the noise around him and pulled Jake forward before smashing him against the wall again. "Did you even talk to her first? Ask her about the watch?"

"Why would I give her a chance to run? It was the watch that was covered in blood, probably *Macy's* blood, and she had it!"

"She was with *me* when you were shot, so that couldn't have been her. And to just assume that the blood is Macy's, that Tilly was involved, shows you don't know a fucking thing about her!"

"Let him go, Kayden," Eastern said from behind. "*Now*, or I swear to God, I'll cuff you."

Jake's mouth opened and closed. "I was just trying to do the right thing!"

"You made a big fucking mistake." One more shove, and he released the asshole's shirt.

Eastern tugged him into his office and slammed the door after him. "What the hell was that?"

Kayden spun on his brother. "You're asking *me* that? You *arrested* Tilly without telling me. Where the hell is she?"

"I didn't arrest her. I asked her to come in and she agreed. She's in a room being questioned."

Kayden stepped closer, his voice lowering to a dangerous level. "Get her out of here. She had nothing to do with Macy's murder."

"Kayden, you need to let me do my job. I don't think she did it either, but that watch was in her possession, and it still had blood on it. It's being tested right now to see if the blood matches Macy's."

"And if it does, what? It's automatically her? You arrest her for fucking murder?"

A muscle in Eastern's jaw clenched.

"You know this wasn't her," Kayden pushed. "The person who shot Jake took the watch. *She* couldn't have shot him because she was with me. And why the hell would she keep something that incriminates her for murder in her desk at work?"

"Like I said, I'm not saying she did it. But others may assume she had a partner...a partner who needs money. And when Macy caught her stealing, she was chased down and killed, then her partner saw Jake with the watch in the mountains that day and shot him."

Kayden flinched like his brother had hit him. "You're talking about her father. You think people will assume she worked with her father to rob the visitors center and kill Macy. Do you know how fucking ridiculous that sounds?"

"But that's the thing, it doesn't sound ridiculous to other people in this town. I can't wear my brother hat right now, Kay. I have to wear my sheriff's hat and do my due diligence to at least question her. Her father's return combined with knowing he needs money, and now the watch being in her possession, isn't good. The fact that she spent so much time with Jake in the hospital too, almost like she was waiting to see if he remembered anything, doesn't help."

God, this was unbelievable. Kayden wanted to punch something. To feel something other than this raging anger and frustration. "Who's questioning her?"

"Paxley."

Good. At least she was fair. There were some officers here who Kayden knew wouldn't be so kind.

Eastern's phone beeped with a text. He glanced down and his jaw tightened.

"What?" Kayden growled.

Eastern glanced up at him. "That's the lab…the blood type's a match with Macy's."

CHAPTER 25

Tilly's head throbbed. A combination of the hangover, her father's visit, and now being stuck in this interrogation room for what felt like hours.

At first, it hadn't been so bad. A woman who'd introduced herself as Officer Paxley had been interviewing her. Then this guy had stepped in, argued with the female officer before basically forcing her to leave, and he'd started hounding her, asking her the same questions over and over again. He clearly liked her as much as the dirt beneath his shoe.

She dropped her head into her cuffed hands. The guy had put them on her the second the female officer had left, as if she was some kind of felon who'd attempt an escape otherwise. She wasn't under arrest, but when she'd tried to tell him that, it was like he hadn't even heard her.

"I told you," she said, exhaustion ringing in her voice. "I don't know how that watch got into my drawer."

"Yet, it *was* in your drawer, and you were holding it when Jake stepped in."

"Wouldn't you?" she asked, louder than necessary, as she lifted her head to stare at him across the table. "If you opened your drawer and saw something that wasn't yours, that didn't belong there, wouldn't you pick it up and look at it?"

He leaned over and flattened his hands on the surface. "We're not talking about me. We're talking about *you*. The woman who conveniently stepped into town right before a murder takes place. Tell me again where you were the night Macy Hodgkins was stabbed to death?"

God, she wanted to scream. "I was home. I *told you* I was home, and before you ask for the millionth time, no I don't have anyone to corroborate that story because I was by myself."

His phone dinged, and he straightened as he pulled it out to look at the screen. "Well, would you look at that, we have confirmation that the blood type on the watch is a match for Macy's. Won't be long before we find out the blood itself is hers."

The blood drained from her face and a light-headedness took over. What did that mean? That someone was framing her for murder?

The chair scraped opposite her as the officer sat down. "Come on, Matilda, let's be honest with each other. We both know this is mostly your father's doing. You were working together, right? He burned through the money he stole from locals in this town, so he got you to help him steal from the visitors center. Only, Macy saw you, and you and your father chased her down. Maybe he killed her, and you tried to save her, that's how the blood got on your watch." He angled closer. "Tell me this was Martin Taylor, and I'll make sure you get a lighter sentence."

Tears of frustration pressed at her eyes. Everything was a mess. The officer hated her and wanted to convict her of murder, her temple throbbed, and her wrists ached from how tightly this jerk had cuffed her. And the fact that someone, probably Macy's killer and Jake's shooter, had planted that watch in her drawer to set her up for something she didn't do just made everything worse.

At her continued silence, the officer scowled in anger. "Matilda—"

"It's Tilly," she ground out. "And I *didn't* do it. No amount of intimidation from you can make me say otherwise." She swallowed and blinked the tears away, refusing to give this man the satisfaction of seeing her cry. "You know how stupid it sounds, right? That my father would shoot Jake, take the watch, give it back to me, then I'd put it in my drawer at work so I can hold it while Jake steps into my office?"

"Yeah, it does sound stupid." The officer scowled. "But then, the Taylor family hasn't really been known for their smarts."

If she wasn't cuffed, exhausted, and in pain, she'd slug this guy. It wasn't like she had anything to lose, she was already being blamed for goddamn *murder.*

The officer had just risen and begun to ask her another round of questions, when the door behind him opened.

The deputy turned. "I'm not finished with her, Walker. I haven't gotten a confession."

"What the hell are you doing here? I sent Paxley in to question her."

"Yeah, well, I took over."

Fury washed over Eastern's face as he moved into the officer's space. "That's not your call. Get out and I'll deal with you later."

"I still have—"

"Get. Out. *Now.*"

The guy huffed, giving her one final glare before storming out of the room.

Eastern knelt down and undid her cuffs, cursing when he saw the red marks on her wrists. "Fuck. I'm so sorry. I didn't know he was in here. And you shouldn't have been cuffed for questioning."

"I said that." She lifted a hand to massage her temple. "He didn't care that the cuffs weren't necessary or that they were hurting me."

Anger darkened Eastern's features. "I'm sorry. I should have checked on you earlier."

She just nodded, not really having the energy for more words.

"Come on." Gently, he helped her rise, and when she wobbled on her feet, he grabbed her elbow to steady her. "You okay?"

"Yeah. I've got a headache and haven't had any water since I arrived."

Eastern cursed. "I'm gonna kill Jarrad. That's if Kayden doesn't kill me first."

She frowned. "Kayden's here?"

A part of her had wondered whether Kayden had heard about this, and what he thought about it all. Did he wonder if she was guilty like Jake had?

"Yeah, and he's been giving me hell to get you out of here since he arrived." Eastern led her to the kitchen, where he got her a glass of water before taking her to the waiting area.

Kayden was the first person she saw…the only person.

The second his gaze collided with hers, he was marching toward her, like a warrior with eyes only for her.

He stopped right in front of her and lifted a hand to her cheek, his other going to her hip. "Are you okay?"

"Not really." She couldn't even muster a lie. She was too physically and mentally exhausted, and by the look on Kayden's face, he knew it.

His gaze trailed down her body, pausing on her wrists. He lifted her left hand and lightly grazed a thumb over the redness. When she flinched, his eyes turned black as his gaze slid over to Eastern.

"What the fuck is this?"

"I know," Eastern said, his voice low and hard. "Another officer took over her questioning without my knowledge. I'll deal with it."

"You'll *deal* with it? Her wrists are fucking red and raw."

"I said, I know. There will be consequences for the person responsible."

Kayden stepped toward his brother, but Tilly grabbed his arm with one hand and touched her temple with her other. "Kayden… can you just take me home? I'm tired."

His eyes shifted back to her, and whatever he saw made his anger shift to concern. "Yeah, let's go, honey."

* * *

KAYDEN PACED around Tilly's kitchen. She'd been quiet the entire drive home, but then, so had he. The fury was so fucking fierce that he'd wanted to storm back into the station, find the officer responsible for her treatment, and drive his fist into their face.

They'd *hurt* her. Not only that, but she'd been a second away from passing out. Dehydrated. Tired.

A vein throbbed in his temple as he glanced at her half-closed bedroom door.

He'd kept that rage inside him, locked away, because she hadn't needed that. She'd needed comfort. Someone to be by her side and make sure she was looked after.

His brother had called to tell him that the officer had been reprimanded. It wasn't enough. But then, nothing would be.

He tried to hold off going into her bedroom, to give her space, but every minute that ticked by felt like ten. He'd already given her some water and painkillers, but he wanted to do more.

Fuck it.

He pushed off the counter and walked to the bedroom, knocking on the door. When there was no answer, he stepped inside to see the room empty. Was she in the bathroom? The shower didn't sound like it was on.

He moved to the bathroom door and knocked.

There was a short silence before her quiet response. "Yes?"

"Can I come in, honey?"

Another pause, this one longer. "I'm a mess."

He cracked the door open to see her sitting on the edge of the bathtub in her bra and panties. Her eyes were red-rimmed and so sad he could have drowned in them. Had she even showered yet?

His heart cracked, and he crossed the space between them and crouched in front of her. "Tell me what's going on in your head, Till."

If she said one word about that damn officer, Kayden didn't fucking care that the guy was a deputy, he was going down there and laying into him.

Her chin dipped and she stared at her hands in her lap. "I keep telling myself I'm strong enough to do this. To be here. But today…it just kicked my ass and made me question whether that's true." A single tear slipped down her cheek, but it may as well have been a hundred.

He reached up and swiped it away with the pad of his thumb. "You're the strongest person I know. Anyone else would have packed up and left by now."

She slid a finger over the red marks on her wrists. "Someone tried to frame me for murder, Kayden."

The anger in his chest expanded, threatening to tear him in two. He covered her hand with his own. "They did. And I swear to you that we will find the person responsible and make them pay."

Her brows drew together, her gaze finally rising to his, shifting between his eyes. "You fought for me to get out of there."

"Of course I did." God, the very thought of her sitting in an interrogation room, being treated like shit, hurt like a fist around his heart.

"Even when all the evidence was stacked against me."

He reached up and slipped a lock of hair behind her ear. "I told you—I trust you. There is no evidence that could ever make me believe you were involved in murder."

Another tear fell, but this time, before he could swipe it away, she leaned her head forward so her temple touched his shoulder and let her tears soak his shirt. "Thank you."

Without missing a beat, he stood, lifting her into his arms. Her legs wrapped around him and she fit so perfectly in his hold.

He wanted to tear down this town. Make every person who'd hurt her pay, including himself. But for now, he needed to be her comfort. Her sanctuary.

He turned on the shower. When steam began to billow in the room, he lowered her to her feet and tugged off his shirt, then pushed down his jeans and briefs. She didn't move as he reached behind her and unhooked her bra. Or when he slid down her panties.

He lifted her into his arms again, both of them completely bare, before stepping under the stream of water.

She cupped his cheek, her gaze exploring his face. "Thank you for saving me today."

"I didn't save you. I just fought for you."

"You *trusted* me."

"I'm sorry it took me so long. I'm sorry I was so late." He wasn't just talking about today and how long it had taken him to find out what had gone down. He was talking about everything that had happened since she'd arrived in Misty Peak. He should have gotten to this place of trusting her faster.

"But you're here now," she whispered, hearing every one of his unspoken words.

She placed one light kiss to his lips, a kiss that seeped right into his soul. It wasn't sexual—it was so much more than that. Then she placed her head on his chest, trusting him to hold her.

CHAPTER 26

"**K**ayden, stop the car."

He shook his head, a hint of a grin on his face. "No. I told you. Cody said not to bring anything, so we're not bringing anything."

Goddamn this stubborn man. "I am not going to your first family dinner empty-handed. You stop the car right now, or I'm opening my door and ninja rolling onto the sidewalk."

Was that a thing? Did ninjas roll out of cars?

Kayden gave her an assessing look, as if trying to figure out whether she would in fact follow through on her threat.

Of course not. She was nowhere near the adrenaline junkie she'd need to be to do such a thing. But he didn't know that.

"I'm doing it." She touched the door handle.

"Fine." He sighed. "Just, let me park close to Sugar and Spice."

She grinned. "Interesting. I thought I wouldn't win this one."

He pulled over and undid his seat belt, but before climbing out, he leaned over and hovered his lips over hers. "I will always cave for you."

The kiss was far too quick and left her wanting more. A hell of a lot more.

She grumbled as she followed him out of the car but felt better when he slipped his hand into hers.

"How are you feeling today?" he asked as they headed toward Sugar and Spice.

Almost a week had passed since she'd found the watch in her drawer. In that time, she'd hired a lawyer but hadn't been called back into the station. Kayden had been doing an amazing job of keeping her distracted. She'd also been working from home, mostly so she didn't run into Jake. He obviously thought she was involved in Macy's murder and possibly his shooting, so it was easier for everyone for her to keep her distance.

"I'm trying not to think about everything," she said quietly. "I'm trusting my lawyer and the justice system, and hoping your brother finds the real person responsible."

The watch had been tested for prints, and yes, it obviously had hers on it, but also another set of prints. Unfortunately, that someone else wasn't in the system, so there was no way to identify the person.

"Eastern's working overtime on this case," Kayden said as he lifted her hand to his lips and kissed the back of it. "He'll get there."

She gave him a small, slightly nervous smile. "I hope so," she repeated.

They stepped into Sugar and Spice and, like every other time, any tension in Tilly immediately eased, not just because of the smell of sugary dough, or the bright colors, but because this was another place her mother had often taken her. Mrs. Sandler had opened the shop when Tilly was little, and it had become an immediate favorite of her and her mother's.

Mrs. Sandler wasn't in, but that wasn't a surprise. She'd flown to Atlanta for her granddaughter Sadie's wedding.

The young girl behind the counter smiled at them. "Hi, what can I get you?"

Tilly stepped forward. "I need a variety of your best desserts. Maybe a dozen?"

"You got it."

The second she turned to grab a box, Tilly felt Kayden's eyes on her. She glanced at him. "What?" The question was supposed to be innocent, but if the look on Kayden's face was anything to go by, she'd missed the mark.

"A dozen?"

"There are going to be six of us there, one being an eight-year-old with a sweet tooth. Two desserts each probably isn't even enough. I should have asked for eighteen or twenty."

He groaned. "What am I going to do with you?"

"Smile and agree to everything I say?"

He laughed.

"I want to make a good impression at my first family dinner," she added quietly.

Kayden lowered his mouth to her ear. "I like hearing you refer to my family as yours."

Tilly lifted a shoulder. "*You* feel like family, so it makes sense."

He growled and nuzzled her neck. "Hell yes, I am."

The girl placed a closed box onto the counter. "Here you go."

"Thanks." She went to pull out her card, but Kayden beat her to it. "Hey!"

"At least let me pay and get one thing tonight."

She shook her head, a smile on her face as she looked back to the girl. "Do you know when Mrs. Sandler will be back?"

"Well, Sadie's wedding is in a week, so not too long."

"Great."

When they got back in the car, far too many treats in hand, nerves began to tingle Tilly's spine. Harper and Cody had organized the dinner at their new place, and even though Tilly got along with everyone, this felt different. Maybe because Eastern was the sheriff, and a week ago he'd taken her into the station for questioning. Or maybe just because tonight felt important, being a family dinner and all.

She was quiet almost the entire drive but didn't miss Kayden's eyes on her. He parked in front of the house, and it was only on the way to the front door that he leaned down and touched his lips to her ear as he whispered, "Relax."

"I *am* relaxed." Lie. Big fat lie.

And of course Kayden knew that. His arm around her waist tightened, and even though she wore a dress, she felt that graze of his thumb like he'd touched bare skin.

They'd barely knocked when the front door opened, and they both looked down to see Avery standing in front of them. She flung her arms around Kayden and he lifted her up. "How's my favorite niece today?"

She giggled. "Uncle Kay, I'm your only niece."

"What? My only niece? What happened to all the rest?"

She laughed again before looking at Tilly. The eight-year-old opened her mouth but before she could say anything, her gaze lowered to the box and her eyes widened. "Are they from Sugar and Spice?"

"Sure are. I asked for a bit of everything, so hopefully there's at least some of your favorites in here."

Avery gasped and wiggled out of Kayden's arms before running back into the house.

Tilly chuckled as she stepped inside and closed the door. Cody and Harper were in the kitchen preparing food, while Eastern poured drinks.

"Daddy!" Avery cried. "Tilly brought dessert from Sugar and Spice."

Humor glittered in his eyes. "Guess you better eat all your dinner then."

Tilly moved around, giving everyone a hug. When she got to Eastern, the embrace was slightly awkward, but she was certain that was because of her, not him.

She turned to Harper. "What can I do to help?"

"Sit on the couch and relax." Harper barely looked up from where she was chopping tomatoes for the salad.

Tilly wanted to argue, but Kayden slipped the box from her hands before pressing a kiss to her cheek. "Sit. Trust me, Avery will have you up and playing soon, so make the most of it."

She settled on the couch. Kayden was holding Avery again as he talked to Cody and Harper when Eastern brought her a glass of wine. But instead of moving away once she'd taken it, he sat beside her and lowered his voice.

"Hey. I know I said this last week, but I really am sorry about what happened. Jarrad's been suspended for what he did, and we're all working overtime to find the person who put that watch in your drawer."

Her chest expanded with much-needed air. "You believe someone put it there?"

Maybe that was part of the reason she'd felt nervous tonight… because Eastern seemed like an evidence man, and all the evidence was stacked against her.

"Yeah, Tilly. I believe you."

That last bit of nerves eased from her body, and she sank into the couch.

* * *

KAYDEN LEANED back in his seat at the table, his plate empty. He'd eaten far too much and laughed more than he had in a while.

Damn, he loved his family.

This was why he'd come home. This was why, even when he missed his time as a PJ, he didn't even consider going back. He'd already missed too much time with them, and now, watching Tilly fit into his family so easily, like she'd always been a part of it…it did something to him. Shifted and changed something inside him.

She was his, and he wasn't going to forget that for a second.

"All right, time to clean up," Harper said, straightening in her seat.

"Absolutely not." Kayden rose to his feet and started collecting plates. "You cooked, we'll clean."

"And get the desserts?" Avery asked quickly, eyes wide.

Eastern rose and he ruffled his daughter's hair. "Yeah, Princess, we'll get the desserts."

"I'll help," Tilly said, about to rise.

Kayden shook his head. "Nope. You're not lifting a finger tonight."

"Kayden, you've barely let me lift a finger for the last week. I can help."

"No. Rest. Relax." He kissed her before grabbing her plate.

In the kitchen, he put the leftovers into containers while Eastern rinsed the dirty dishes and filled the dishwasher. Tilly was talking to the others when she threw her head back and laughed, and he just…stopped. Because fuck, he liked seeing that. It had taken days for her to even start getting back to her usual self after her trip to the station, and it was only today that she'd begun smiling.

"How's she doing?" Eastern asked quietly as he came to stand beside Kayden.

"Better than she should be after what happened."

"Good." Eastern turned his back to the others. "It's looking more and more like this has to be an inside job. We've looked into everyone who works at the visitors center. Pixie, Theo, and Hendrix have alibis for the night of Macy's stabbing, but Elle doesn't."

Kayden frowned. "You think Elle might have killed Macy? We basically grew up with that woman. She was best friends with Jace and at our house more often than not."

"I don't want to think that. But this person knew about the safe in the visitors center. They also know the mountains and could have been there when Jake found the watch. Sometimes people are capable of more than we realize. Plus, she was close to Macy."

Kayden cursed and ran his fingers through his hair.

"Hey, off topic, but did you see Mrs. Sandler at Sugar and Spice?" Eastern asked.

"Nope, she's in Atlanta for her granddaughter's wedding. Why?"

Eastern sighed. "Thought that was around now. I keep hoping Sadie will come back to visit. Avery misses her."

"Maybe after the honeymoon?"

"Yeah, maybe." Then his brother grinned. "Guess which brother's thinking about coming home?"

Kayden straightened. "You're shitting me? Jace or Lock?"

"Jace. Said he's making plans to get out."

"I didn't think that would ever happen." Jace wasn't just the youngest brother, he'd sought out adventure since the day he was born.

Eastern nodded. "No shit."

Together, they finished cleaning up, then Kayden plated the desserts and set them on the table. Avery jumped in her seat, her eyes so wide Kayden wondered if she was going to leap across and grab everything. She didn't—she'd been raised too well for that. But the second Kayden told people to dig in, she was the first to grab her favorite double chocolate chip cookie.

When everyone had something on their plate, Harper sighed and leaned into Cody's side. "We should do this more often."

Eastern nodded. "I wouldn't say no to that."

Kayden slipped an arm around Tilly's shoulders and tugged her closer, pressing a kiss to her temple. She glanced up at him, her smile so wide and radiant, he couldn't stop his own smile. "You look happy."

Her features softened. "I am. It's crazy, isn't it, with everything going on, that I can smile and laugh and feel good?"

"Not crazy, honey. You deserve to be happy."

"Are you? Happy?"

"Happier than I've been in a long time." Possibly ever.

CHAPTER 27

illy sighed as she pulled up in front of her parents' house. She'd spent all day at the library studying for her final exams.

She was almost there, then she'd have her business degree and could finally get a full-time job. Maybe then she'd move out of her childhood home.

Ha. Yeah, right. Leave her mom? That wasn't something she was ready to do...not just yet, anyway. Some people were close to friends from high school. Some had siblings or partners they barely separated from. Her mother was her best friend, and she wouldn't have it any other way.

Grabbing her bag from the passenger seat, she climbed out of the car, frowning when she saw her father's car wasn't in the driveway. Strange. Most days he worked from home and was almost always here, especially in the evenings.

Maybe he was out with friends. He often went to the bar with Harry or Ted.

She climbed onto the porch and stepped into the house, the frown deepening when she saw most of the lights were off. Not only that, but the place was cold. Had her mother not turned the heat on? She always had the heat on. Sometimes Tilly joked that she made this place a sauna.

"Mom?"

Nothing.

With slow steps, she moved into the living room, then the kitchen. Empty. Where was everyone?

She dropped her bag onto the kitchen island before moving to the bedroom. The second the door opened, she stopped.

Her mother stood by the window. Her back was unnaturally straight, and she had a phone pressed to her ear.

"Mom?"

One more beat of silence, and her mother finally turned, eyes red-rimmed, face blotchy...she'd been crying.

"Tilly, baby, you're home early."

Tilly glanced across at the clock on the bedside table. "It's almost six." If anything, she was late.

"It is?" Her mother looked at the clock. "It is! Gosh, time got away from me. I should start dinner."

She started across the room, but Tilly stepped in front of her, gently wrapping her fingers around her mother's arm. "Mom, talk to me. What's wrong? Why are you crying?"

Her mother never cried. Not when they'd lost family pets. Not when Tilly had gotten pneumonia and been rushed to the hospital.

Her mom shook her head. "Let's eat first."

"No. I can see something's very wrong. Please tell me."

New tears sprang to her mother's pale green eyes. She took a quick breath before whispering, "He's gone."

Tilly's heart thudded, a chill sweeping over her skin. "Who's gone?" Even though she asked the question, a part of her knew. The missing car, the quiet house...

"Your father. I, um...I got home, and all his things were gone. His car, everything from the safe...even my jewelry."

Tilly was shaking her head before her mother had finished speaking. "No. That's...why would he empty the safe and take your jewelry?" Her *father was an absentee dad and husband, and a workaholic, sure, but he would never take everything they had and desert them. He would never steal from her mother.*

"He left a note." Her mother's fingers trembled as she lifted a small piece of paper off the bed and handed it to Tilly.

"I'm sorry," Tilly read, her gaze running over the two words again and again.

"He also emptied our shared bank account," her mother continued.

Tilly looked up to see pain on her mother's face. Not just pain. Agony. And heartache...so much heartache.

Her mother had always loved her father more than he'd loved her. It was something Tilly had come to recognize very early on in her life.

But this?

"Mom...this doesn't make sense."

Her mother swallowed, her head lowering. "Your father has always had this...unhealthy obsession with money. He came from a very poor upbringing. I assumed we were doing well enough. That we were happy. But if he's stolen from us, I think...I fear he might have taken money from other people as well."

Her heart gave a little twist. "What are you talking about?"

"A lot of people in this town have trusted your dad with their money. If he's gone..."

When her mother couldn't finish the sentence, Tilly put the pieces together. "You think he took their money and ran."

"Oh God." Her mother's chest heaved too quickly, panic tugging and pulling at her face. "What will we tell people? How will we tell them he's gone? That their money is gone?"

"Mom, it's going to be okay."

"No, it's not. If he's done what I think he's done, nothing will be okay!" Suddenly, her mother's knees gave way. Tilly only just caught her. Both of them slid to the floor.

Her mother's pain was loud and heartbreaking. Tilly just held her, listening to the woman who'd never cried a tear in front of her as she wept...all the while thinking if this was true, if her father really had done what her mother suspected, then everything was about to change.

* * *

Tilly's eyes shot open, her heart still pounding and her lungs panting too quickly.

A dream. It was just a dream.

But it wasn't. It was a memory.

Her gaze shifted to the spot on the floor where she'd held her crying mother. It was right here in this room, beside the bed, and even though it was years ago, it may as well have been yesterday, she remembered it so well. The pain. The heartache. And the hurt that her father had inflicted.

She scrunched her eyes in an attempt to fight off the array of emotions rippling inside her. She hated remembering that day. She hated everything about it.

Turning her head, she looked at Kayden. While she lay on her back, breaths whooshing in and out of her lungs, he lay on his side, arm heavy across her waist, looking so unbelievably peaceful.

Her fingers itched to touch him. Let his calm slip inside her and wipe away the unrest.

She just stopped herself.

Carefully, she slipped out from under his arm, doing her best not to wake him.

In the kitchen, she filled a glass with water and stood by the window. Seeing her mother in pieces that day...God, it had hurt. Her father had never deserved her mother's love. He'd never deserved either of them.

She'd just finished her water and was lowering the glass to the sink when hands slipped around her waist. She gasped, her heart jumping into her throat, but then warm breath brushed over her neck.

"Hey. It's me. Are you okay?"

The air flowed out of her in a long breath before she turned and looked up into Kayden's beautiful ocean-blue eyes. "Yeah, I just had a bad dream."

His brows slashed together. "Want to talk about it?"

Did she? She'd had the dream so many times but had never spoken about it out loud. "I dreamed about the day I got home and Mom told me Dad was gone. That he'd emptied their savings and stolen from us."

The fingers tightened on her waist. "That would have been hard."

"I remember not feeling hurt or scared for me, just for Mom. Because I knew she loved him. And she loved this town, and we both knew what he'd done was going to ruin everything."

He reached up and cupped her cheek, his thumb immediately grazing her skin. "Why didn't you feel hurt for you?"

"Because he'd never been much of a father. From a young age, I realized how selfish he was, only wanting to do things for himself, to better *his* life. I never understood why my mother loved him so much."

"Sometimes love blinds us from a person's faults."

"That's true." She shook her head. "I hated that day. And every day that passed after it until we left Misty Peak. But even in Ohio, my mother's pain didn't go away. And I understood why. We'd run from the problem my father had created, hoping a change would fix everything, but it didn't."

"It shouldn't have been your problem to fix or run from."

"This town *made* it our problem."

Something akin to pain crossed his face. "I'm—"

She touched a finger to his lips, silencing him. "Don't say you're sorry. People are responsible for their own actions. You can't change how I've been treated."

He kissed her finger, his hand leaving her face to slip around her wrist. "I wasn't much better than everyone else when you first got here. It's something I'll always regret." He kissed her palm. "I shouldn't have tried to pin your father's crimes on you. I should have seen past the connection."

His mouth shifted to the inside of her wrist, and an involuntary shudder rolled down her spine.

"You're nothing like him," he whispered, his kisses now moving down her arm, nearing her shoulder. "You're good, and you deserved better from your dad."

Her breaths started to shorten again, but this time for a different reason. At his closeness. His breath against her skin… his lips. When his mouth reached her shoulder, she trailed her hands up his bare chest, feeling every hard ridge…so much strength.

He nibbled her neck, and she moaned, tilting her head to give him better access. "Kayden…"

"Tell me you're mine, Tilly. Tell me it's you and me and that's all we need."

He found a sensitive spot behind her ear and sucked, making it so she could barely get words out. But she did…just.

"I'm yours, Kayden. It's you and me."

* * *

His. She'd just admitted that she was his, and that was fucking everything.

His mouth crashed to hers, his tongue slipping between her lips, tangling and stroking.

She groaned and leaned into him, her breasts pressing against his chest.

With a growl, he lifted her from the floor and set her onto the kitchen counter. Then his fingers were at the base of her shirt. A shirt that was his, and every time she wore it, all he wanted to do was tear it off.

He pulled it over her head and immediately reached for one

of her perfect breasts, cupping her. Palming. The sounds she made when he touched her drove him wild. Made him want to lose himself in her and never be found.

He ran his thumb around her nipple in a circular motion before thrumming the hard bud back and forth.

"Your breasts are so fucking perfect," he growled. Just like the rest of her.

He lowered his head and wrapped his lips around the nipple, and her fingers clenched in his hair. The whimpers and cries that slipped from her mouth pushed him to keep going. He sucked and tugged at her nipple, running his tongue over the bud before releasing it with a pop.

He swapped to her other breast, doing the same thing, licking and sucking, while his hand trailed down her belly and slipped into her panties. The second he stroked her, her thighs widened, her fingers lowering to his shoulders and digging into his skin.

"Kayden…" His name was a breathy whisper on her lips, and it made him want more. It made him want to hear his name said in that exact way a hundred times over.

He trailed his mouth back up her chest and neck before claiming her mouth again. God, she tasted good. Always sweet, and so infinitely unique.

He slipped a finger inside her to find her wet and so fucking ready for him. But before he could do anything, she reached for him, slipping her hand into the waistband of his briefs, and pulling out his cock.

His growl rippled and tumbled throughout the room at the feel of her fingers around him. At the way she explored his length from base to tip. Thickening him. Making him so fucking crazy, a buzzing started between his ears, blocking out every other sound.

"Tilly, when you touch me like that, I want to lose all control."

Her mouth skimmed across his cheek before nipping his ear. "So lose control."

Fuck. He tugged her to the edge of the counter, slipped her thong to the side, and thrust inside her, her walls stretching around him, driving him right to the fucking edge.

Her head flew back, a scream wrenching from her throat, but he slipped a hand behind her neck and tugged her back to him. His mouth crashed to hers as his tongue dove straight inside and he began to thrust, pulling almost completely out of her before pushing back in.

He did it again and again, and every time he returned to her, he felt that thing. The coming home. The returning to where he was meant to be.

When it wasn't enough, he lifted her from the counter and turned. Her legs immediately slipped around his waist as he pressed her against the nearest wall. Then he thrust harder. Deeper. And her cries became louder, slicing through the otherwise quiet house.

Reaching between them, he stroked her clit, and when her head once again fell back, her eyes scrunching closed, he couldn't look away. She was fucking gorgeous and free and *his*. He ran his thumb in a circle around her clit as he continued to thrust, rubbing and stroking.

Until finally, she screamed, and her walls closed around his cock as she broke. He kept thrusting. Kept watching, so fucking lost in her, until he too shattered, growling as he took her mouth one more time, falling into the abyss that was Tilly.

CHAPTER 28

H ome time. Finally.

Tilly had been sitting in front of this damn screen all day, to the point that everything on it was starting to blur. She should have left over an hour ago. Everyone else had except Jake. He'd actually offered to stick close to the building as he worked outside. She had a feeling it was a way of trying to make up for what he'd done. He'd already apologized, but she honestly had no idea how she felt about that.

He could have gone to her that day. Spoken to her about what she was holding instead of going behind her back and calling Eastern.

But, at the same time, what was done was done, and it couldn't be changed. At least he was trying to make amends by offering to remain late with her. She'd stay on her own, but with everything that had happened in these mountains, that wasn't an option.

Kayden had had to leave early to pick up Avery from school because Eastern had unexpectedly had to work late.

Finally, she shut down the computer and grabbed her bag. Before leaving, she sent a quick text to Jake.

Tilly: Just leaving now. Thanks for staying back with me.

The office was quiet and dark around her as she walked outside, then crossed the parking lot. She'd almost reached her car when her phone buzzed with a text. She expected it to be Jake, but it wasn't.

Kayden: Hey, sorry, still at Eastern's. Whatever he's got going on at the station is taking him longer than he thought.

Tilly: You're fine. I'm actually just leaving work now anyway.

Kayden: Everything okay?

Tilly: Yeah, there were a million fires to put out and they all turned up at four p.m. I'm grateful Jake offered to stay with me. Want me to pick up dinner?

She added the part about Jake to remind him that she wasn't here alone, knowing he'd lose his mind if he thought she was.

Kayden: I'll grab us something on my way home. Be safe.

Tilly: I knew there was a reason I liked you.

Kayden: I knew it was because I feed you. Don't take long or I'm coming to find you.

Yeah, he probably would too.

She'd just taken out her keys to open her car, when she suddenly remembered the invoice she had to pay. Crap. She'd told the guys working on the skywalk that she'd pay it by the end of the day.

With a sigh, she moved back toward the building. She was almost at the door when a sound had her pausing and turning. It almost sounded like a footstep. She scanned the parking lot as cool evening air slipped over her skin, the quiet almost feeling eerie now.

She lifted her phone to text Jake again.

Tilly: Hey. I left something in the office, just going back inside. Everything okay with you?

Once the text was sent, she slotted the key into the door and stepped inside. Quickly, she jogged to her office and shuffled through everything on her desk.

Jesus, why was everything so disorganized right now? She wasn't a disorganized person. Hell, she usually prided herself on having her shit together. But with the increasing busyness of the center and the mess that had been her life the last few weeks, she'd been slipping.

Where was it? Wait, Pixie had told her she'd print the invoice, but had she ever actually given it to Tilly?

Frowning, she went out to Pixie's desk and started shuffling through a stack of printed documents on the desk. At least her stuff appeared organized, not that it was helping Tilly find what she needed.

When she didn't find it on the desk, she opened the first drawer, noticing it was just stationery, before trying the second. It was in the third drawer that she found another pile of papers.

Tilly pulled them out…frowning at what looked to be medical bills. Dozens of them. Were these for Pixie's father when he'd been alive? Why would she still have them?

She was about to put them back into the drawer when she noticed the framed photo that was beneath them. It was of Pixie and an older man, maybe her dad.

Tilly remembered this photo. It had been sitting on Pixie's desk on Tilly's first day. She'd even looked at it when Pixie told her about her father's passing.

Why would she have hidden it away in a drawer?

Something in the photo caught Tilly's attention.

Wait…was that…

Tilly gasped.

The watch. Pixie was wearing the watch Jake had found in the mountains.

The same watch that had been planted in Tilly's drawer and tested positive for Macy's blood.

She dropped the framed photo like it had burned her, barely hearing the crack of glass. Had Pixie been the one who'd robbed the visitors center safe, then killed Macy? Had she also tried to frame Tilly?

Her breaths were whooshing in and out of her when something sounded from the deck.

Jake. She had to tell him.

She ran toward the door to the deck and opened it, just as the door to the café closed.

Why was he going in there?

She stepped out onto the deck and headed toward the café. She was halfway there when she pulled out her phone and called Kayden. Maybe because she wanted to hear his voice. Maybe because she wanted someone to tell her that the watch in the photo couldn't possibly be the same one with Macy's blood on it.

But instead of Kayden answering the call, she got his voice mail.

"You've reached Kayden's phone, leave a message."

"Hey, it's Tilly. This is going to sound crazy, but I found something in Pixie's desk drawer. It was a photo of her wearing the watch." He'd know which watch she was talking about. She opened her mouth to tell him she was calling the police, only to stop when she stepped into the café to see, not Jake but Pixie, standing by the back wall. A large painting had been taken down, and behind it was a safe. One that looked just like the safe that had been broken into in the other building. It was open, and there was cash inside. A lot of cash.

Tilly gasped, the hand with the phone in it falling to her side.

Pixie spun—gun in hand. "Tilly? What are you doing here?"

For a moment, Tilly couldn't speak. All she could do was stare down the barrel of the pistol that was pointed right at her chest. She opened and closed her mouth, but no words came out...not a single one.

"Tilly! Answer my goddamn question. Why are you here?"

Pixie's shouted words pulled Tilly out of her shock and had her retreating half a step. "I, um, forgot something so went back to the office. When I heard something in here, I thought you were Jake."

"Jake? Why would you think I was Jake?" Her gaze moved behind Tilly.

Had she not seen Jake on her way in here? Where was he?

Pixie shook her head and stepped forward, gun unwavering. "It doesn't matter. The point is, you shouldn't have come in here."

"It was you," she whispered. "You stole from the safe in the office."

"I guess it's too late for me to deny it. Yeah, it was me."

"Why?"

"*Why?*" The word almost sounded manic from the other woman's lips. "Because cancer took everything from my father, both physically and financially. It took everything from *both* of us. I helped him pay his medical bills, and now I have *nothing*. I don't have my father. I don't have money to get out of this godforsaken town, where he's everywhere I look. I deserve more than working in a place like this. And when he died, I decided that if no one was going to give it to me, I was going to take it."

And she couldn't have just worked hard to save up to leave, like other people? "You killed Macy."

"I didn't want to. The woman came into the office and saw what I was doing. She was going to call the police. I told her not to, but she'd already pulled her phone out! All I had was a knife, so I pulled it out and told her to drop the phone. She ran. I chased her."

"And you stabbed her to death."

"When you see your future about to disappear, you do what you have to do to survive."

She shook her head. No...most people drew a line at murder. "You tried to frame me."

Pixie lifted a shoulder like it was no big deal. "People in this town already hate you. Your father stole from everyone, so I assumed people wouldn't bat an eye at the idea of you stealing from the safe in the visitors center."

Only, she hadn't been counting on Kayden's belief in her. On Eastern doing what was right.

Tilly's gaze rose to the safe behind her. "How did you know about these safes?"

She still couldn't believe there was a second one. Where had they come from? Where was the money from?

"Linda was *always* forgetting things. Work with her as long as *I* did, and you realize the woman has early-onset dementia. I wasn't surprised when she didn't even remember the first safe existed."

Tilly frowned. "So the money was hers?"

"She got a huge life insurance payout when her husband died. She confided in me one day that she didn't trust banks and was splitting the money into two safes right here on the center's property. I thought it was fucking weird, but, hey, that was Linda. I knew where the first safe was, but not the second. I searched this place high and low but never found it, until yesterday, it finally dawned on me. If it wasn't in the foyer, your office, or the eco center...maybe it was here, in the café."

God, all this time, this woman had known Linda held a huge sum of money in this center, and all she wanted was to take it for herself. "How did you know the code?"

Pixie scoffed. "Every code and password that old woman ever had was the same. Always the birthday of her late husband. But that doesn't matter. What matters is that I get this money, get the hell out of here, and make sure no one knows what you saw tonight."

A chill swept over Tilly's skin, her gaze darting to the barrel of the gun before rising to Pixie once more. "What are you going to do? Shoot me?"

"Why not? Can you imagine the story of Martin Taylor and his daughter robbing the local visitors center? Only, Martin got greedy yet again. Killed his daughter to keep it all for himself and ran."

Tilly swallowed the lump of fear in her throat. "Pixie, don't do this."

"It's already done."

In one life-altering moment, a large body dropped Tilly to the ground as the gun went off. Tilly screamed and looked up as her father pushed to his feet and lunged toward Pixie.

Jesus. Where had he come from?

"Run, Tilly!"

It took a fraction of a second for her father's shouted words to compute in her head. Then another to force herself to her feet just as the gun fired again, this time getting her father in the gut. Tilly gasped, bile rising in her throat as she stumbled back a step.

"Dad!" She wanted to run to her father and see if he was okay so she could do what she could to help.

Pixie also stumbled back, like she couldn't believe what she'd done. Then she turned hate-filled eyes on Tilly.

That's when Tilly ran.

* * *

"You know, you don't have to watch this with me, Uncle Kay."

Kayden's lips twitched as he shifted his gaze from the TV to Avery. "I love watching animated shows with talking dogs."

Avery lifted a brow at him, and damn, she looked ten years older than her eight years.

"Okay, I don't," he admitted. "What I love is spending time with my niece."

He wrapped an arm around her shoulders and pulled her into his side. Eastern would be home soon, and as much as he adored his niece, it couldn't be soon enough. All he wanted to do was see Tilly. Touch her. Hear her voice.

He glanced at the setting sun outside. If her earlier texts were anything to go by, she should be home by now. He didn't like that she'd left so late, not with everything going on right now, but the only way he was okay with it was that Jake was there and under strict instructions to remain close to the center. He should text her and check that she'd gotten home safely.

His phone was on the charger in the kitchen.

He was about to go grab it when the door opened and Eastern walked in. Avery squealed before jumping to her feet and propelling her small body into his arms.

Eastern lifted her. "Hey, Princess, have you had a good afternoon with Uncle Kay?"

"Yep, he made me spaghetti for dinner and watched my shows with me."

Eastern's brows rose. "Really? My big brother cooking a meal and watching kids' shows?"

Kayden lifted a shoulder as he rose from the couch. "I'm the favorite for a reason."

Eastern laughed as he set his daughter on her feet. "Ave, I'm just gonna talk to Uncle Kay in the kitchen for a sec. Won't be long."

"Okay." She ran back to the couch.

Kayden frowned as they moved out of the living room. The living and kitchen were open plan, but with lowered voices, he was sure Avery wouldn't hear, not with her cartoon taking up her attention.

"Everything okay?" Kayden asked in a hushed voice.

"Just when I thought one fire was put out, another pops up."

Kayden braced his hands on the kitchen island. "What happened?"

"I had to visit your friend Theo's apartment this afternoon, after he called in a domestic assault."

"A domestic assault? You're saying someone assaulted *him*?" Kayden hadn't even known the guy was dating anyone.

"Yeah. Pixie."

Kayden straightened. "*Pixie*, as in—"

"Pixie who works at the front desk of the visitors center, Pixie. Yeah. Apparently the two of them have an on-and-off relationship. Very explosive. He was pissed. Said he was done with her. That she assaulted him. Threw a vase at his head. He said he wants a restraining order."

"Shit."

"Yep. Interestingly, he also said he lied to us about Pixie being with him the night of Macy's murder."

Kayden's back straightened. "Why would he do that?"

"Because Pixie asked him to. He also told us that at the time Jake was shot, she wasn't in the office. She took a half hour break from the desk and wasn't there when they locked down the center."

A ball fisted in his gut. "You think it was her?"

"Don't know, we haven't been able to find the woman to question her. She's not home and not answering her phone, but we have officers stationed on her street."

Suddenly, all Kayden could think about was getting to Tilly. It was all too connected to the visitors center, and he wanted to be with her right the hell now.

He grabbed his phone—only to stop at the sight of the voice mail.

Putting the phone to his ear, he listened to Tilly's voice.

"Hey, this is going to sound crazy, but I found something in Pixie's desk drawer. It was a photo of her wearing the watch." Suddenly, there was a gasp, and a beat later, a new voice sounded. The words were too muffled to make out...but he was almost certain he recognized the voice.

Kayden's gaze shot up to his brother, fear settling inside him, weaving and poisoning.

"What is it?" Eastern asked.

"Call your deputies to the visitors center. Tilly's in trouble."

CHAPTER 29

illy's breaths whooshed in and out of her chest as her feet sank into the dirt on each step.

She'd had to choose—run back to the visitors center and hope like hell she made it to her car without receiving a bullet to the back or head into the mountains.

She'd wanted to choose her car. God, she'd wanted to drive to safety so badly. But the chance Pixie would have caught her before getting there was too high, and then she'd have been trapped. Either that, or the woman could have blocked her way out of the parking lot and shot at her car.

So she'd chosen the mountains, where she could slip between trees, maybe hide or use them as shields.

A shudder ran down her spine as she pushed for more speed. She could hear Pixie's footsteps behind her. They didn't sound like they were gaining on her, but she wasn't creating any more distance either.

Pixie was a *thief*. A *murderer*. Jesus, it didn't feel real. Not only had she killed Macy, she'd shot both Jake and now her father.

Was her dad alive? She didn't even have her phone to call for help—it had flown from her fingers when her father had shoved her to the floor.

She rounded a tree, her foot catching on a root and sending her to the ground. She groaned as her cheek hit something hard, pain radiating throughout her skull. When the breaking of a branch sounded behind her, she forced the pain to the back of her mind and shoved back to her feet.

"I can fucking hear you!" Pixie shouted, causing Tilly's throat to close. "You're a dead woman!"

She forced herself to focus. Had Kayden heard her voice message? Had he heard Pixie's words and understood what was going on?

Every second that ticked by had the sky getting darker around her, to the point she could barely see the ground beneath her feet. Would the dark be a help or a hindrance?

She stepped on a rock at a bad angle and cried out as she went down, the twist of her ankle sending pain shooting up her leg.

Quickly, she crawled behind the closest tree and grabbed her calf in an attempt to stem the pain flowing up her leg. When she glanced up, she finally realized where she was...right near the edge of one of the mountain drop-offs. It was a foggy area of the mountains that people rarely visited, just because of how steep the trails were.

Jesus, it would be so easy for Pixie to corner her here.

As if the universe heard her fear and laughed, Pixie's voice sounded again. "I heard you, Tilly. I know you're here. What happened? You fall and hurt yourself?"

She was close, and she'd stopped moving, which meant it wouldn't be long before Pixie found her.

"You know, I never wanted any of this to turn out the way it did," Pixie said, voice almost defeated. "I'm just desperate to get out of here and *live*. Like, *really* live. Watching someone you love die before your eyes changes you. And having all your money drained by medical bills, only for your loved one to die anyway, makes you realize you deserve so much more."

Deserve more? So she felt *entitled* to everything she'd stolen from Linda?

Slow footsteps drew closer. "I thought that taking money wouldn't hurt anyone. Linda doesn't even remember putting it there. If only fucking Macy hadn't walked in on me."

None of that gave her the right to kill someone.

"I was searching for the second safe in your office the day you walked in on me. I didn't have a weapon, so I shoved you. When I couldn't find the second safe, I robbed the hardware store," Pixie continued. "But I didn't get hardly anything."

More footsteps. God, Tilly wished she had a weapon.

"I still have nightmares about the way I stabbed her, you know," Pixie said softly. "But every time the darkness tries to close in on me, I remind myself why I'm doing this. I deserve a ticket out of this town. I *deserve* to be happy."

Even if that happiness came at the cost of others' lives. She was sick.

"When I realized I lost my watch, I took a break in the middle of every shift to search for it. Someone was looking out for me that day when I stumbled upon Jake looking at it in the dirt." Pixie's footsteps stopped. "I can see the patch in the dirt where you fell, Tilly, and marks where you crawled behind that tree. Just come out. Don't make this harder than it has to be."

Tilly's heart slammed against her ribs. The woman wanted to make killing her easy? Her mind scrambled to come up with a plan, anything to save herself.

But it was too late. Pixie moved around the tree, gun aimed. "Get up."

Tilly was slow to rise to her feet. "It doesn't have to be like this, Pixie. I can help you."

"I don't need help. I just need all of this to be someone else's fault so I can take my money and get out."

"We'll pin it on my father," Tilly pushed desperately, her mind working a million miles a minute. "We'll say that we caught him stealing from the safe and he attacked us. One of us was able to jump on him, take his gun, and our only option was to shoot him."

Her brows pinched. "Why would you do that to your own father?"

She wouldn't, no matter how badly he'd hurt her. But Pixie didn't realize that. "Because it wasn't just this town he hurt. He took my mother's savings, her jewelry, everything of hers and mine that was worth *anything*, and he ran, deserting us. His actions forced my mother and I to leave our home. And now, even though I'm back, I'm certainly not welcome."

Pixie's frown started to smooth out. Was she actually considering it?

"Come on, Pixie." Tilly worked hard to keep the desperation out of her voice. "I can see you don't want to hurt anyone else. And you don't have to. Plus, I can help you. I already have Kayden and Eastern on my side, and they hate my father. If you let me tell this story, they'll believe me."

Pixie's eyes flickered between hers, and in that moment, Tilly couldn't breathe—because the woman was deciding between letting Tilly live or die.

"How do I trust that you'll stick to your story?" Pixie asked.

"Why wouldn't I? This town only blames me for what my father did because they have to blame *someone*. But if we let the town know what he did, and he's here to arrest, then the blame will go back to him, where it belongs, and I can finally live my life in peace." She inched forward a step. "Plus, I've been waiting five years to get revenge on him for what he did to me and my mother. And what a perfect revenge this would be."

When still Pixie looked unsure, Tilly took another hesitant step forward. "While you've only ever wanted to leave, all *I've* ever wanted was to come home. This is where I grew up. Where all the memories of my mother and I were made. I don't want to leave. And maybe now, with your help, I might be able to stay."

Several beats of silence passed, and every one of them had Tilly's hands growing clammier…until finally, Pixie lowered the gun. "We need to get our stories straight."

* * *

EVERY MUSCLE in Kayden's body was tense as Eastern drove them to the visitors center. He'd gotten his neighbor to look after Avery and had called his deputies to get down to the mountains. Kayden had also called Theo and Hendrix in case they were needed, because they knew these mountains better than anyone.

But where the hell was Jake? He'd called his damn number a dozen times and it kept going to voice mail.

A part of him hoped the team wasn't necessary. That she'd gotten away from Pixie. Out of the visitors center. That he and Eastern would drive up to an empty parking lot.

Fuck, such a big part of him hoped for that. But the second they pulled into the parking lot, he knew that hadn't happened, because there sat Tilly's blue Honda.

She was still here. She hadn't gotten away.

He lifted the gun in his lap.

"I shouldn't let you go in there—"

"I'm going," Kayden growled, cutting off his brother's words before climbing out of the car.

"Thought so."

Kayden ran toward the entrance to find the door to the center closed but unlocked. He stepped inside. Empty.

"Tilly?" He called her name, but at the silence, ran into her office to find it as empty as the entrance. Shit. He ran back out as his brother stepped inside. "She's not in here."

Kayden ran out onto the deck, Eastern's footsteps echoing

behind him. The café door was open and when he stepped inside, he felt raw and open.

Because there, on the floor, was a pool of blood.

"It might not be hers," Eastern said quickly, hearing the unspoken fears in Kayden's head. Eastern stepped around him and walked over to the empty wall safe. "Did you know this was here?"

Kayden shook his head. "No, but I didn't know about the last one that was broken into either." Suddenly, he spotted something on the floor. He lowered and lifted the cell phone. Tilly's phone.

Eastern checked around the counter and in the back room before returning and shaking his head. "There's no one here."

Kayden stepped back out onto the deck.

If she hadn't gone back to the visitors center, then she had to have gone up the trails.

When he got to the end of the deck, there were prints in the dirt that went either way. Smaller ones that led into the forest, and larger ones that led toward the street.

"I'll follow the larger ones," Eastern said quickly. "Keep your phone on you in case I need to call."

Eastern took off, and Kayden took a few steps when something behind a tree caught his attention. Frowning, he moved over to it, only to growl when he saw what it was.

Jake. He lay on his back, head bleeding. Someone had hit him. *Shit.*

He ran over to the other man and touched his pulse. Alive.

His eyes rose just as Eastern jogged back. "Whoever was bleeding took off in a car they parked under some trees down there." He looked down, cursing before pulling out his radio and calling for an ambulance.

Kayden didn't wait for his brother. He took off into the mountains at a run. He needed to find her before it was too late.

CHAPTER 30

"*I* don't know if I can do this."

Tilly stopped at Pixie's words, her heart pounding. They hadn't been walking for long, maybe a couple of minutes, and Pixie had forced them to stick to the cliffside trail, claiming there was less chance someone might find them.

Her ankle throbbed, but she was pushing through the pain, telling herself with every step it was just a little farther.

"Can't do what?" Tilly asked, trying to sound calm, when in reality, every part of her was in turmoil.

"I barely know you. You could easily turn on me. Hell, you could tell Kayden and Eastern the truth the second we get back."

Tilly stepped closer. "Pixie, I'm *not* lying, and I'm *not* going to turn on you. I have no reason to tell them the truth and every reason to go along with the story. I told you, I *need* my father to pay. This *town* needs my father to pay."

The other woman's eyes darted around the area.

"Pixie…if you kill me and run, they'll look for a third person. They'll look for *you*."

Pixie eyes were wide and wild. "I could just kill you…tell the police I had no choice—it was you or me."

The beats of her heart stumbled over each other, but Tilly was careful to keep the fear off her face. "Pixie—"

"Wait…you had a phone in your hand when you stepped into the café, and the screen was on. Shit! I can't believe I'm only just remembering. Were you talking to someone?"

Crap. "No. I was just searching for something on my phone." The excuse sounded as weak out loud as it did in her head.

Pixie stepped forward, gun once again raised. "You're lying."

"No, I—"

A branch snapped somewhere close by. Immediately, Pixie spun behind Tilly, grabbed her by the throat, and pressed the barrel of the gun to her temple. "Who was that?"

"I don't know," Tilly forced out.

"You do! Kayden knows about me, doesn't he? That's why when you stepped into the café you looked scared but not surprised. Is he here right now?"

"Please, I—"

"Put the gun down, Pixie."

Tilly's heart crashed into her ribs. *Kayden?*

He stepped out from behind a tree, gun in hand, and the air rushed out of Tilly's chest so fast she almost sagged.

Pixie's breath stuttered. "She told you about me."

He shook his head. "No. Theo called Eastern. Said he lied about being your alibi, both during Macy's murder *and* Jake's shooting."

The arm around Tilly's throat tightened. "But Tilly confirmed it was me."

"It's over, Pixie. Let Tilly go and turn yourself in. It's the only way."

A flicker of movement from Tilly's left had her eyes shifting to the side.

Eastern? He sat behind some bushes—and had a gun aimed right at Pixie.

"None of this was meant to happen!" Pixie cried, hysteria in her voice. "I just meant to get out and live my life."

Her chest heaved behind Tilly, her arm still tight around her throat. When she tugged Tilly back a step, her skin chilled as she whispered, "Pixie, stop. We're too close to the edge."

"If I can't get out, what's the point in any of this? I don't want to rot in a cell!"

What was she saying? That she was going to jump?

"Let her go," Kayden growled, a bit of fear lacing into his words now, "and you can do whatever you want."

"But I can't, can I? I'll either go to prison, or get sick, or live in poverty my entire life. And if I can't get out, I may as well take the woman who took my chance at freedom down with me."

"No!" Kayden shouted.

A gun fired. Tilly screamed but didn't feel the pain of a bullet.

Kayden sprinted toward her as the gun fell away from her temple, but as Pixie toppled back, her arm was still around Tilly's throat—and she tugged them both back and over the edge of the mountain together.

* * *

Tilly was yanked back, and Kayden's world stopped.

He sprinted toward the cliff's edge, everything narrowing to pinpoint focus as he looked over the side.

While Pixie's body lay still at the bottom, Tilly had grabbed onto a sharp rock ledge several yards down.

The air whooshed from his chest. Alive! She was alive—for now. But he could already see her hold on the rock was precarious.

"Hold on," Kayden shouted. "I'm gonna get you out of there, Tilly."

Eastern ran toward him. "Fuck." He looked over the edge, the air whooshing from his chest. "I radioed our location to the others the second we found them. Hendrix and my officers are there. Help shouldn't be long, and Theo will bring the gear."

He pulled the radio from Eastern's hold. "Hendrix, you pack the rappelling gear?"

"I did. Almost there."

Now he just had to pray the man made it in time.

Thirty seconds, maybe less. That's all it took for him to arrive, but the entire time, Kayden didn't take his eyes off Tilly. Every second felt like ten.

When Hendrix dropped the gear behind them, Tilly's fingers were slipping.

Shit.

"Hold on, Till! I'm coming down."

As Eastern and Hendrix worked together to wrap the rope around a tree as an anchor, Kayden slipped on a harness. His skin itched to go. Get down there. But he pushed his impatience aside, forcing himself to remember his training. He had to be smart.

When the anchor and knot were secure, Kayden stepped backward off the edge of the drop-off. He'd done rescues like this a million times during his career as a PJ, but this was different. This was Tilly's life on the line. It was personal.

He rappelled down the mountain quickly.

"Kayden..." Tilly's pained voice floated up to him. "I can't...hold on..."

He moved faster and had just reached her when her fingers slipped from the rock edge. He grabbed her wrist with his free hand, catching her in his tight hold.

He growled as he tugged her up, using every scrap of strength he had to get her into his arms. When she was high enough, she wrapped her arms around his shoulders and her legs around his waist.

It was the relief he needed to take his first full breath.

"Kayden..." she whispered.

"I've got you, honey. You're safe."

CHAPTER 31

Kayden stood by Tilly's side as the paramedics looked her over. Her skin was pale and her eyes too wide, but that wasn't what had fury simmering inside him.

She'd almost died tonight. Hell, if he'd reached her a second later, one damn second, she'd be gone.

His hold on her tightened. His team was getting Pixie's body from the bottom of the mountain, but there was no way she'd survived that fall. Not a fucking chance. She'd been too still, and the angle she'd been lying at had been all wrong.

He hadn't left Tilly's side since getting to her. He'd carried her down the trail and waited for the ambulance with her…not that they'd taken long.

His muscles tightened when Tilly flinched from the paramedic touching her ankle. It had changed to a purple color and was so swollen it looked like there was a tennis ball on the side.

He wished he could take her pain away, while at the same time, was so damn grateful it was just her ankle that was hurt, aside from some scrapes and bruises.

"Okay, Miss Taylor, all done." The paramedic finally pulled off his gloves and stepped back. "Based on your range of movement, the ankle doesn't appear to be broken. You're welcome to go to the hospital and get an x-ray if you want, but I think it's just a bad sprain, made worse by the walking you did on it."

"I don't want to go to the hospital," she said quickly, leaning into Kayden's side. "I just want to go home."

"Well, plenty of rest and ice is my advice then."

She nodded as the paramedic walked away. Kayden was about to help Tilly up when Eastern came over to them.

"Hey." His brother studied Tilly's face. "How are you feeling?"

"Tired."

"That's understandable. I'm sorry to ask you to do this, but I need you to take me through what happened tonight."

Kayden growled. "Can't it wait until tomorrow?" She was exhausted.

Eastern opened his mouth, but Tilly touched a hand to Kayden's chest.

"It's okay." She took a breath before looking at Eastern. "I was about to leave for the day when I realized I had an urgent invoice to pay. I went back in but I couldn't find it on my desk, so I searched Pixie's. That's when I found the framed photo in her bottom drawer, of her wearing the watch that had Macy's blood on it."

Eastern nodded. "The framed photo with the broken glass."

Tilly cringed. "The broken glass was me… I was so shocked, I dropped it. I was going to leave, but I heard something on the deck. I thought it was Jake." Her lips turned down. They'd already told her about how they'd found Jake and how paramedics had rushed him to the hospital. "I saw the door to the café close."

"That's when you called me?" Kayden asked.

She nodded. "Yeah, and then I walked in to see Pixie standing at the safe. She pulled a gun on me. Told me she helped her father pay his medical bills and it drained all her money. That his death made her want to get out of here and live her life. She admitted to killing Macy because Macy caught her stealing from the first safe. And shooting Jake. She said the money was Linda's."

A shudder coursed down her spine, and he pulled her closer.

"How did you get away without her shooting you?" Eastern asked.

"My dad—" She straightened, eyes widening. "Oh my God, my dad! I completely forgot! He was here. He came out of nowhere and tackled me. He saved me from being shot, but then *he* was shot in the stomach. Is he okay? God, please tell me he's not dead."

Her father had been the source of the blood. The person who'd run.

Kayden and Eastern exchanged a look. A look Tilly obviously caught.

"What?" she asked.

Kayden cleared his throat. "The café was empty when we got there...and so was the safe."

She frowned. "You mean he was able to take the money and get away after being *shot*?"

Seemed to be the case. Looked like not much stopped the guy from seizing an opportunity to take money that wasn't his.

"I've had an APB out for his arrest since we found out he was in town," Eastern said, pulling out his radio. "And local hospitals will notify my office if they treat a gunshot wound." He looked back at Tilly. "Go home. Get some rest. We can chat some more tomorrow. Are you sure you're okay?"

She nodded, but no part of Kayden believed that.

The second his brother left, he stepped in front of Tilly and cupped her cheek. "How are you really doing?"

"It was Pixie. All this time, the murderer the entire town was looking for, Jake's shooter, and the person who framed me...she was sitting right outside my office and I didn't even know."

"None of us knew." But damn, he wished he had. He should be better than that.

"Thank you," she whispered. "You saved me."

"No, honey. I almost lost you. But I'm so fucking glad you're okay." He tugged her against his chest and just held her. Let her warmth slip inside him, smooth the frayed edges and put back together the parts of him that had torn apart tonight.

When he finally gained the strength to release her, he only did so for a second before slipping his arms behind her back and legs and lifting her.

She gasped. "Kayden, I can walk."

"Not happening." Not when her ankle looked like it did. "I just need to hold you, honey. To remind myself that you're here and alive."

She sighed but didn't argue. And when she leaned her head against his chest, all he could do was breathe her in.

* * *

Tilly watched the trees pass through the window. The moonlight as it cast a dim glow over the road. Everything from tonight felt like a blur. Pixie. Her father. Falling off the mountain edge and Kayden rappelling down to save her. It didn't feel real.

She knew she was still in shock. Probably would be for a while.

Kayden reached over and took hold of her hand. "What are you thinking about, honey?"

"Is it crazy that for a split second after my father saved me, I thought maybe he'd changed? That maybe there was a part of him that *did* love me, or at least, cared about *me* more than money."

Hell, he got *shot* in an attempt to help her escape. That had to mean something. But then to run with stolen money, without even calling for help for her, when he knew a woman with a gun was chasing after her?

No. That wasn't love.

She glanced down at her hands. "It's like he's so greedy, he chooses money at every opportunity over everything and anything else." Even his family…*especially* his family.

"It's not crazy to hope that someone who's supposed to love you will do better and then feel disappointed when they don't," Kayden said quietly. "One day, he'll look back and realize he chose wrong."

She looked over him. "You think so?"

"How could he not? Money doesn't bring happiness. People do. Relationships. Being loved and loving in return."

Her heart rippled in her chest at the mention of love…because she loved Kayden. She hadn't told him, and right now didn't feel like the right moment, but she did.

There was a fear inside her that when she eventually did say those words, he wouldn't return them. After all, they hadn't been dating very long, and the start of their relationship had been so rocky.

He lifted her hand and kissed the back before pulling up at her house.

"I can't believe Pixie's gone," she whispered, more to herself than to Kayden.

She hadn't been able to look down to the bottom of that cliff because she'd known what she'd see. The fall had been too high for anyone to survive. And yes, Pixie was terrible for everything she'd done and had gotten herself into that position tonight, but she'd paid the price with her life.

Kayden's jaw visibly clenched. "I'm just pissed that even in the last moment, when she could have chosen just to take herself down, she tried to take you with her."

"She was bitter about not getting out of here." Tilly shook her head. "How ironic, that she was trying to get away from everything I've been trying to return to."

"Not trying…you *have* returned. Misty Peak is your home. It will always be your home."

She caressed the back of his hand. "You make me feel like it's home."

"Good."

As Kayden climbed out of the car, Tilly took off her seat belt and opened her door. That's as far as she got before Kayden came around to her side and lifted her out.

She opened her mouth to yet again tell him she could walk, but honestly, the feel of his strong arms around her, his heart beating against her ear, was too comforting to put a stop to. She pulled her key from her pocket and unlocked and opened the door while Kayden shoved it the rest of the way open with his shoulder.

They'd just stepped into the living room when Kayden stopped, his brows tugging together. Slowly, he moved to the couch and lowered her.

She frowned up at him. "What—"

He touched a finger to her mouth. "Do you feel that?" he whispered.

For a moment, she had no idea what he was talking about… then she felt the breeze. The cool air on her skin.

Was it coming from the kitchen?

When Kayden rose, he pulled the gun from his holster.

Her pulse pounded, little flickers of fear coming alive in her chest. Kayden reached the kitchen and turned, his gun aimed as he shouted, "What the hell are you doing here?"

Whoever he spoke to was hidden behind a wall.

"I need…help."

Tilly gasped.

Ignoring the pain in her ankle, she shot to her feet and hobbled over to Kayden. That's when she saw him.

"Dad?"

The glass on the back door was broken, and it stood wide open, with her father right beside it, gun in hand and pointed at Kayden. But he was holding his wound with his other hand, blood soaked into his clothes and running through his fingers. Even in the semi-darkness, she could see how pale he was. He looked a second away from collapsing.

She went to step forward, but Kayden shot an arm out, pushing her behind him. "Kayden—"

"Lower the gun, Martin, and we'll help you."

"After what I did to your father?" her dad growled. "I don't trust you not to kill me."

"Really? Then what are you doing here?"

"I had nowhere else to go." Her father coughed, blood spluttering from between his lips.

She frowned. "Kayden isn't a murderer, Dad. He won't hurt you."

"She's right," Kayden agreed. "I love your daughter too much to do that."

Despite everything, her heart thumped. *Love?* He'd just said he loved her.

"Put the gun down," Kayden pushed quietly. "And I'll help you."

"I can't…I can't go to the hospital. They'll arrest me."

"Dad," Tilly tried again. "Put the gun away and let us get you some help. It's either that…or die." She was sure if he didn't get immediate medical attention, he wouldn't survive the night.

"I—" Her father stopped speaking, and his eyes shuttered. Then he dropped to the floor.

"Dad!"

Kayden raced across the kitchen, holstering his weapon before dropping to her father's side and starting first aid. Tilly pulled out her phone, only able to hope the ambulance arrived in time.

CHAPTER 32

"I'm nervous." The words fell from Tilly's lips before she could stop them.

They'd just pulled up in front of the hospital, and for the life of her, she could not get out of the car.

Kayden slid his hand over hers. "Why are you nervous?"

She could have laughed. "I'm so angry at him for so many reasons. And he's probably angry at *me* for calling an ambulance and being the reason he's cuffed to a hospital bed. Because I have questions for him that I don't think I'll like the answers to." In fact, she was certain she wouldn't like the answer, yet something inside her still needed to ask. When he'd just left town five years ago, she hadn't gotten the closure she'd needed.

"I'll be right there in the hall, waiting for you."

He'd offered to stay in the room with her and her father, but something inside her had known that this was something she needed to do on her own...even if it scared her.

They'd found out it had been her father who'd knocked Jake out for the simple reason of he hadn't wanted to be seen.

It wasn't a surprise. Pixie probably would have just shot him. So Jake was lucky in a terrible sense. And God, she'd been so grateful when he'd been released from the hospital with a concussion.

They'd also recovered the money her dad had stolen from the safe. Once Linda finished her cruise, that money would be returned to her.

When she still just sat there in the passenger seat of Kayden's truck, he didn't rush her. In fact, other than the occasional swipe of his thumb against her hand, he was completely still and silent beside her, as if he'd sit and wait with her all day if that was what she needed.

Finally, she sucked in a long breath and wrapped her fingers around the door handle before climbing out. Cool, crisp air blew through her hair, the morning sun barely visible behind the clouds.

"Are you okay to walk?" Kayden asked, already standing beside her.

"Yeah, my ankle's not feeling too bad today." It had been just over a week since everything had happened, and even though she still had a lot of swelling and bruising in her ankle, she'd been able to bear a bit more weight. Which was good, considering how awkward it would be for Kayden to have to carry her everywhere. She'd rented some crutches, but they were just annoying.

At the front desk, a girl Tilly had never seen before smiled at her. "Hi, how can I help you today?"

"I'm here to visit Martin Taylor. I'm his daughter, Matilda Taylor."

The smile didn't falter as she turned to her computer and typed something in. "Room twenty-eight. It's at the end of this hall to my right."

"Thank you."

As they neared the room, Tilly realized she probably hadn't needed the number. The officer stationed outside the door was a good giveaway to which room was his.

She stopped in front of the officer, offering the man a small smile. "Hi, I'm—"

"Tilly, I know. Eastern said you'd come. You're welcome to go in."

She nodded before turning to Kayden. "I'll be back in a sec."

He stepped closer and pressed one gentle kiss to her lips. "I'll be right here waiting for you."

"I know you will."

Turning, she sucked in a final breath of courage before stepping into the room.

Her father lay in the center of the hospital bed, one hand cuffed to the railing, his head turned as he stared out the window. He shifted to look at her, but if he was surprised to see her, he didn't show it.

"I was wondering when you'd come to see me, Matilda."

She stopped a foot away from his bed. "How did you know I'd come at all?"

"Because you never got to ask me why I did it. That's why you're here, isn't it? You've had five years to stew on the question."

It was surprising that her father would know that. In the end, she didn't ask. She asked another question that she'd been wondering for just as long.

"Was it worth it?"

He frowned. "Was what worth it?"

He knew, but if he wanted her to spell it out, then she would. "Was the money you stole from this town worth what you lost? The friends. The community. Me and Mom." Her voice almost broke on that last bit, but she held herself together…just.

Her father glanced down at the cuff around his wrist, as if that would somehow give him the answer. "I was never deserving of you, your mother, or this town, Matilda. Especially your mother. For some reason, she loved me. *Me.* A man who'd grown up with nothing. A man who had nothing to give."

"You could have given her your love. Your trust and loyalty." There was so much more to give a person than money.

"It's hard to give someone your love when you don't feel worthy of theirs." Finally, he looked up. "No. It wasn't worth it. But by the time I figured that out, it was far too late."

"It's never too late. You could have come back. Returned the money and turned yourself in."

"But that would require me to be selfless, something I've never been good at. Besides, I owed people a lot of money. Most of it was gone within a week."

Tears stung her eyes. Because everything her father said was what she already knew, and yet a part of her had been hoping he'd tell her something different. What, exactly, she wasn't sure.

"Despite what you might think," he said quietly, "I did love you and your mother."

"You just loved money more."

"And look where that's gotten me." He shook his head. "I wish I was different. I wish I was a better man."

"You could have been. You chose not to be."

"That's true. But maybe the best thing I ever did was let your mother raise you. You're just like her, you know. Strong and courageous and full of integrity. Maybe that's why I came to you the other night, after being shot. Because I couldn't turn myself in, even if it meant saving my own life…but I knew *you* could. And at least now, the latest people who are hounding me for money won't be able to get to me."

So he'd pissed off the wrong people, and he'd wanted Tilly to fix it with the sale of her house.

"I wish you'd realized that you don't always need to be reaching for more," Tilly said quietly. "More happiness. More stuff. Sometimes, to be happy is just to appreciate what you have. You always needed more…even when you already had everything."

Her father's eyes flared, a mixture of sadness and regret

swirling in their depths. He did regret what he'd done. She could see it. He knew he was a selfish person. He knew he should have done better. He'd just never been able to change.

"Good luck, Dad."

He nodded, emotion darkening his eyes. "You too, baby."

* * *

KAYDEN SHOVED his hands into his pocket. Shit, he was nervous. He wanted to be in there, with Tilly, making sure she was okay. But this was something she needed to do on her own, and as much as he hated that, he understood it.

He was pacing the hall, forcing calmness into his mind, when his phone rang. He pulled it out, frowning when he saw who was calling. Flint Matthews. The man who'd bought his father's home all those years ago. The man who'd told him that he planned to knock it down.

"Flint?"

"Kayden. How are you?"

"Considering everything that's happened lately, not as great as I should be, but I'm getting there." And Flint definitely hadn't helped that, but the destruction of the house seemed almost insignificant in comparison to almost losing Tilly.

"I heard there was a rough patch. I'm sorry about the trouble at the visitors center."

"Thanks."

Wind blew over the line before Matthews spoke. "Look, I'm just calling to let you know I'm not knocking down the house."

Kayden stopped pacing. "You're not?"

"No. I'm getting older, nearing retirement, and my son's just told me he's not interested in taking over the farm, something about wanting to explore the world." He sighed. "So, I have no reason to expand. I'm going to sell...and I thought I'd check in with you and your family to see if anyone would like to buy it back before I put it on the market."

Something inside Kayden lifted. A big weight that had been pressing down on his chest, making him feel far too heavy for so long. "You'll sell us the house?"

"If you want it."

Yes. Hell yes. "We want it. Let me talk to my brothers and see who'd like to purchase it or whether we'll all go in together. Jace may be coming back, so he may be interested."

"Great. And Kayden…I'm sorry my original plans to knock it down hurt you. I know how important that place was…*is*…to you and your family."

"You had to do what was right for you. But I'm glad your plans have changed."

He was just hanging up when Tilly stepped out of the room, her eyes red and the hint of tears shining in them. He shoved his phone into his pocket and crossed the space between them.

"Hey, are you okay?" If her father had hurt her—

"I'm okay. He acknowledged that he didn't make great choices but said he didn't feel capable of making better ones. He told me everything he gave up for money wasn't worth it."

He brushed some hair from her face. "And how do you feel about that?"

"I'm not sure. I'm glad that he recognized what he lost five years ago. Nothing will ever change the past, but at least he acknowledged that Mom and I deserved better. That this town deserved better."

"I'm glad you got your answers."

"Me too."

He cupped her neck. "What do you want to do now?"

"I am *so* in need of some Sugar and Spice to lift my mood. Maybe we could take some cupcakes and iced coffees to the mountains?"

A damn perfect afternoon. "Done."

When they were in the car and driving, Kayden shot a glance across at her. "Do you feel better after speaking to him?"

"I do, actually. I guess because he left without any explanation all those years ago, I never got any closure, but now, in a way, I have. And maybe the town will stop hating me so much because they can hate him in prison instead."

His fingers tightened around the wheel. Jesus, he hated remembering what this town had put her through. It was getting better though, and it would keep improving.

"Were you on the phone when I came out?" she asked, reminding him of his chat with Matthews.

"Yeah, Flint Matthews called me, the farmer who bought my family home." He felt her muscles tense but attempted to smooth them out with a graze of his thumb on the back of her hand. "He's going to sell the property, and he asked if my brothers or I wanted to buy it from him."

Tilly gasped. "Really?"

"Yeah. And one of us will. Or all of us. We'll figure it out."

"You'll finally get your family home back."

"We will." He pulled into a parking spot near Sugar and Spice, then turned to face her. "I can show you the home we grew up in, where all our memories were made."

Her features softened. "I can't wait."

They'd just climbed out of the car as Harry Jacobs, the local electrician, was walking past. The same man who'd intimidated Tilly at the visitors center and exploded on her the night they'd celebrated Cody's birthday.

Jacobs stopped in front of her. "Tilly."

Kayden moved quickly around the car to Tilly's side and inched in front of her. "What do you want, Harry?"

The older man lifted his hands. "I'm not here to cause a scene or fight. I just…I heard about what happened with Pixie and Martin, and I want to say sorry."

"Sorry?" Tilly asked, sounding confused.

"Yeah. It was your father who stole from me, and that's where the blame always belonged—on him, not you. I shouldn't have treated you like I did. It was just that when I saw you, it brought it all back and I took it out on you."

There was a small pause before Tilly responded. "Thank you for apologizing. I appreciate it."

"I'll do better. And I'll make sure my boys do better too. If you ever need anything, don't hesitate to ask."

Tilly nodded, and they both watched as Harry walked away.

She looked up at Kayden, smiling. "I got Harry on my side."

"You did."

"Maybe others will come around too."

"There's no maybe about it, Till. Everyone will love you." He wrapped his arms around her waist. "This is your home."

She nibbled her bottom lip, something clearly rolling around her mind. He didn't push her to speak, just waited for what was coming.

"This is probably the wrong place to mention this." She laughed. "Outside Sugar and Spice and in the middle of the street, but...that night, when my father was in the kitchen, you said... well...you said you loved me. Is that true?"

His heart jumped in his chest. He *had* said that. And he'd meant it. Neither of them had brought it up again since that night because they'd had so much going on. "It wasn't the way I wanted to tell you. I wanted there to be candles and music and pasta."

"Pasta?"

He lifted a shoulder. "That's just what people eat when they make declarations of love, isn't it?" She laughed, and he tugged her closer. "But maybe that's where I'm wrong. Because I don't need that stuff. All I need is you. I love you, Tilly. I've loved you for a while, and I hate that it took me so long to tell you."

Tears filled her eyes, but they didn't fall. "You're right. We don't need that stuff. We just need each other." She cupped his cheek. "I love you too, Kayden Walker. You slipped into my life and made a *person* feel like home for me, rather than a place."

There it was. The final weight lifted off his chest. Gone. Because of her.

He lowered his head and kissed her, let everything she was slip inside him and become a part of him.

Tilly completed him, and he'd remind her of how important she was to him every damn day.

CHAPTER 33

"Can we get ice cream?"

Eastern's lips twitched at his daughter's question. They were in the grocery store, and he'd been waiting for it since they stepped foot inside. He was surprised she'd held off until the basket was half-full. "Ice cream, huh?"

"Please, Daddy? And we can put sprinkles on top while we have a movie night."

The sneaky kid. She knew he couldn't say no to a movie night. Every opportunity he got to spend with his daughter was a gift, and he didn't take them for granted for a second.

"Okay. Peppermint flavor."

She scrunched up her nose. "But chocolate chip is so much better."

"How about we compromise on mint chocolate chip?"

She seemed to take a moment to consider it before giving one decisive nod. "Deal."

When had his baby girl turned into a little adult who was negotiating deals with him? He needed time to slow the hell down.

They stopped at the freezer section, and Avery opened the

door to pull out a tub of mint chocolate chip. "You know, Amber told me her dad doesn't like ice cream."

"There's obviously something wrong with him."

Avery giggled, and the sound was music to his ears. God, he loved his kid. Being away from her for long stretches during his time as a SEAL had been hard, but he'd done it because he loved to serve his country and had assumed she was well looked after by her mother.

Not the case.

Fuck, he wanted to kick his own ass for not realizing his ex, her mother, had a drinking problem. That she'd barely been caring for their daughter in the end, had let go of their nanny, Sadie, and was passing out in the middle of the day. And then to just run off?

The only thing that helped him get through all that was the knowledge that Avery was safe and with him now, and that was the way it would stay. He'd applied for full custody and the hearing had been brief—because Jamie had never bothered to show up. Avery was officially his.

"He also doesn't let her have any sprinkles," Avery added.

Eastern feigned a gasp. "No sprinkles?"

"I know. I told her I'd sneak her some."

He bit back the laugh. His daughter, the sprinkle smuggler. "Maybe that's not a good idea, Ave. If her dad says no…"

"Wouldn't you want someone to get sprinkles to me if Mom said no?"

A muscle in his jaw clicked at the mention of her mother. He tried not to show it. Damn, he tried so hard every time she mentioned her mother, but he never seemed able to control his reaction.

"I'd always want to make sure you had access to sprinkles, Princess."

She beamed at him.

Eastern was just rounding a corner when a woman with her

head down, eyes on her phone, ran straight into him. She gasped, grabbing onto his arm.

He gripped her waist to steady her. "Whoa, you okay there?"

Her eyes shot up—beautiful dark eyes, almost black. Right now, they looked sad, with a hint of tears and redness, as if she'd already cried a bunch of tears.

She opened her mouth, but before she could get a word out, a scream sounded behind him, then Avery threw her arms around the woman's legs.

"Sadie, you're here!"

Sadie? Her former nanny? Eastern had met her once or twice over the years, but she'd been younger then. The young lady he remembered looked *nothing* like this woman.

Wait—why was she here? Shouldn't she have just married that guy in Atlanta?

Sadie blinked a few times before visibly forcing a smile to her lips and lowering to her haunches. "Oh, Avery, sweetie, I've missed you so much, baby girl!" She pulled Avery into a hug, and the two just held each other for a long moment.

"I've missed you too," Avery whispered.

There was so much emotion in their embrace...in the way both of them spoke. Eastern had known his daughter loved Sadie, given how much she spoke about her, but this really confirmed it.

When they parted, Sadie remained crouched, brushing some hair from Avery's face. "How have you been?"

"Terrible! I've had no one to tell all my problems to, and there have been *so many*."

Sadie gave Avery a sweet smile as Eastern cleared his throat. His eight-going-on-sixteen-year-old rolled her eyes.

"I mean, I've had no girls to tell, Dad."

Sadie tilted her head. "Well, I'm back now."

She looked at Avery with such love and affection, Eastern suddenly regretted not getting to know her previously.

"For good?" Avery asked, hope in her voice.

"Yeah, sweetie, for good."

Avery threw her arms around Sadie again.

If she was here to live, did that mean her husband was here too?

When Sadie rose, her dark eyes glistened with tears, but she blinked them back as she looked up at him. "It's good to see you again, Eastern."

He dipped his head. Sadie had worked for Avery's mother, not him. He could probably count on one hand the number of times he'd met her, the first time being when she was only a teenager. "You too." For some reason, he couldn't stop staring at those big black eyes. There was so much sadness in them, but also, a bit of light. After seeing Avery?

"Are you working at Sugar and Spice?" Avery asked.

"I am. I'm helping my grandmother with the shop again, but if your dad ever needs someone to look after you, I'll always make myself available."

Avery gasped and spun, tugging at Eastern's shirt. "Oh, please, Daddy? I love Sadie!"

Yeah, he knew that. His daughter had mentioned her almost every day since he'd returned from the Navy. "Avery and I would both love to have your help, on occasions when you're free."

Hope lit Sadie's eyes. "Great." Then she frowned as she patted her pockets. "Where's my phone?"

They both saw it on the floor and reached for it at the same time, bumping into each other again.

He grabbed her arm so she wouldn't fall back. "Shit, sorry."

Sadie looked up at him, so close he could feel her breath on his skin. See the tiny laugh lines beside her eyes. "That's okay."

He was still fixated on her when Avery's voice cut through the silence. "Daddy…you owe the swear jar a dollar."

Sadie laughed, and he bit back a groan. Trust his daughter to cut through whatever the hell was going on in his head with something like that.

He lifted her phone, noticing she'd been in the middle of responding to a text. When she took it from his fingers and looked at the text, worry slipped over her face.

"Everything okay?" he asked quietly.

"It's fine."

In his line of work, those two words spoken so quickly rarely meant things were fine.

They both rose and she clicked a few keys before handing her phone back to him. "If you pop in your number, I'll text you so you have mine, then you can let me know when you need me."

As he took her phone, he noticed both her hands were bare of any rings. *Interesting.* He put his number into her phone, and the second she had it back, his phone dinged with a message.

"Great," Sadie said quietly. "Text any time."

"He will!" Avery was almost jumping with excitement. "Have you and Scott moved back into your old place? Can I visit?"

Sadie swallowed, and Eastern suddenly knew the answer before she spoke the words. "It's just me, honey. Scott's not coming back."

Avery frowned, but before she could ask another question, Sadie grazed her cheek. "It was so good to see you again, sweetie, and I'm glad I'm back so I can see you regularly."

She gave them each one final smile before walking away, and Eastern was left wondering why the hell that smile knocked the breath out of his chest.

Order book three in the series, RECKLESS FALL, featuring Eastern and Sadie, NOW!

ALSO BY NYSSA KATHRYN

PROJECT ARMA SERIES

Uncovering Project Arma

Luca

Eden

Asher

Mason

Wyatt

Bodie

Oliver

Kye

BLUE HALO SERIES

Logan

Jason

Blake

Flynn

Aidan

Tyler

Callum

Liam

MERCY RING

Jackson

Declan

Cole

Ryker

BEAUTIFUL PIECES

Erik's Salvation

Erik's Redemption

Erik's Refuge

SHORT CHRISTMAS STORY

Hidden Shadows

RECKLESS SERIES

(series ongoing)

Reckless Hope

Reckless Trust

Reckless Fall

Reckless Faith

Reckless Love

JOIN my newsletter and be the first to find out about sales and new releases! CLICK HERE

ABOUT THE AUTHOR

Nyssa Kathryn is a romantic suspense author. She lives in South Australia with her daughter and hubby and takes every chance she can to be plotting and writing. Always an avid reader of romance novels, she considers alpha males and happily-ever-afters to be her jam.

Don't forget to follow Nyssa and never miss another release.

Facebook | Instagram | Amazon | Goodreads